THE
SURVIVORS
CLUB

Praise for *The Survivors Club*

"An utterly engrossing thriller. *The Survivors Club* grips us from the very start and simply doesn't let go. The novel seamlessly achieves that rarity in crime fiction: making our palms sweat while bringing the characters and their stories straight into our hearts. Bravo!"
—Jeffery Deaver, *New York Times* Bestselling author of *The Kill Room*

"Welcome to *The Survivors Club* – where cheating death just once may not be enough. J. Carson Black's latest thriller takes you into a whirlpool of conspiracy, blackmail, and betrayal, where no one can be sure who is the hunter and who is the prey—a game of blood whose outcome may leave no survivors."
—Michael Prescott, author of *Cold Around the Heart*

"J. Carson Black's *The Survivors Club* is a twisted, diabolical cat and mouse game that will keep you riveted."
—CJ Lyons, *New York Times* Bestselling author of *Hollow Bones*

"Black serves up a breezy thriller with a killer premise: What if people who cheated death once weren't so lucky the second time around? By the time the plot snakes through twist after twist, you'll be asking yourself . . . do you feel lucky?"
—Brian Freeman, Bestselling Author of *Spilled Blood*

"J. Carson Black delivers desert heat with her latest cool thriller, *The Survivors Club*. Detective Tess McCrae shows us again why she's the southwest's top cop."
—Alan Jacobson, National Bestselling Author of *No Way Out*

THE
SURVIVORS
CLUB

BY J. CARSON BLACK

THOMAS & MERCER

Published by Thomas & Mercer, Seattle

www.apub.com

ISBN-13: 9781612182711
ISBN-10: 1612182712

Library of Congress Control Number: 2013906870

To my mother, Mary Falk, and my aunt, Evelyn Ridgway, with all my love. You two always did love a good conspiracy.

SEPTEMBER 2012
The Hilton Atlanta

Alec Sheppard rested his hands on his knees and took a few breaths before turning to walk clockwise around the hotel's running track. The late September sun turned sultry, the golden light flaring off the windows of the convention center across the way. It had taken him a long time to come back from the accident, but he'd been put together pretty well, and while he wasn't the runner he once was, he could still keep up a good clip. As he walked, he gazed out at the downtown Atlanta skyline. The sun was sinking, an orange ball in the sky. He looked down at the building below him—a down-in-the-mouth bar.

His wife had left him. He didn't blame her. She couldn't understand his "obsession with skydiving." Didn't understand why a few weeks after he fell into that swamp in Florida he was already thinking about it. She said he was like a kid, and not in a good way. How could they begin to think about having children when he was like a cocked gun, ready to explode in her face at any minute? Annette was not a risk taker. He'd known that when they got married a couple of years ago. What had seemed an interesting conversation piece when she was his girlfriend had turned into reality. He lived, ate, breathed, and slept risk. He was risky in his investments (that didn't turn out too well early on, but he was on the rebound and his presence here in Atlanta was proof of that), and according to Annette he had a risky lifestyle—he was an adrenaline junkie.

Two weeks ago she'd left, wrestling two suitcases to the front door, her face a cold mask. And then the mask crumpled and she cried in long, jagged sobs. He remembered then the reason he'd married her, how much he had loved her, and reached out to steady her by the shoulders, to hold her, to comfort her, as he had done so many times before.

She'd slapped him across the face and said the last words she spoke to him face-to-face. "You!" she said. "You, you . . ." And turned and walked out into the sunshine, toward her car and the moving van that would take everything away and leave his house and soul empty.

Yet here he was, the blood pumping through him, every sense alive, reveling in the moment. What a bastard. But he could *run.* He'd been pounding it out on the oval track running around the edge of the hotel, feeling free again and thinking about another jump. Not for a while yet—he had to be in good shape—but he was thinking about it. He even knew where he wanted to go: SkyView Jump Center in Houston. He lived in Houston, so it was the obvious place to start back.

He felt a twinge in his hip. The hairline fracture of the pelvis wasn't back to a hundred percent, and he wouldn't be jumping for a while. But he would.

He couldn't wait to get back in the air.

As Alec walked through the reddening gloom, the sun torching the buildings one more time before going under, he was aware of someone coming at him. A jogger, the rhythmic sound of his running shoes hitting the ground—one-two, one-two. Alec nodded to him as they were about to pass each other, and suddenly something slapped his chest.

Stunned, he watched as the guy kept jogging, one-two, one-two, one-two. Already just a figure in the gloom. Had the jogger assaulted him? Slapped him? Hit him? He looked down, half expecting to see blood from a bullet wound. Shock, he thought. I'm too shocked to know I'm hit. And yes, there was red there, on the center of his chest. But it wasn't blood.

It was a red sticker. The kind you might see on a broken-down car's back window to indicate it needed to be towed.

The only thing on it was a number.

Five.

He peeled the sticker off his T-shirt and looked in the direction of the hotel door. Aware that he'd heard the door open and close while he was still feeling his chest for blood. Also aware that his heart was thumping much harder than it ever did before he jumped out of an airplane.

The sticky stuff on the back adhered to his knuckles, and it took him a minute to fold the thing up so it didn't stick to his fingers. Now what?

He started back along the track, feeling a slight chill now as the sun disappeared. Squinting in the gloom. He stopped by the door and peered at the roof. Nobody here now. The jogger was gone.

He left the rooftop and took the elevator down to his floor. Holding the sticker away from his body, his stomach roiling. He didn't know why, but he felt like a marked man.

3

CHAPTER 1

APRIL 2013
The Ghost Town of Credo, Arizona

Santa Cruz Sheriff's Detective Tess McCrae saw everything.

She saw everything and remembered everything.

Right now she was seeing a sixty-eight-year-old Caucasian male named George Hanley, shot to pieces. Thirty rounds from an AK-47. Brass everywhere—she'd come close to stepping on one of the casings, which had lodged into the spongy wood porch of the ruined cabin.

Careful not to touch *anything*, not with hands or feet or body or clothing.

George Hanley had that clumsy inanimate look corpses get—caved to the side like a grain sack that had fallen off a shelf, propped up against the blood-stained interior wall as if someone had pushed him there.

His bloodied DL had been thrown on his stomach like a playing card. The wallet they'd found nearby, tossed into a corner of the cabin.

4

He wore a flannel shirt, tan chinos, and running shoes.

Tess had to hunker down close and squint hard at the license, had to read it through the dark red stain, read it aloud to her partner.

She took photos of the corpse and the graffiti-covered Sheetrock wall. Although in truth, she didn't need to.

She saw the crime scene in every indelible detail, and she would remember it that way. Every bloody flap of skin, every jagged crater—many of them so close together they made one cavernous, many-chambered wound.

Blood soaked into the floor as if someone in a rage had stomped hard on a crateful of blackberry Popsicles.

His torso had been turned into a sieve. Thirty rounds from an AK-47 will do that. From his crotch to his throat, he was riddled with bullets. He'd been shot through each eye, and the duct tape affixed to his mouth.

She had a whole gallery of gruesome images inside her skull, but this was the worst.

Overkill.

No—

Overkill squared.

Tess had what her new partner, Danny, liked to call "The Supah Power." Her memory, virtually photographic, was a parlor trick to the people she worked with, a topic of conversation but also something her fellow cops liked to have her utilize on their own cases.

She was the most popular girl in school.

But already there were too many suspects. This homicide, in the rickety old ghost town of Credo right on the border between the United States and Mexico, looked like a hit. It looked like a hit by an enforcer for one of the Mexican cartels—either Sinaloa, which owned this part of the world, or the Zetas, or the violent upstart group, Alacrán—Spanish for "scorpion."

George Hanley had been riddled with bullets and then "silenced" by duct tape. All of this pointed to a message being sent.

But to whom?

"What d'ya think?" Danny Rojas said behind her.

"What do *you* think?"

"Looks like a cartel hit to me."

"A sixty-eight-year-old white guy?"

"A sixty-eight-year-old white guy who used to be a homicide dick." Danny held up his smartphone. "I looked him up. If it's the same guy, and I think he is, he was shot up before."

"He was?" Tess stepped carefully to peer over Danny's shoulder. She had to squint. Jesus, those screens were small.

"See? He was on a reality show—*The Ultimate Survivor.*"

"Huh."

"And this. You're not going to believe this. This is why." He pulled up the article for her.

She read the headline.

"Kind of weird, huh, *guera*?" Danny said.

Pronounced "Wetda." He called her *"guera,"* which could mean anything from "blonde" to "Anglo" to "white," ostensibly to get under her skin. But in the couple of months they'd worked together, it had become more of a pet name.

Danny said, "I mean, look. He won the lottery. A three-hundred-thousand-dollar payout. The guy sure was lucky."

"Until he wasn't." Tess grabbed his phone and scrolled through the article. In 1991, Hanley, then a veteran homicide detective with Phoenix Metro PD, was shot multiple times in a gun battle with a street gang. He died twice on the operating table, but was resuscitated. He returned to work but had to take a desk job. Eventually, he worked his way up to lieutenant.

"The lottery, man," Danny said. "Three hundred thousand dollars. He gave most of it away to the Humane Society."

Tess was barely listening. She was reading the part where ten-year-old George Hanley had been home sick the day his mother drove his sister four blocks to the elementary school. The car had been T-boned on the passenger side, his sister was paralyzed.

"Lucky Lohrke," Tess muttered.

"Who?"

"Somebody else who was lucky."

CHAPTER 2

"So who was this Lucky Looky guy?" Danny asked as they drove back the way they'd come, bumping over the bone-jarring wash-board road. They'd finished up at the crime scene late in the day, seen the techs to their cars, and closed up. They'd padlocked the gate to the ghost town, even though the border here was porous and anyone who could crawl through a four-strand fence could get in.

"*Lohrke*," Tess said. "Not Looky."

"Who is *he*? Somebody who was lucky, eh?"

"He was a baseball player," Tess said.

"You like baseball?"

"Nope. I just saw his obit in a magazine."

"Bet you don't like soccer, either."

"You're batting a thousand today."

"So let me guess. You remember every detail of this obit, am I right?"

"Yup."

"Weren't you, like diagnosed or something? What's it called? Super-autographical—"

"Superautobiographical memory."

"Yeah, that. If I give you a date you can tell me what day it was and what you were doing."

"True."

On May 2, 2009, she'd picked up a *Time* magazine. It was a Monday in Albuquerque, sunny with a few high clouds. She'd stopped at the Coyote Springs Safeway to pick up a few things she'd run out of—milk, bread, toothpaste, and a packet of hairpins. She'd been working a particularly ugly homicide—Yolanda Ochs, beaten, and her throat slit—and was on the way home. As Tess waited in the checkout line, she flipped through the magazine, and that was when she saw it.

Jack "Lucky" Lohrke's obituary.

"So what made this Lorhke so damn lucky?" Danny asked her.

"In World War II, the two guys on each side of him were shot and killed."

"So? That doesn't sound so unusual."

"Okay. After the war, he was bumped from a transport flight home by a high-ranking officer at the last minute . . ."

"Just him, right?"

"I dunno. Probably."

"So let me guess . . . the plane crashed."

"Killed everyone aboard. But that wasn't all."

"Oh, do tell!" Danny using his Carmen Miranda voice. "Choo don' mean there's more, do you?"

"Your accent needs work."

Danny pulled the sun visor down against the blinding sun—a fiery orange ball low in the sky. "My wife says I do gay perfectly."

"That's her problem. You want the rest of the story or not?"

"Oh, yeah, don't stop now, *chiltepin*."

Little chili pepper. Jeeze. "Let's stick with *guera*, okay? Fast-forward to 1946," Tess said. "Jack Lohrke played Triple A Baseball with the Spokane Indians. That's good, right? Triple A?"

"Oh, yeah, that's good. Which you'd know if you liked baseball."

"So Lohrke got word on the road that he was just traded to the San Diego Padres. They stopped to eat at a diner. He decided right then and there he'd hitch a ride and join up with his new team. So he left them there."

"This does not bode well."

"Nope."

"So what happened?"

"They were about to drive up into the Cascade Mountains. It was snowing up on the Snoqualmie Pass. The team bus went off the road, through a guardrail, and crashed down the mountain. Burst into flames. The manager and nine members of the team were killed. The survivors were in bad shape, too."

"Holy shit. He really *was* lucky."

"I'd say so."

"Like George Hanley," Danny added. "Except *his* luck ran out."

~

The sun was low in the sky by the time they reached Rio Rico, where George Hanley's daughter and her husband lived. They waited at the door of an older brick ranch in a nice neighborhood. You knew it was a nice neighborhood because there was open space between the houses, and because the houses were on top of a hill for a valley view.

Danny looked at Tess. "How are we gonna do this?"

"Very carefully."

They'd both said it at once.

Danny said, "That gave me the creeps."

"Me, too. Let's not do that again."

The outdoor light came on.

Tess cleared her throat.

They were both aware of the politics involved. The deceased was an ex-cop. The shooting looked like a cartel hit. Not to mention Hanley's death could spur widespread fear among the retired people who populated this area.

As they waited, Tess said, "I don't think we go into the extent of his injuries right now."

"Yeah," Dan replied. "Dead's dead."

So they played it that way.

The door opened.

The daughter, Pat—she was in her midfifties—took it hard. Her husband, not so much. He seemed more annoyed than anything.

Pat Scofield started weeping, saying she should never have asked her father to move here, it was all her fault, who would do something like that?

Bert Scofield had been watching a baseball game and his gaze kept straying to the TV set, which his wife had turned down.

He did look up every now and then to ask a question. Was it someone his father-in-law knew? Was it in his apartment? "When was he killed?"

"We're not sure. Sometime yesterday," Danny said.

"At that ghost town, right? Why would he go there?"

"We don't know."

"You don't know much, do you? You say he was shot? I've told him he shouldn't be going out there, you never know who you're gonna run into. All those drug smugglers, wetbacks, place is riddled with 'em. I hope he was carrying."

He was, of course—Hanley was a retired cop. He had a snub-nosed .38 on his hip and a knife strapped to his ankle. He didn't have a chance to draw either.

The commercial was over and the game was on again. Bert stood up—the meeting was at an end. "So what now?"

Tess addressed Pat. "Your father's body is at the medical examiner's office. We'll get in touch with you when he's released."

Pat looked up from where she had been sitting, her face slack with shock. "You mean that's it?"

Tess knew what she meant. Someone comes to your house and tells you your loved one is dead, and that is all there is to it. There's nothing you can do. You've been delivered the bad news that so-and-so's never coming back, and then the detective leaves and gets into his car and drives away and you close the door and you're alone. Or with someone as shell-shocked as you are.

"Can't we come down and identify him?" Pat asked.

This was the tricky part. "It's okay, ma'am," Danny said, holding her hands in his. "Your father's already been identified."

He didn't mention that the DL was soaked through with blood and it was hard to be sure. But the empirical evidence, the torched car's VIN number, what could be seen of the DL, and other pieces of identification, his guns and his knife—everything came back to

George Hanley. She said, "Can you let us have a photo? Something recent? People don't have to go down there in person anymore—"

"But we should go down there, shouldn't we, Bert? He's my *father*."

Bert looked up from the television. "I think we should do what they say, Pat."

She marched over to him, grabbed the remote, and shot it at the screen. The screen went black. "Goddammit, my *father* has been *killed!* And all you can think about is a *baseball* game? I want to see him. Can't I go see him?" She started to cry again.

Tess took her hands in her own. She looked into the woman's eyes, willing her to meet her own gaze. "Pat, honestly, I don't think you should see him right now. They'll release him in the next day or two. I've seen a lot of people who have lost loved ones, and it never helps." *Lie.* "You want to be prepared for when you see him." *Half lie.* "You have to trust me when I tell you that this is only going to hurt. You need time to get used to the idea."

Pat's eyes took on a furtive shine. "What are you hiding from me?"

"We're not—"

"What happened? You said he was shot. Is that true? I just want to see him!"

Tess looked at Danny and Danny looked at Tess.

She'd know sooner or later, anyway.

Tess held Pat's eyes with her own. "He was shot multiple times. You don't want to see him like that."

"Mul-multiple times?"

"Yes."

"Like before? When he was living in Phoenix?" There was hope in her voice.

Thinking that maybe he survived again.

Tess held her hands steady. Held her eyes. "No, I'm afraid he's gone. You don't want to see him right now."

Tess saw it come home to the woman. The shock turned her face pale. She stared, but could barely move her lips. Her eyes took on a glazed shine.

She bolted for the bathroom, and Tess and Danny looked uncomfortably at Bert as they heard her retch.

But she didn't insist on going with them.

CHAPTER 3

It was going on eleven p.m. by the time Tess sat down to write her initial report for the George Hanley murder book.

She and Danny Rojas had split up. Danny returned to the scene to supervise the removal of George Hanley's vehicle, a 2005 Yukon Denali, while Tess worked on the report back at the Santa Cruz County Sheriff's Office.

Earlier, deputies had been dispatched to secure the possible secondary crime scene—Hanley's apartment.

One of them—Javits—called to tell her the door to the apartment was locked when they arrived. It had taken them a while to get there because there was a car accident at a nearby intersection and they had stopped to render aid. They'd reached the apartment by 9:47 and saw nothing amiss. He reported that the area around the room—the walkway, the curb, the parking lot—was free of trash.

They secured the scene by sealing the door with crime scene tape and extending the tape out to the pillars of the walkway.

"Did you knock on doors?"

"We did, both sides of his apartment and the place above, but nobody answered. It appeared quiet. The lock had not been tampered with."

Hanley's keys—and Tess assumed the key to the apartment was included— had been left in the ignition of the burned car.

Her phone chirped—Danny. Tess ended her call with the deputy.

"The Yukon's on the flatbed on its way to forensics," Danny said. "Took a long time to winch it up out of that ravine. Burned to a crisp."

"How far was it from the ghost town?"

"Maybe a half mile, like we thought. The closest place to dump it."

They would give it a thorough going-over.

"It was torched big-time," Danny said. "Don't know what kind of evidence they'll be able to recover. Still, gotta try."

"Hopefully there's something."

"Yeah, hopefully." But he sounded gloomy. Or maybe he was just tired.

Tess stared at her monitor and tapped her fingers on her desk. There was one other detective in the room, Derek Little, a guy she didn't know well. He was at his own desk, which faced away from hers, talking on the phone. Tess got the impression he didn't like her, probably because she came in with Bonny, the new undersheriff.

She knew a lot of the Ds she worked with considered her to be a teacher's pet.

Nothing I can do about that.

Back to George Hanley. So he was a retired cop who came down here from the Phoenix area to be near his daughter. Nothing unusual about that scenario. They hadn't learned much from Pat and Bert, except that George Hanley led tours of the ghost town, Credo, once or twice a week. His mother had been born in the town, and he had memories of visiting the ghost town as a child.

The only thing she could think of: if he went down there often, he might have seen something. Something a retired cop might notice.

Border crossers, drug smugglers, and gun runners passed through that area all the time. Even though it was rugged country, the border around there was porous. Where there was opportunity, there was also activity.

Her cell vibrated. She was surprised to see the US Immigration and Customs Enforcement Agency, ICE come up on her readout at this hour.

The agent returning her call, Tony Versailles, explained that he'd been on a raid and was too jazzed to sleep. "What do you want to know?"

Tess ran it down for him, asked him if there was anything on George Hanley.

"Offhand, I can't remember anyone like that," Versailles said. "It's kind of unusual."

"His age, you mean."

"You'd be surprised at some of the old folks we've dealt with. There are old guys involved, sure, but they're usually the brains of the outfit and stay clear of the day-to-day operation. Some of the prominent community leaders around here are up to their necks in organized crime, but they're hard to nail down. I call 'em the Godfathers. Let me take a look and I'll call you back."

He called her twenty minutes later. "I don't see anything here. That doesn't mean there isn't something. But the guy's an Anglo. He doesn't really fit the profile."

"He's an ex-cop," Tess said.

"Yeah. Could be something there. But we haven't come across him. I'll keep checking, though."

"Thanks," Tess said.

"No problem. Keep me posted—you never know where this could lead."

She became aware that Derek Little was staring at her from across the room. When she caught his eye, he looked back at his computer monitor. Concentrated on it for a moment.

Then he rolled his chair out from the desk and stood up.

He walked in her direction. Derek was tall and skinny, the way Tess envisioned Ichabod Crane.

He stooped over her.

Cleared his throat.

"I have a question for you." When he spoke, she got the impression it was like trying to pull a sliver out of his hand with a pair of tweezers.

She looked up at him. Wasn't about to stand up.

He cleared his throat again. "You remember the Sanchez case?"

"That wasn't mine."

"But we were all looking for him, right?"

Yes. Bonny had put his picture up on the projector. He had beaten his wife to death and was on the run.

"I have a photo here, came off a surveillance camera." He shoved it under her nose. "Is that him?"

She looked at the guy. "Where was this?"

"Outside Appliance City."

It was blurry. A night photo. Tess said, "Yes, it's him."

"Uh. How do you know? It's blurry and you can see less than half his face."

"It's him."

"You sure?"

"I'm sure."

"Okay. Then . . . thanks." He remained where he was.

"And?"

He slapped the photo back on the desk. "What kind of car is that? Behind him. See?"

Just the fender. No, just half the fender. Fortunately, it was the part with the headlight.

Tess had seen a car just like it the other day. "It's a Ford Fusion."

"Thanks."

He picked up the photo and walked back to his desk.

The Magic Show was over.

~

Twenty past midnight, Tess gave it up and headed for home. She had a twenty-mile drive on a winding two-lane road to her place in Patagonia and she was already falling asleep.

Hanley's apartment was sealed.

It could wait.

CHAPTER 4

Orchard Apartments near Rio Rico was a two-story tan stucco, faded with age. The only landscaping was two spindly agaves ringed with cement blocks. The blacktop edged up to the wild yellow grassland that seemed to take over everything in sight. A large banner had been tied across part of the second story with the legend: MOVE-IN SPECIAL $499 A MONTH - FURNISHED. Across the road was a convenience store, and beyond that, a Motel 6.

Tess met Danny there midmorning. He'd already been up in the Atascosas, driving around talking to potential witnesses.

"You canvassed the whole area?"

"Uh-huh."

"How'd it go?"

"I made it back to the car alive, so I'd have to say it was a success."

Danny liked to joke but this time he was serious.

"That bad?"

"It's like *Blade Runner* out there." He added, "If you're going to Credo, check them out—I wanna know what you think."

He looked at the apartments and grimaced. "What's a retired cop who won the lottery doing living in a dump like this?"

"He gave most of the money to the Humane Society," Tess reminded him.

"Bet his daughter liked that."

They'd had to wait for a warrant, so it was midmorning by the time they reached the apartments. Danny rousted the apartment manager from her desk and followed her as she scuttled down the walkway to his door. She'd taken note of their badges and Tess could tell she wanted to ask questions, but Danny just thanked her and closed the door behind them.

They gloved up and started looking around. At first, Tess folded her arms under her armpits and looked at everything without touching.

George Hanley was a neat man. A bachelor's two-cup coffee-maker sat on the counter, lined up with the toaster. Issues of gun and fishing magazines were stacked neatly on the veneered-oak side table by the chair. Everything in the bathroom was lined up on shelves with military precision. Clean towels, spotless floors.

Tess noticed this because she did the same thing.

Danny took the kitchen while Tess took the bedroom. Again, she looked at everything, taking mental snapshots of the room layout and contents.

Next, she checked the desk by the sliding-glass door in his bedroom. The sun poured in, throwing a lozenge of light on the carpet. The desk top was completely clean, except for a jar of pens and pencils. She went through the desk drawers and found the usual stuff—from Post-its to a stapler to erasers and other detritus that didn't warrant being seen in the open.

A MacBook Pro laptop sat on the bedside table. Tess called out to Danny. He came in.

He whistled. "Could be a goldmine," he said.

"If we get it to forensics soon—"

"It'll probably be a week before they get to it. They're backed up, what with Guzman."

The Guzman case was a big one. Several members of a prominent Nogales family had been gunned down during a wedding. The patriarch, Alejandro Guzman, owned several legitimate businesses and was a household name in Nogales for thirty years. But it was widely known that he played both sides of the street. He'd been careful to keep his illicit operations separate from his sweet old grandfather image. But he'd laundered money for the Alacrán.

It had caught up with him in March, when he was shot once through the eye and once through the heart as he toasted his daughter's wedding.

"They just confiscated about a dozen racehorses," Danny said. "They're gonna be busy for a while."

"Probably," Tess said. *Welcome to the Arizona-Mexico border.* She looked at the laptop. She was gloved. The laptop was exactly like her own. She could open the lid, fire it up, and take a look.

Danny hung back in the doorway. They looked at each other.

"I guess we bag it and hope for the best," Tess said.

"Probably has a password."

"Yeah."

"Crap."

"Double crap with a cherry on top."

"A fucking crap flambé."

They both laughed at that.

"I'm gonna go back to his pantry," Danny said. "Guy must have bought out Costco."

Hanley had a four-drawer file cabinet. Folders were neatly marked with his credit card bills—one Visa and one American Express card—and several folders holding information on what appeared to be old crimes. Newspaper clippings and printouts, mostly, some of him at homicide scenes. Hanley was meticulous in his filing system. Tess also noticed he held no balance on his credit cards, paying in full every month. She found his rental agreement and a number of other business records. Tess photographed them all in situ and then stacked them and put them in the evidence box she'd brought.

George Hanley was a deliberate man.

She looked through the wall calendar and saw a few notations.

"Danny, check this out."

Danny ducked his head in. "What?"

She motioned to the calendar. "Nice handwriting. What is that? The Palmer Method? My dad wrote like that."

One on April 8, with the notation: "finance adv."

"Financial advisor?" Danny said.

Another notation at the end of April: "SABEL."

"What's that?" Danny asked.

Tess typed the letters into her phone and got the answer. "Southern Arizona Buffelgrass Eradication League. Says here it's a group 'dedicated to ridding southern Arizona of a highly flammable invasive species of grass.'"

"Jesus. That's a mouthful."

"He must have belonged to the group." Tess photographed the calendar and then took it down. They went through each month, Danny peering over her shoulder.

There were several notations. In January, there was a line across three days and the word "Conference." In May, another line through three days, and the notation, "LA." And under that, "look at wading pool."

"Wading pool?" Danny looked at Tess. "You think . . .?"

"I dunno."

"Hey, I know he's old, but they say that never goes away. You think he was hanging out around the city wading pool trolling for kids?"

"It could mean anything. Maybe he has grandkids, and he was planning on buying them a wading pool for Christmas."

"Do Pat and Bert have kids?"

Something else to ask them.

Their search went downhill from there. They switched rooms. Now Tess took the living room and kitchen and Danny took the bedroom, bathroom, and linen closet.

The first thing Tess saw was a dog's water bowl and dish, both empty and sitting in the kitchen sink. "He had a dog?" she called to Danny.

"Looks like it. He's not here now."

Tess called the Scofield residence and Bert answered.

"Your father-in-law has a dog."

"Adele. I took her to the pound this morning."

"This morning?"

"I picked her up last night."

Before the crime scene tape went up. "That was quick."

"I couldn't leave her there. She was my responsibility."

"And you took her to the pound today?" Tess was hardly ever surprised at the things people did. Still, this was cold.

Bert must have sensed her disapproval, because he said, "Pat's allergic to dogs. I don't know what you think we should have done."

Then he disconnected.

Tess looked at the bowls sitting in the sink, and thought how fortune can change at a moment's notice. One minute the dog had an owner who apparently adored her. The next, she was in the dog pound, facing death.

Tess hadn't liked the Scofields before. Now she disliked them even more.

Danny was in the hallway. "What was that?"

"Bert took Hanley's dog to the pound."

"Oh? That was quick."

It wasn't her job to like the survivors of a homicide. Her job was to serve justice.

Her job was to get the bad guys. As she stepped out onto the walkway for some air, a cool breeze hit. Down at the far end of the building, she saw a young man holding a bag of trash coming down the steps. He headed out across the parking lot to the Dumpster.

Nobody heard or saw anything. Some people had known Hanley to say "hi" to, but he was so recent to the apartments that he had made little, if any, impression.

Tess stared out at the freeway, trying to figure out what an old man like George Hanley would have to do with drug runners or *coyotes*.

Thirty rounds fired from a rifle—probably an AK-47, the weapon of choice for all of them—Sinaloa, Alacrán, Zetas, the Javelinas—and he'd been shot from five feet away.

Why use so much firepower on an old man?

"So, what you think, *guera?*"

"You know what it looks like."

Danny nodded.

The killer or killers had left footprints—mostly sneaker prints, called "running w's" because of the tread. There had been no attempt to cover up the footprints, because whoever killed Hanley didn't care. Whoever killed Hanley had left the casings—all thirty of them—because he didn't care.

He wasn't covering up anything.

In fact, it was just the opposite.

Whoever did this appeared to be making an example of George Hanley. Everything played into that—the thirty rounds, the spent casings, the footprints all over the place, and God knew, there were probably fingerprints, too—somewhere. More than that, there was the duct tape on George Hanley's mouth—to shut him up.

Don't talk. A message.

"What do you think about the duct tape?" Tess asked Danny.

Danny kept his eyes forward, tracking the tractor-trailer rigs slowing down on the freeway for the exit. Their engines growling through the gears. "My guess, the guy put it on him after he was dead."

Tess agreed. She thought the tape had been affixed to Hanley's mouth as an exclamation point.

"I think the guy who killed him was ready for him," Danny added. "Maybe caught him by the doorway and walked toward him, shooting."

That was how Tess saw it, Hanley being pushed back by the hail of bullets and falling into the wall of the ruin.

Then whoever killed Hanley drove his car to a ravine a half mile down the road from the ghost town, rolled it to the edge, pushed it over, and torched it. Accelerant had been used. Tess made a note to ask any ranchers or squatters in the neighborhood if they saw the fire the night before. No one had called it in, but the people around here minded their own business.

The object of this kind of killing was to terrorize. But who was there to terrorize in this situation?

George Hanley was a retired cop who owned a dog and gave tours of Credo. What would anyone in a group like Alacrán or Sinaloa want with him?

"*Plata o plomo*," Danny said.

Plata o plomo. Tess had heard the popular *narcocorrido* before—a song that glorified the drug runners and cartels. *Plata o plomo* was the choice in Mexico: silver or lead. Go along with us and you will be paid handsomely; go against us and you will get bullets.

A wind sprang up out of nowhere, blowing sand across the empty parking lot and making the yellow tape shiver. Then it was gone. Another semi shifted down, the sound familiar in the west and comforting. Tess glanced at Danny. "How's Theresa?"

"*Nada*. The doc might induce labor if it goes on much longer."

"Fingers crossed," Tess said.

"One way or the other, *guera*," Danny said. "You know what they say: what goes in's gotta come out."

The warped humor of Danny Rojas.

CHAPTER 5

They split up. Danny would be testifying at a homicide trial just before lunch, and would probably be gone for most of the day.

Tess followed Ruby Road to the end of the blacktop and her plain-wrap Tahoe clunked over the washboard road. It was a long, bone-jarring drive.

This was Border Patrol country. It was rare for Santa Cruz County to send anyone out here—certainly not on patrol. She was alone.

She passed the gate to the ghost town of Credo on the left. The gate was a continuation of wire fence. A wire loop held the gate and the fence post together. The ranch gate could be unlooped and dragged across the road to make way for cars.

Tess noticed a van from the medical examiner inside the fence. She decided to come back when they were gone. When she went back to the crime scene she wanted quiet and a chance to think. She drove around the bend and up another hill.

Around another bend there would be a couple of trailers and an even more primitive camp.

Tess slowed at the sight of an old travel trailer backed into a rocky hill. It sat on a spur off an old ranch lane. Thirty yards beyond the trailer, where the road bottomed out in the streambed, a couple of tree-limb posts were strung with two strands of wire across the wash. Tess noticed that tin cans had been stuck on top of the limbs, and they'd been shot to pieces.

The travel trailer was shaded by a camo tarp. The sixties seemed to be a theme here: a faded Game & Fish truck, pale green, stood out front, the emblem painted over. A campfire ring and a make-shift table made out of scrapwood kept a cheap kitchen chair company under the tarp.

There was a stake and a chain, too—for a dog.

She had a bad feeling about this, partly because of the way the place looked, but also because of Danny's *Blade Runner* comment.

As Tess pulled up, the trailer door squeaked open and a tall tanned man stepped out.

Two things she noticed right off the bat: First, he was really tanned.

The second thing: he was armed with a Winchester repeating rifle.

And it was aimed at her vehicle. "What do you want?" the man yelled.

Tess took him in: he was tall and the color of beef jerky. Gray-blond hair in a ponytail. Flip-flops.

He wore a dirty guayabera shirt and nylon running shorts circa 1970.

"Who the hell are you? What do you want with me?"

Tess buzzed down her window and said, "Santa Cruz County Sheriff's Office. I want to ask you about a fire the day before yesterday."

He lowered his rifle an inch. "Fire?"

Tess kept her hands up and palms out. "May I get out of the car?"

"Stay where you are!"

Tess had parked diagonally to the clearing, so if she got out, the engine block of the SUV would be between her and the trailer. She opened the door and held her hands up.

"Come out from behind there," he said, motioning with his weapon.

"No. You need to put down your rifle. Otherwise, you'll be facing a lot more law enforcement than just me, and I don't want us to get off on the wrong foot."

"I have the right to defend my property."

The ownership of the property was doubtful, but Tess ignored that. "You have nothing to fear from me. Lay down your weapon and let's talk." At the same time, she slid out of the car, canting her body so that her right side was hidden. She inched her hand down to her side, unsnapped the holster, and drew her SIG Sauer. She called out, "Did you see the fire?"

"Fire?" he said again.

"A car was burned about fifteen miles down the road. You must have seen it."

"I did not! Cease and desist! You are trespassing on my property!"

"Can't we talk?"

"You can't be the sheriff! I talked to the sheriff yesterday. He looked nothing like you!"

"That was my partner, Danny."

"Danny?" He was puzzled. "Another one? How many are there of you? Why are you harassing me? Throw your weapon out. Do it now or I won't be responsible for what I might do! A man has a right to defend his life and his property."

"I can't do that."

There was a pause. "Okay. Leave your weapon in the car."

"I will," Tess lied. She watched as he lowered his rifle again and scratched an ear.

"Okay, then." He took a deep breath.

"I just want to talk to you. Like the other guy, Danny. Remember? He came by and talked to you and then he drove away."

"Okay," he said again. He'd made a one-eighty-degree turnaround in a split second. "I don't want any trouble. You have backup? They're not on their way, are they?"

"No. I'm just here to ask you about the fire. Like my partner Danny was. You remember he just asked you some questions and left? Please put down your rifle."

He lowered his rifle all the way, then walked out from under the tarp and set his rifle carefully on the ground. He stepped back.

"Thank you," Tess said, easing her SIG Sauer P226 back into her holster but keeping her hand close. "Thank you."

He nodded. Suddenly he looked shy. "You can't come in, though. The place is a mess."

"That's fine. We can talk out here." Tess did not move from behind the door and the engine block. "Anybody else live with you? Anyone inside the trailer?"

"No. I ride alone."

"Did you see the fire?"

"Of course I saw the fire." Another one-eighty.

"Do you remember what time it was, Mr. . . . ?"

31

"Name's Peter. Peter Deuteronomy. Rhymes with lobotomy."
He giggled at his own joke.

"You believe in the Bible," Tess said. "That's good."

He smiled. "You a Christian?"

"Yes." She was, and she wasn't, depending on the things she saw on any day. But right now she was a true believer. He hadn't shot her, for which she was thankful.

"Some of us around here, we have a Bible study. I could ask them, if you want to join."

"Thank you, but I have my own. What night do you guys meet?"

"Tuesdays at seven o'clock p.m. Over at Matty Thompson's house."

"Oh. That's when we meet, too."

His face fell. "Too bad, but at least you're washed in the blood of the Lamb."

Tess nodded. "So can I ask you about the fire? You saw it? Do you remember what time that was, Peter?"

He looked down at the ground, shifted his feet on the rocks. "I think it was during *Pickers*. I saw it over that hill." He pointed. "Just a light, but I could tell it was flames. And smoke."

"So that would be what time?"

"It was a rerun. They had the *American Pickers* marathon. So I can't rightly remember. It was still light, though."

"Evening?"

"No. Dusk."

"Dusk. Like around six p.m.?"

"Uh-huh. You want to hear about the shooting, too?"

"I would, yes."

"Somebody must've been shot up bad. Maybe it was the guy you're looking for. It was an automatic weapon—an AK-47, I'll bet. Rat-tat-tat-tat-tat-tat! Like that!"

"How long was it between the shooting and the fire?"

"You think the same guy who was shooting set the fire?"

"Could be."

He looked down at his own rifle. Tess hoped he didn't have second thoughts. She eased one hand down to her own unsnapped holster.

"How long, do you think?" Tess asked again.

He frowned. "I dunno. Maybe a half hour?"

"Did you call the police?"

"Nope. People are always shooting around here. There are a lot of bad guys. That's why I tell intruders I shoot first and ask questions later."

Comforting. "So you think the fire was around six-thirty p.m.?"

"Sounds about right." He was staring at his weapon again, even took a step toward it. Tess didn't think he wanted to shoot her. She hoped it was because he just didn't want to be away from it very long.

He said, "I heard someone start up a car and drive away after the shooting. Then I saw the fire."

"All this happened between five and six-thirty at night?"

"Pretty sure. Can I get my rifle now?"

"Tell you what. I'm going to get into my car and drive away. Let me get back in the car, okay? And when I drive around that hill, you go pick up your rifle."

"Sounds fair." But she could see his hand itching. He was looking at the rifle the way a dog looks at a ball he can't quite get to.

~

Tess went to three other squatter camps in the Atascosa Mountains. No one answered at two of them, and an older gentleman in a newer travel trailer invited her in for iced tea and a grilled cheese sandwich. He remembered seeing a light in the sky, but it was too far away for him to hear anything. He, too, thought the time was around sunset.

She had a time frame.

By the time Tess got back to Credo, the place was deserted.

The ghost town looked the same as it did yesterday: adobe dwellings slumping into the earth, wood shacks bent out of shape by the elements, corrugated steel roofs were a patchwork of silver and rust. In mid-April, the mesquite was just budding out in halos of bright green.

The crime scene tape was still wrapped around the falling-down cabin, strung out to include two white oaks.

The Tahoe bumped along the dirt track and she parked behind the stone foundation of the stamp mill. The oaks and mesquite grew wild there, and Tess knew the vehicle couldn't be seen from the road. It wasn't an overt act of concealment, but Tess didn't want to attract the attention of anyone driving along the road. Tourists and hikers used this road, and she didn't want to deal with anyone today.

As she'd done the first time, she started seventy yards or so away from the cabin where Hanley had died and walked all the way around. As she walked, she looked down at the ground, but also at the hills and mountains and mining buildings of Credo, paying particular attention to windows, doorways, and trees. With her eyes, she tracked the cabin where Hanley was shot and killed, getting closer with each circuit.

Found "high sign" on an animal path coming down one hill.

Strands of burlap clung to the bushes and mesquite. Burlap meant someone had been moving drugs—most likely marijuana. She found a thread of flannel, as well. Flannel was a good shirt for early spring. The fabric breathed, it could be cool or it could be warm, and repelled burrs and thorns. That was why border crossers often wore flannel shirts.

Tess had a few small plastic evidence bags with her, and tweezers. She took a few samples of the flannel and burlap, and photographed the bush they'd been caught on. Plenty of footprints—maybe even more than last time.

Even though the road was blocked by a padlocked gate, anyone could come through here on foot, or even on horseback. Anyone with wire cutters could get through a four-strand wire fence with horses or mules, or slip in on foot.

She worked her way to the cabin.

Every shell casing—all thirty of them—had been circled with iridescent orange paint before being taken for evidence.

Tess couldn't think of one instance of an enforcer for one of the cartels killing a US citizen on this side of the border.

She crossed her arms and rested her hands under each armpit, so she would not be tempted to touch anything. She stepped up onto the cabin's porch. Even at this time of the day, a chill emanated from the doorless entry.

Tess paused outside the doorway. The smell of musty adobe overlaid the membranes of her mouth and nostrils. She peered into the darkness at the opposite wall. Blood everywhere. Geysers of it on what was left of the chalk-like gypsum board.

From the trajectories and blood spatter and the way Hanley was found, Tess was sure her theory was correct: he had been pushed back by the assault, and stumbled backward until he hit the wall.

She closed her eyes. And saw him.

Grouped shots, mostly center mass, Hanley's neck turned into pudding. Two shots to the face—both eyes.

The duct tape pasted across his mouth.

Hanley's Denali was a burned-out husk—there would be little, if any, evidence. They'd identified it by the VIN number. Plaster casts had been taken of the tire treads near the place where the Denali had been driven off the road, as well as shoe prints. But they would need something to match them to.

Tess looked around the cabin. There were long sections of the rafters open to the sky, sun and shadow striping the concrete floor.

He'd had a weapon, but didn't draw it. This surprised Tess. You'd think that out here he would hear someone coming. There was no way someone would be able to sneak up on an ex-cop. Tess knew Hanley would have kept the careful habits that had seen him through his sixty-eight years. If she were him, coming out here late in the day like that, she would have scouted the area. She would have looked for trouble ahead of time.

Looking for trouble was what cops did. Didn't matter if you'd been out of the life for years. Old habits die hard.

A dove in the rafters shifted and cooed.

It came to Tess just like that, and she knew it was true.

He was meeting someone.

A clatter above, and the dove took off, its wings whickering as it sped away.

Tess froze. She was here alone, in a place known as part of the smuggling corridor.

She heard footsteps on the sand and rock.

Careful to keep away from the stripes of sunlight, Tess stood back from the paneless window and looked in the direction of the footsteps.

A man was walking down the lane toward the ghost town. He'd left his vehicle, an older model Range Rover, near the gate, and had just slipped through the wire.

Looked like a hiker. Hiking boots, the thick socks, the ballcap, the sunglasses, the cargo shorts. He carried a bladder of water on his back, and a drinking tube snaked around to lie on his chest, not far from his lips.

"Stay there!" Tess called. "This is a crime scene."

The guy looked at her quizzically, but kept coming, his hiking boots skating a little on the rocks as he came down the hill.

"This is private property and a crime scene!" Tess shouted. Aware of her weapon, her hand close. "You are not allowed to be here!"

The guy raised a hand in greeting and kept coming.

He was carrying; a small gun, might be a .32, on his left side— a lefty.

Tess spread her stance. She unsnapped her holster and drew her SIG Sauer—the second time today. As she'd done earlier, she kept it hidden behind her hip. "Sir—I am giving you a warning. Stay where you are."

He stopped and held up his hands. *I'm harmless.*

"Is that the cabin where George Hanley was shot?" he said. "Looks like it."

"Do you know George Hanley?"

"May I approach?" His hands still up.

He was a good-looking man, lean and sinewy, somewhere in his mid-to-late thirties. The dark aviator shades made her think of a model in one of those fashion magazines. They also covered his eyes.

"Do you know anything about Mr. Hanley?" Tess repeated. "Are you a friend of his?"

Hands still up. "Can I approach?" He crunched forward and came within fifteen yards of her, saw her face, and then stopped. Whipped off his sunglasses. "Look, I understand why you'd want me to keep my distance—I know that's standard police procedure. You're just being a good cop."

What a strange thing to say. The man did not strike her as cop material, but he spoke about her copness—for want of a better word—with a familiarity that seemed real. She was usually good at pegging people, so this took her aback.

"I'm one of the good guys," he said. "I work for Pima County Sheriff's. May I approach? Maybe I could shed a little light here."

She motioned him the last few yards.

He came fast. Tess stepped back, ready, her eye on his left hand. He kept his hands raised high, nowhere near his weapon.

Still. Her hand closed tighter around the butt of her SIG Sauer.

"Hey! I didn't mean to startle you. Are you working the Hanley case?"

Now he was too close—infringing on her space. She felt like taking another step back, but didn't. Pushed her own body forward. "Will you step back, sir?"

He did.

"Do you know anything about what happened here?"

"Not personally, no. You think it was one of the cartels?"

She said nothing.

He grinned. He had a crooked mouth, the only thing that marred his good looks. He didn't show his teeth.

"If you know anything about this, you need to tell me," Tess said.

"No, not this particular case, but it might be similar to what I've been working on. That's why I came down here today."

"In your capacity with the Pima County Sheriff's? What capacity is that?"

"They depend on me to do a number of things. Recently, I've been named to an administrative investigator position."

That sounded political—made up to keep him or someone he knew happy. She could picture him measuring crime scenes.

He looked beyond her at the cabin. "It says in the paper he was shot multiple times. How many?"

"Sir, I cannot share any details of this case with you. As someone who works in law enforcement, you understand that this is a crime scene, and you need to leave now."

He stepped toward her. "Hey, look. I'm not trying to steal your case. I'm here to help. I just asked you a question. It said 'multiple gunshots' in the paper. I'm just trying to ascertain if that's true."

Tess drew her weapon and held it down low behind her back— the second time today. "You need to walk up to your car and go, now."

"I can see it on your face! It's true. He *was* shot multiple times. I read they burned his car, too."

"I can't speak to that, sir." The phrase "returning to the scene of the crime" was a cliché, but it was also an accurate predictor of suspects in those crimes. Many times a bad guy *did* return to the crime scene, sometimes to gloat. And this guy was a blue-ribbon gloater.

Tess could almost feel the restrained violence in him.

He loomed over her, grinning like a parrot. Now she could see the teeth he'd tried to hide. They peeked out under the crack of his lips—

tiny teeth. They didn't go with the rest of him, his good looks. The expensive hiking outfit.

Manic energy.

Tess said, "You need to walk up the road, get into your car, and drive away. This is the last time I will tell you that."

"Or what?"

She traded her SIG for cuffs. Cuffed one hand, shoved him, and while he was off balance, cuffed the other.

"You can't do this! I'm a citizen!"

"This is a crime scene and you are not allowed to be here. You are interfering with an active investigation." She pushed him in the direction of the gate. "I'll escort you to the road, sir."

"I just want to know how many times he was shot! Were they multiple gunshot wounds?"

"Multiple gunshots? What do you mean by that?"

He shut up.

Tess continued to push him up the path.

They reached the gate, and Tess used one hand to pull the loop over, shoved the fence pole sideways to the right so the gate fell into the dirt. She marched him over the strands of the gate and aimed him toward the Range Rover. Pulled him to a stop just shy of the car and felt in his pockets and came up with his wallet and checked his DL. His name was Steve Barkman, thirty-six years old.

"This your car?"

He shut up. He said nothing when she uncuffed him and told him to get into his vehicle. He did as he was told.

She watched him drive away.

She waited for him to turn around and come back.

The sun warm on her head, bearing down on her.

The brightness in her eyes. She watched the hill he'd driven around.

Multiple gunshots.

Why'd he ask her *that*?

CHAPTER 6

Before heading back to the Santa Cruz County Sheriff's Office, Tess drove past the exit and turned on W. Mariposa and worked her way over to Animal Control. She badged the woman behind the glass and was buzzed in to the office.

"I'm looking for a dog named Adele," Tess said, giving her the names of both George Hanley and Bert Scofield.

"I'm sorry, but number 014489 was adopted already."

"She was? When was she adopted?"

"Right after she came in. We didn't even have time to process her."

"Who adopted her?"

"I don't think we can give that out."

"This is a homicide investigation," Tess lied. "The dog is important to the case. Did the person who adopted 014489 look at any other dogs?"

Wondering why it was important to her.

"I wasn't here. I could ask, but I don't know if Sally would remember."

"Sally was the one who adopted the dog out?"

"Yes."

"Is she here now?"

"I'll get her."

Tess waited. The intake papers were on the desk, and Tess looked at them. Adele was five years old, an "Aussie mix." There was a place to clip a photo, but it was blank. They didn't even have enough time to even take a picture?

When the woman returned, another woman wearing a similar knit shirt and khakis but with considerable more girth nodded to her shyly.

Tess asked her about the person who came in.

"I barely put her in her run before someone asked about her."

"They asked to see an Aussie mix?"

"Yes. Probably, they walked around and saw her. That's what most people do. I was out on the floor, hosing down the runs, and the woman wanted to adopt the dog. So I took her up to do the paperwork, and then we went back and got the dog."

Tess craned her neck to read the name. Bernadette Colvin.

"This is her address, right?"

"Uh-huh." The woman pulled the card back, worried that there was a confidentiality issue. Tess could have pressed her to give her the card, but decided it was unnecessary.

Tess was still unclear why she had felt compelled to come here. To see the dog, or to rescue her? But now that she was here, she had more questions. The quickness with which someone adopted the dog seemed fortuitous, if not downright strange.

Maybe Colvin was a friend of Hanley's. Maybe, since she adopted the dog, they had been close.

The address for Bernadette Colvin was nearby—just ten minutes out of her way. Tess drove to Walnut Tree Place, a uniformly beige townhome in a housing division full of them. The homes and garages presented blank faces to the street, and Ms. Colvin's house was no different.

Tess pushed the bell. No answer. Hard to tell if anyone was there, with the drapes drawn. She remembered the phone number on the card, used her cell phone, and got voice mail. She left a message, asking for Bernadette Colvin to call her.

~

Tess was walking toward the homicide room when Bonny poked his head out of his office. "When you're in, why don't you come by."

He sounded grim.

Tess dumped her briefcase by her desk and walked down the short hallway to Bonny's office. She noticed his nameplate was finally up next to the door: "Thaddeus Bonneville, Undersheriff." Bonny hadn't made much headway in setting up his office. There were boxes and files on every chair and file cabinet. He was still moving in, having taken over as the Santa Cruz County undersheriff when his good friend of forty years died in harness two months ago.

Bonny had brought Tess with him. He looked like he was regretting it, now. "I just got a call from the sheriff," he said.

The sheriff was on vacation, so this was a big deal.

"John's not happy. You know what you did? You handcuffed the son of a sitting federal judge."

Tess opened her mouth to protest. Bonny held up a hand. "Not just any judge. Geneva Rees."

Tess had heard of Geneva Rees. She was the kind of judge who loved the spotlight, especially when it came to border issues. Tess was already acquainted with some of her virulent lectures from the bench.

Rees was also a girlhood friend of the governor.

Tess said, "Barkman presented a potential danger to me."

"I'm sure you felt that way. But you know how Geneva Rees can hold a grudge. And see, the deal is, little Stevie Wonderboy out there is her only child."

Tess could feel the trail narrowing, and it was lined with thorns. "He's from Judge Rees's first marriage."

"Yes."

Tess cleared her throat. "To the governor's brother."

"That pretty much covers it. Judge Rees and her ex are still on very friendly terms, so I hear. And you know her and the governor are like that." He crossed his fingers. "But that's not all. She's a Democrat—'big D.' Our boss is not going to like this."

Tess knew what he meant. The sheriff of Santa Cruz County was influential in party politics—in fact he made sure the party was run like a well-oiled machine. She said, "Her son needs to learn some manners."

"That may be, but you got to remember we have two political parties in this state. One's all brains and no principle, and the other is all principle and no brains. But this county is Democrat and this is how the game is played. Barkman's got a dipshitty little job researching minor crime scenes, which makes his mama happy, and that makes all of us happy. He does the legwork they can't afford to do, and one hand washes the other. So you see my problem. Now suppose you tell me your side of the story."

Tess told him.

"Can't blame you, considering where you were. Hell, just going out there you should get combat pay. I have no problem with what you did, but the sheriff thinks you should send Barkman a written apology."

Tess felt her stubborn coming on. For a moment she thought about digging her toes in, but in the scheme of things—considering what they were faced with—it wasn't worth it. "Sure, I'll send him a note."

"I'm gonna want to see it when you're done."

"Fine."

"Good." He leaned back in his chair and started swiveling—something he'd always done when he had something hard to think about. "So what's your take on this? On Hanley?"

"I'm not sure."

He rested a cowboy-booted foot over the other knee, clasped his hands over his stomach. Bonny had a bad back, and liked to keep at least one leg up high for relief to his lower spine.

He turned his pale blue eyes on her. "Your theory?"

"I don't have one yet."

"You don't have one yet."

She cleared her throat. "It has all the earmarks of an execution. Like they made an example of him."

"They."

"'They' or 'he' or 'it.' I don't know what else to call them."

"So your suspects are everybody and nobody."

"That sums it up."

"You think they're in Mexico?"

"I don't know, sir."

"They could be in Mexico. They could be here in the state. I read the report, but I want to hear it in your own words. Tell me what you've got."

Tess went over it for him. Her theory that Hanley was meeting someone. "I doubt someone could sneak up on an ex-cop like that. Plus, the time of day. So late."

"Doing something illegal," murmured Bonny.

"Could be."

A sixty-eight-year-old man who came down here to be near his daughter. A guy who had a dog and liked fishing and kept to himself and was civic-minded enough to belong to a buffelgrass eradication group.

But you never knew about people.

Bonny scratched his head. Dandruff ensued. "You're telling me that he was, what? Running drugs? Guiding crossers? Gunrunning?"

"His death fits with any of that."

"But?"

"I can't see it. At least, it's hard for me to see it. I suppose the money . . . I guess anyone can fall prey to that."

Bonny said nothing.

"Another thing. He had a dog. The same day the dog went to the pound—yesterday—a woman adopted her. Snapped her up. It might not mean anything, but—"

"You can't be saying you think the dog was evidence in some way? Like he was smuggling drugs in the dog?"

"It's happened."

"You believe that's the case here?"

47

Tess thought about the man's credit cards, paid in full every month. His monastic lifestyle. The fact that he gave a large portion of his lottery check to the Humane Society. She thought about the pet products—dog shampoo, doggie treats, prescription diet food, grooming brushes, toys, matching leash and collar.

"No."

"Where does that leave us?"

"I don't know. But it looks like *somebody* wanted to make an example of him."

Silence.

When Tess was in her late teens, she'd go with her friends to a city park in Albuquerque at night. They'd done the usual things, including ride a teeter-totter in the dark, hang out on the picnic tables, sometimes there were makeout sessions, and once or twice, more than that. Some of them smoking and some of them drinking. Kids at a loose end. They were the only ones in the small park.

And then she'd felt it. Just sitting there on the aluminum seat of the picnic table. She'd felt something dark and menacing brush past them. There was no cold air, but Tess had felt cold inside. It was there. Evil.

She'd looked at the kids she was with. She didn't know some of them that well. Three males and another female.

But it hadn't been coming from them. At least she didn't think so.

It was as if a door had opened and something bad had come through and passed them by.

Tess felt that way now.

"The way things are going, what's happening these days, is too much," Bonny said into the silence. "Sometimes I wonder why we bother. Why the Border Patrol keeps rolling that rock uphill. The people in Mexico and the people here—we're outnumbered and out-gunned. Look at Mexico—even the good guys have to become bad guys just to survive. Shit, that's the norm for down here."

They sat there, the feeling that they had been enveloped by something bigger than both of them: an evil that was palpable. It was a sunny day outside. Blue sky. Cars in the parking lot, sunlight bouncing off chrome. Heartbreakingly beautiful blue mountains in the distance, blond grassland rising up to them like pale surf.

But they were underwater. They were sinking under a deluge that seemed to spread. The killings. The torture. The burnings. Beheadings.

Obscene.

Tess rubbed her arms, feeling the air conditioning cold on them.

It was just like the park.

~

Tess typed up what she had and added it to the murder book. She copied the new information to the report that would circulate to her superiors.

She left early. It was time to find out about the rest of George Hanley's life—the one that seemed so normal. She would start by going over to interview the head of SABEL, a woman named Jaimie Wolfe. Jaimie's place was on State Route 82 outside Patagonia, where Tess lived.

She stopped at the Circle K on her way out of Nogales, bought an energy bar, and roamed the tabloid racks. This time she saw something new—Max Conroy sharing a split page with an actress in a bikini, the droplets from her dip in the ocean accentuating her beautiful body. One hand held back the dark tangle of her hair and water beaded on her perfect breasts. She had exotic eyes.

The headline said, "Max's Mermaid?"

The woman's full name was Suri Riya, but she was one of those stars who went by one name: Suri. Her bikini wouldn't cover a tea-cup Chihuahua. Make that two teacup Chihuahuas.

Tess opened the back door to the SUV and dumped the tabloid on top of the others—the *Globe, Star* magazine, *Celebrity NOW*—all of them thrown into a cardboard box. One of these days maybe, she'd get around to looking at them.

She drove out onto the highway headed in the direction of Jaimie Wolfe's place.

CHAPTER 7

The sign out front said Wolfe Manor Performance Horses and featured the silhouettes of a prancing horse and a jumper with the words English - Western - Performance Horses For Sale underneath. The property was in a natural bowl of land surrounded by the Patagonia foothills, not ten miles from where Tess lived.

Tess parked near a riding ring with low jumps. Three girls that Tess pegged to be between the ages of twelve and eighteen were riding around the edge of the ring, posting up and down in their English saddles. The horses were massive and obviously pricey—muscular animals that seemed much too large for the girls riding them. A woman stood in the center of the ring. She was as thin and breedy as a whippet. She wore vanilla-colored breeches and a black tank top that showed off her dark tan. Her long sun-bronzed hair was pulled back into a ponytail that poked through the back of a blinding white visor. Riding boots finished the ensemble—casual, elegant, and expensive.

Money.

The woman glanced in her direction, sun bouncing off her dark glasses, then turned away and yelled something to one of the girls. The girl sat up straighter and tilted her chin up. She seemed self-conscious.

The woman called out instructions for another fifteen minutes, ignoring Tess. Finally, she told them to cool down their horses and walked toward the fence. A pack of dogs materialized from the stable area—mutts and purebreds. The dogs joined up with the woman in the ring and accompanied her to where Tess stood.

"If you're looking for the riding stable, it's back off Highway 83," the woman said. Tess knew Jaimie Wolfe was thirty-four years old, but she looked older. The sun had already done its damage.

"Jaimie Wolfe?"

She woman turned to look at her. "Is this about George's death?" She pushed her sunglasses up on her head. "I wondered when you'd get around to me. You want some iced tea?"

Tails wagging, the dogs trotted along beside them *en masse* as they walked to the house. Jaimie talked as they walked. "I can't believe what happened. He was such a nice man. Absolutely dedicated to ridding this part of Santa Cruz County of buffelgrass, and even put a lot of his own money into it. He worked like a longshoreman."

"You mean digging out the grass?"

"Yeah, but also getting the news out. He'd give talks, he did the newsletter. Never missed a meeting, and I guess that's why I wondered if something was wrong . . ."

"That would be, when?"

"Day before yesterday? Yeah, we were going to touch base. It all seems so unreal." They stepped up onto the porch. Latticework corralled the porch and yellow jasmine gave off a heavenly scent.

"You go ahead and sit down and I'll get us some iced tea." She slipped through the screen door and was gone.

Tess watched the girls at the stable. One had her giant steed in a wash rack and was spraying him with a hose.

Jaimie Wolfe came back out with the iced tea, handed one to Tess, and sat down, tipping back and resting her booted feet up on the railing. "So what else do you want to know? I'll do what I can to help."

Tess said, "Did he talk about anything besides buffelgrass eradication?"

Jaimie cocked her head. "For instance?"

"For instance, if anything was bothering him?"

"Bothering him?" She seemed confused. "I don't think so."

"He didn't have anything on his mind? Anything that might have been weighing on him?"

"No. But really, I didn't spend that much time with him. Just the SABEL stuff."

"By the way, do you have a list of SABEL members?"

Jaimie said, "Yes, but it's on my computer. Give me your e-mail address and I'll send it to you."

"Did he get along well with everybody on the SABEL board?"

"From what I could tell, yes."

Tess looked into Jaimie Wolfe's eyes. "You know how he was killed?"

Jaimie looked away. "I saw it in the paper today—I can read between the lines. Awful." She shuddered. "I can't imagine who would do something like that. Nobody *I'd* know." Abruptly, she stood up and yelled at one of the girls. "Don't let him do that! If you're not careful, he's going to step right on your foot. Put your boots back on until you're done with him. Flip-flops, for fuck sake!" Turned back to Tess. "You're asking if he had any enemies? Let me think. He took the spread of buffelgrass very seriously." She launched into a description of how the invasive, flammable African species came to the country, leaving the Sonoran Desert susceptible to wild-fires. "Everything could go up, and fast," she said, waving at the golden hills around them. "He was a true believer. He was also worried about his daughter and his son-in-law. He thinks—thought—they're headed for divorce."

Tess said, "Have you met them?"

"A couple times. That was enough for me."

"What do you think of Bert Scofield?"

"What I *know* about Bert Scofield is that he came on to me. It was at one of our get-togethers we had here at the ranch about three months ago. I was in the kitchen and he kind of had me trapped between the door and the kitchen table."

"What did you do?"

"I stomped on his instep. And I told him if he pulled that crap again, I would tell his wife."

"What was his response?"

She shrugged. "He said he was gonna leave her anyway. He also said she didn't care."

"How would you characterize his relationship with his father-in-law?"

"I only met them socially, they weren't the least bit interested in SABEL or anything that didn't include eating—the two of them really put it away, a pair of greedy-guts—and I noticed she was

sneaking leftovers from the spread into her purse. I didn't say anything, because I loved George. I felt so sorry for him."

"Why?"

"He pulled up stakes to come here to be near her. But she always
seemed like a sour old ingrate, to me. Hate to say it, but sometimes
I think the wrong daughter died."

"You're talking about her sister? Karen?" Tess asked. In Tess's
research, she'd learned that Pat wasn't George Hanley's only daughter. Years ago, his other daughter had been shot and killed during a
holdup at a convenience store.

"Yeah, that was a long time ago, apparently." Jaimie stood up
and bracketed her mouth with her hands. "Alison," she shouted. "Is
your mom coming soon?"

One of the girls looked up from where she'd been sitting on a
chair outside the barn and yelled, "After she gets off work!"

"I want to talk to her, so don't sneak off, okay?" Jaimie said to
Tess, "That woman owes me for two months board, plus lessons. I
know it's hard times for everybody, but she should pay at least *something*. I try hard to keep these kids going, but this is an expensive
business."

"Riding lessons?"

"Oh, it's much more than that. *Showing*. Big money, you
wouldn't believe how much those warmbloods cost. Alison's mom
has a good job, but she doesn't have anywhere near the money she
needs for them to compete on the highest level. The sad thing is,
Alison has the talent. She could go all the way."

"I got the impression it was George's daughter who wanted him
to come out here."

"You got that right. But then he did and she ignored him. She's
a cold one. Don't get me wrong. She's needy, and kind of weak, but

it's all about her. She wanted her dad to come down here but once he was here, it was like, she had *that* box checked. Pat's such an insecure person. She knows down deep what a disgusting creep her husband is, but she wants to hold on to him. Why, I don't know. She's the type that only grabs on if she thinks she's going to lose you. You could tell George thought he'd made a mistake coming down here, but that only made her tighten her grip. And when he did come over to her place, she just got in arguments with him."

"You seem to know them pretty well."

"Don't forget—I saw them in action. George asked me to go with him on more than a few occasions, kind of as backup. I knew he was unhappy. Pulling up stakes like that and coming all the way here. I'm divorced myself, and I know what a drain the wrong kind of person can be. Now I'm free as a lark, and doing what I love to do."

"But it's an expensive hobby."

"Oh, yeah. But I come from money, and even though I have a lot less than I used to, I'm doing all right."

"Was anything bothering George Hanley, besides his family situation? Anything you saw?"

"I dunno. He was such a gracious man. Old-fashioned that way. I guess you could say he was a gentleman."

"Did he ever mention planning a trip to LA?"

"I don't think so." Jaimie stood up, her eyes on the barn. "There's Alison's mom. I've got to talk to her. Anything else?"

"Did he talk much about the tours he led in Credo?"

"I have to talk to her," Jaimie said, starting down the steps.

Tess moved fast to catch up with her. "Did he? Talk about the tours in Credo?"

"He mentioned how much he enjoyed them. He was worried about illegals, all the drug running, stuff like that, but who isn't, around here? It was such a remote place." Her pace quickened. "Janine!" she called to the mother, who was just getting out of her Cadillac. Jaimie Wolfe darted a glance back at Tess. "Look, I've got to get this straightened out. I'm paying fricking alimony to my *ex*, if you can believe it, the bastard thinks because I'm a DeKoven I'm rolling in it. Which is *not* the case at all. Plus, it's the principle of the thing. I'm one of the best there is in this business."

"Anything," Tess said, "that could shine a light on who might have wanted to kill him?"

"I'd start with Bert," she said. "He really didn't like having George around. Selfish bastard."

She walked away.

DeKoven. It didn't occur to Tess what that meant until she'd driven off the property. She was new to Santa Cruz County. But Tess had been living in Arizona long enough to have heard the name.

Jaimie Wolfe was a DeKoven?

CHAPTER 8

Tess rented a house on Harshaw Road. Harshaw Road was a poorly maintained stretch of asphalt outside Patagonia proper—a mixed population of old houses jammed together on dead-end streets, and small ranchettes.

Tess's place was just about where the houses thinned out to a few acres per landowner.

She turned left onto the one-acre lot, the Tahoe's tires rumbling across the cattle guard, and parked on the narrow lane that ended next to the house. The place needed paint. It needed a lot of things. But there was a voluptuous pistachio tree in the front yard, one of two remaining from a long-ago orchard, complete with a tire swing.

That, along with the cheap rent and the great view, was what sold her on the place.

From the deep porch (and the porch swing left by its previous residents) Tess could watch horses graze in the field across the way.

She often watched the day time-lapse away on the hill across the road, the emerald mesquites catching the last rays, the sun torching them Day-Glo green before the shadows advanced and transformed them to the color of ashes.

It was peaceful and quiet here, except when the coyotes awoke her at dawn. She liked hearing them, as long as the cat was inside.

Her house: two swings but no dryer.

The cat wasn't waiting for her at the door. Sometimes he did, sometimes he didn't; depended on his mood. It seemed to her he distrusted her ever since she'd bundled him off to the vet to be fixed.

Tess unlocked the door to the house.

The sun stole across the display case near the big window. Someone had attempted to give the picture window an arch, but this one looked like something you'd carve out of a cardboard box.

The display case made up for it. She'd bought the curved-glass and wood display case at a local antique store. It had come from a museum and cost her one whole paycheck.

Tess grew up as an only child, but her two best friends were the twin daughters who lived next door. Her mother and their neighbor, Celia, were very close too. They took the three girls—Tess, Beth, and Jennifer—to theme parks and movies. Tess learned quickly that Beth and Jennifer were well-acquainted with the term "souvenir," a word she didn't know. To the twins, it meant getting their mother to buy them something—usually something kitschy, although she noticed Jennifer held out for more expensive swag. Everywhere they went, Beth and Jennifer clamored for souvenirs. Tess caught on quickly, and did the same.

Fast-forward to her work as a homicide detective. Tess had tracked a serial killer once in her career, the hardest type of killer to find. She'd gotten lucky and made an arrest. That was all it was—luck. What she saw in his house had been expected, but Tess was not prepared for how it affected her.

The killer had kept trophies from the twelve women and girls he'd killed. A hairbrush, a pair of earrings, panties. Even one girl's asthma inhaler.

That got to her more than anything else. She could imagine the girl's fear as he choked her—a girl who knew what it was like to require air and fight for it.

That was when it occurred to her that *someone* had to mark the scoreboard for the good guys.

So every time Tess solved a case, every time a bad guy was put away, she picked out a souvenir that had some meaning to the case. *To remember them.* To remember the victims. Not as victims, but for the people they were.

Tess's souvenirs were distributed across three shelves, and placed before each of them was a card, neatly labeled. Right now there were six victims and six symbols of what had meaning for them: a baby's rattle; a rodeo buckle; a bottle of Juicy Couture perfume; a bottle of CK One cologne; a Genesis CD; and a healing crystal from the Desert Oasis Healing Center.

Her gaze lingered on the healing crystal. She thought of all the bad things that had been generated by the Desert Oasis Healing Center.

And the one good thing that came out of it.

Max Conroy.

CHAPTER 9

When Brayden got to Le Bar this evening, *he* was there, waiting for her.

Going out with her friends was supposed to be fun.

He was strange. Good-looking—really good-looking—but he was way too familiar. The way some guys are, you know the type. But this was different.

He scared her. And Brayden did not scare easily.

Her instincts were good, and alarm bells were going off.

He was a handsome guy, really, but his grin was crooked with just a hint of his teeth, little teeth. Just thinking about it sent shivers up her spine.

And he leaned too close.

Two days ago, they'd perched on stools by the long bar near the dance floor, a place that funneled the cute guys through. The place was just a zoo, tons of people. Brayden was with her two friends from college and work, Melinda and Daffy (they called Daphne

Daffy because she kind of was.) Brayden had been divorced for five months, and it was nice to get back out again in public. Nice to flirt a little.

Frankly, it would be nice to sleep with someone again, without having to share the rest of her life with them. After Justin she could go without marriage for the rest of her life.

But this guy, Steve, bothered her. It was almost as if he'd targeted her. She knew that Melinda and Daffy were hotter than she was. And better at flirting, too, because they hadn't been out of commission for seven years. So why didn't he go after Daffy, who was slim and stunning and had boobs to die for?

(They were fake.)

When he'd first stared at her across the bar, she couldn't believe it. He was absolutely gorgeous. Only when he came over to talk to her did she feel uneasy.

Really, like he was targeting her. Like a predator who wanted to eat her.

That creepy smile of his.

But it wasn't just that.

He gave her the impression he'd studied up on her. He had a familiarity with her family—at least that was how it sounded. He didn't come right out and talk about her little girl, or her ex, or her family, or what she did. But she got the idea from context that he knew stuff.

When he went off to the bathroom, she decided to grab her purse, pay her part of the tab, and get out.

The next day, he'd called her.

Mel had given him her number.

Brayden made some excuse, managed to get off the phone.

When Mel and Daffy wanted to get together tonight, she'd thought about saying no. But they were going someplace else, way on the other side of town, and while Tucson wasn't a big city, it had plenty of bars.

When she got there, he was sitting with them.

She was about to turn around and walk out when Mel saw her and waved.

His back was to her—he hadn't seen her. Brayden ignored Mel's waving and slipped into the crowd—so many people at the bar tonight—and worked her way through and out the door. Out into the cool night, the moon riding high in the sky.

Walked briskly to her car.

"Hey, Brayden!"

She kept walking. Only fifty yards or so and she would be there. She heard his footsteps quicken.

"Hey," he said, grabbing her arm. "What's the hurry?"

"I have to get home."

He got up close to her. Infringing on her space, his face looming over hers. "What's the matter? You seem spooked."

He looked puzzled, but Brayden knew his puzzlement was a fake. Like everything else about him.

"I have to go." She dug into her purse for the alarm remote. What if he accosted her here in the parking lot?

She heard him jog a couple of steps to keep up with her. His breath on her neck as he touched her arm again.

She said, "Look. I have a boyfriend—"

"No you don't." He grinned his crooked grin, his face close. "Don't you want to know where I saw you?"

"What?"

"Where I saw you."

She shook her head. "I've got to go."

"Atlanta. Ring any bells?"

Her heart seized up for a second. "That wasn't me. I don't know what you're talking about."

"Okay," he said. "I wasn't there. Maybe it wasn't you, but you know what I'm talking about." He leaned in close to her. "We have a lot to talk about."

She managed to pull away. Fumbled at the remote button, unlocked the car.

As she slid onto the seat he rested his arm on the roof. "We really should talk."

She turned the key to the ignition but it didn't seem to catch so she turned it again—the grinding clash of gears shrieked across her nerves. But the engine was running. She put the car in gear and it lurched forward. Barkman stepped back.

Brayden floored it, and watched him in the rearview mirror.

He was laughing.

CHAPTER 10

Tess at home: Feed the cat. Decide what to eat for dinner. Watch the sun set from her porch swing, watch the lights wink on in the house across the way.

Before she figured out which frozen dinner to heat up in the microwave, the phone rang.

She knew it was him even before she saw the readout.

Max said, "I miss *you*."

"I miss you."

"I miss you more."

Tess said, "God, we're annoying."

"We should live in the same place," Max said. "Then we wouldn't be annoying."

"You can move in with me. You want me to call the moving van company?"

"Sure. Can you put up the cast and crew?"

Tess looked around. The living room to her rented house was small, and the kitchen was smaller. "It'll be tight. We'd have to stack them like cordwood."

"They're used to it. The orgies."

"I forgot."

"How can you forget? Hosting orgies—it's one of my best assets."

"I thought your strong chin was your best asset."

"Nah, it's gotta be the orgies. Unless it's my entourage."

"You have an entourage?"

"Okay. I don't have an entourage. I'm down to one lonely, dorky guy—all I've got is my sidekick."

Tess smiled. By now she'd seen most of his movies. Max's characters *always* had a sidekick. All of Max's sidekicks were a little on the homely side, but lovable. She said, "Is he lovable? Does he have soulful eyes?"

"How would I know? I'm a guy."

"But he's your wingman."

"Guess you could call him that."

"Is he secretly in love with me?"

"Oh, yeah. You know the type. Guy's always moping around, just hoping to get a glimpse of you. I guess he still thinks he has a shot."

"He doesn't. Even though you don't really appreciate me the way you should, and your sidekick . . ." Tess fished around and came up with: "Marshal."

"Marshal?"

"Marshal."

"You sure?"

"That's his name."

"I would have named him Ned, but okay. *Marshal* worships you from afar. He gets to know the real you, because I'm too busy squiring famous actresses to events to notice the love of my life right under my nose."

"It's true—poor Marshal and I spend most of our downtime together."

"Meanwhile," Max said, "I go on my merry way, doing my own thing, not knowing that every day in every way I'm—"

"Breaking my heart?"

Silence.

Tess wished she hadn't said that.

Max said: *"Am* I breaking your heart?"

"No, not really. Could be I'm already beginning to forget you."

"Forget me? How is such a thing possible? I'm the leading man."

"I have the tabloids so at least I can remember what you look like."

There was another pause. He said, "I can fly out. Next week, it would have to be quick. Overnight—or you could come here."

Tess thought about Bonny, new here as undersheriff. Bringing her to Santa Cruz County with him. She was his right hand. And there would be Danny's merciless teasing. Razzed unmercifully about the "movie star." She wouldn't mind being razzed. She wanted so badly to see Max right now, this minute, but Tess also knew she had to concentrate on this case. She'd be gone long hours. She only had a limited window of opportunity on Hanley—the longer without a break there was, the more unlikely the case would ever be solved. Still, Max would be here.

Tess said, "You can't really get away, can you? You're on a schedule."

"I could call it an emergency."

"You know you can't do that."

He sighed. She knew he was thinking there was no getting away from responsibility. So many people depended on him. And she couldn't go there.

And yet the physical yearning was almost unbearable.

He said, "When can you come out here?"

"Not now."

Quiet for a moment. "We can plan for something later. We're both too busy."

"Yes."

"But it doesn't mean this won't work out," he added.

"No." She remembered how thin and pale he'd been in the hospital after the shooting. Max Conroy, star of stage and screen, kidnapped and held for ransom in her county. In Bonny's county.

And Tess had ended up in the middle of a deadly romantic triangle, trying to help a displaced movie star on the run from kidnappers and a scheming wife who would have been happy to play the part of a grieving widow.

Max had been damaged. Badly. But he had survived, and somehow they had ended up together.

Except he lived in California and she lived here, on the border between Arizona and Mexico and loneliness.

Tess remembered waiting for the paramedics. She remembered the blood. She didn't know for sure, but she'd thought that he had died. When she was alone with him for those few frantic seconds, as she tried to compress the wound.

Maybe he hadn't died. But he had been slipping away. Max heard her voice, and she still felt that this was what made the difference. She knew he believed it, too.

Sometimes she wondered if he loved her at all—or if he just felt he owed her.

He said, "I miss you."

"I miss you, too." She wanted to add that it was an almost physical pain.

They talked for a while and covered the waterfront—her case, his TV series, even beautiful Suri. Tess could tell from his voice that she was just what she always knew the woman was: his costar.

No worries.

But when she put the phone down, she was aware of the ache. It was the ache of a woman whose husband is gone, his side of the bed empty.

~

When her cell rang a moment later, Tess answered, "What did you forget?"

But it wasn't Max. "Is this Detective McCrae?"

She recognized the voice—it belonged to Steve Barkman, the guy who'd accosted her in Credo. "How did you get my number?"

His mother was a powerful judge, but Tess suspected it was somebody with Pima County Sheriff's—a noncommissioned employee with a high degree of suck-uppiness.

"I figured you're home for the day."

Tess tried not to be creeped out. "What do you want, Mr. Barkman?"

"Just wanted to talk about the Hanley case."

"I don't talk about my cases."

"Wait! Could we meet? I need to know about the shooting. I heard he was shot multiple times. Can you confirm that?"

"I'm not telling you anything pertaining to this investigation. I am going to hang up now."

"Listen, just give me verification."

Tess had second thoughts about hanging up. "What's your interest in this, Mr. Barkman?"

"I'm a concerned citizen."

Tess said, "Mr. Barkman, do you know anything about this?"

"You're not accusing me of anything, are you? Because you don't have a leg to stand on if you're trying to pull that intimidation shit."

Defensive. Angry. But underneath, she sensed he was gloating. Tess thought he knew more than he was giving away, and she guessed he wanted to show her that he was important, that he knew details about the investigation.

"Mr. Barkman, I didn't mean to come off sounding like that. I'm just curious if you have some inside knowledge about this that might be able to help us out."

"I might be willing to trade."

"Trade?"

"I'd want all the information you have on the case."

"I can't do that, Mr. Barkman. You're working for the sheriff's office in Pima County. You ought to know that I can't tell you anything. But if you have information that could help us you could—"

"If you're not going to wash my hand, I'm not washing yours. You'll regret this, but that's your choice."

And he hung up.

Tess stared at the phone. She'd memorized his number from the readout, punched in his number. Got his voice mail.

She pushed the door open and walked out onto the porch. The air was cool now that the sun was down. Cool enough for a long-sleeved shirt. She hugged herself, staring at the moon sailing above the cut-out hills.

Closing her eyes, she willed the air to stir behind her, to hear his step, to smell Max's cologne as he put his hands on her arms and put his face against her neck.

But Max was far away. In a galaxy far away, a place completely foreign to her.

A dog barked. Tess shook off the feeling of Max standing beside her, the phantom closeness that made her melt inside.

Steve Barkman figured into this somehow. Either he was taunting her about his knowledge of her case, or he was trying to pump her for information.

She brought out her laptop, and under the yellow stain of the porch light she searched for the website of the *Arizona Daily Star*. She found the article and read it through.

It was a very short piece, not even an article. More like a paragraph, and it read like a follow-up to an earlier story, probably from the previous day.

No mention of multiple gunshots.

Yet Barkman was sure Hanley had sustained massive firepower. Why?

Maybe somebody with Pima County Sheriff's Office told him. She could picture someone he worked with saying that the man found in Credo was shot up badly.

She stared at the hill across the way.

Shot multiple times.

"Why is it so important to you?" she said to the invisible Steve Barkman. But the only ones who heard her were the stray cat and the crickets and the dark.

CHAPTER 11

The next morning, Danny pulled into the parking lot the same time as Tess did.

"Autopsy results," he called out. "Including photos!" He waggled a thumb drive.

Inside, they went over the report and the photos.

The photos were gruesome.

Tess had taken many photos of George Hanley at the scene. He was only recognizable as a human being by his legs, arms, and the shape of his head.

"Look at this." Danny opened up one of the autopsy photos—George Hanley, naked on the autopsy table, his wounds cleaned up and looking as if he'd been attacked by dark red leeches. But this photo focused on Hanley's lap.

Tess had looked at and photographed the body. She'd marked evidence, but hadn't touched him. There was always a risk that her own clothing lint, her own skin or hair follicles, her own DNA, could end up on the victim, especially one as torn up as this one was.

Tess could see exactly what Hanley looked like on the floor of the cabin. She could see the crime scene techs as they took Hanley away, could run it on a reel in her mind. They almost had to scrape him off the floor of the cabin to get him into the body bag. He was a blood-soaked bag of grain. The cloth of his knit polo shirt and chinos had been enmeshed in his flesh.

So Tess had not seen then what she saw now.

His genitals were fully intact.

"That's right," Danny said. "He's still got his balls. And here's Exhibit B." Another photo of Hanley's mouth. "They didn't stuff them in his mouth."

Tess hadn't stripped away the duct tape. There was no way she could do that at the scene. But she had wondered . . .

She'd wondered, as she knew Danny had wondered, if anything had been jammed down Hanley's throat, his lips sealed by the tape after the fact.

That didn't happen.

Both Tess and Danny knew what this meant.

When it came to looking like a drug-related or cartel killing, Hanley's death had walked like a duck. It had walked like a duck, and talked like a duck.

But it wasn't a duck.

"Somebody didn't do his homework," Danny said. "They sure didn't know about the latest fashion accessory. You gotta wonder who would work so hard to make it look that way."

The focus on the case had changed. It was quite possible that whoever killed George Hanley had tried to make it look like a drug-related hit.

~

Tess and Danny attended George Hanley's funeral.

They went to pay their respects to a fallen cop—no matter how long he'd been out of the job he would always be one of them—but also to see who might show up.

The funeral was held at the Lois Maderas Memorial Park outside Nogales. The only people who attended were George Hanley's daughter Pat; her husband, Bert; and a handful of people Tess put in two categories: a couple of Hanley's neighbors at the apartment he'd been staying in, and a sprinkling of well-off people in middle age. Judging from the bumper stickers on their big SUVs, Tess pegged them as environmentally conscious members of SABEL. Jaimie Wolfe did not attend.

Tess and Danny kept an eye out for anything unusual, and chatted up the SABEL people and neighbors when they could. But they could only do so much. They had to keep it respectful—this was not the time to grill anyone. Mostly, they were here to watch and learn.

And to document with photos of the mourners—both Danny and Tess were adept at taking photos with their cell phones without their subjects being the wiser.

Before the service began, Tess walked to the main building under the pretext of using the restroom, and from there she watched the mourners.

Sometimes killers attended funerals. It was always wise for a detective to attend the funeral of the victim if he could. Some killers were loved ones—domestics were common as dirt. The bad guy came because he (or she) had to show up as part of the family.

Sometimes, they came out of guilt. There were also instances where killers came to see their handiwork—what they had wrought.

They came to gloat.

But Tess saw no unusual behavior.

It looked mostly like people attended because they either wanted to pay their respects, or they felt they had to.

She walked back to the graveside.

Pat Scofield looked as if someone had taken a baseball bat to her—stunned. Her face and eyes were red from crying. She wore thick hose with a chunky-looking dress that was years out of date. Her husband was turned out surprisingly well in a bespoke suit.

"The odd couple," Danny whispered, nodding at Pat and Bert. "Think I'll go for a walk up on that hill."

His turn to watch the mourners.

~

After the funeral, Tess asked Danny if he'd like to go with her to check out Jaimie Wolfe. Tess still hadn't gotten the list of SABEL members. She'd called Jaimie twice and left messages.

"Sure," Danny said. "I got some things I have to do—some cleanup on Roscoe, but later this afternoon, I'm available."

Roscoe was a sad story—a woman had neglected and starved her little son to death. Tess knew the case haunted Danny, what with his own firstborn coming soon.

They split up after agreeing to drive out to visit Jaimie at the end of their shift.

CHAPTER 12

The best thing about the Lois Maderas Memorial Park: the hills and windbreak of trees at the top of one of them. The shade here was dark, and he was far enough away that even a sharp-eyed cop wouldn't see him. He lay on his stomach on the grass, watching.

He didn't come to watch the mourners.

He came because he knew the cops would be there, and he wanted to see who they were.

They were easy to spot. Dressed professionally, but casual. Even if they didn't dress like cops, he would know them anywhere.

Because of what they were looking at.

They weren't watching the coffin as it was lowered into the earth.

They were looking *out*. Out at the people surrounding the grave. Their faces impassive behind dark glasses. Quiet and contained, they kept their eyes on the mourners, and now and then they scanned the surrounding hills.

He didn't use his binocs because he didn't want to catch a reflection.

The woman in particular interested him. She wore a navy jacket over a pale blouse and chino-type slacks. He could see the rectangle under her jacket on her left hip. The woman was a cop all the way. Her dark blonde hair pulled into a neat ponytail. The dark glasses. The calm around her.

And the other guy—the spic.

He was a little more restless. Full of energy. Looking for trouble. When he looked toward the hills, it was almost with X-ray vision.

The watcher knew he couldn't be seen, but still . . .

He knew that killers often showed up at funerals to gloat. Or out of nervousness, because they couldn't stay away. Maybe they were worried about some loose end, maybe they had a compulsion.

But *he* came to watch the cops watching for him.

CHAPTER 13

This time there were no girls or horses in the riding ring.

Tess stood back while Danny knocked.

It took a while, but Jaimie finally came to the door. She wore a similar outfit to the one she'd worn last time—except for the cowboy boots, which were beat up, but expensive.

"I'm busy today," Jaimie said, her voice abrupt.

"Just a couple more questions," Danny said.

"Who are you?"

Tess stepped up close to Jaimie. "This is Danny Rojas, my partner."

"Your 'partner?' With the sheriff's office? Or are you lovers?"

Danny gave her his best sexy grin. "We're negotiating on that."

Tess thought about stomping on his foot, but the moment passed.

Jaimie came out on the porch and closed the door behind her. "All right, you can ask your damn questions! I just hope it won't take long."

She seemed completely different from the way she'd been before. Last time she'd at least given the appearance of being forthcoming, and volunteered information. This time she folded her arms and stood on the porch. "What do you want to know?"

"First, I need the names of the SABEL members," Tess said.

"Fine." She walked inside and closed the door.

"You have a way with people," Danny observed.

They waited. The smell of alfalfa, horse urine, and manure drifted up to them.

A couple of minutes later, Jaimie Wolfe returned with a sheet of paper. "Names and phone numbers," she said, her voice brisk.

Only eight people on the list. Apparently eradicating buffelgrass wasn't a popular pastime around here.

"Do you have any theories as to why George Hanley moved down here?"

Jaimie shrugged. "He *said*, to be with his daughter."

"He never mentioned an additional reason to you?"

"I don't think so. Look, he wasn't crazy about his daughter, but she was related to him. There are problems in any relationship. Now if you'll excuse me, I've got things to do."

Tess said, "What did he tell you about leading the tours at Credo?"

"I think he said his grandmother grew up there, when it was a real town."

"Have you ever been there?"

"Nope. I've trailered my horses out into the Atascosas and rode some trails, but that was a long time ago. Back before things got really bad. Now I wouldn't go there if you paid me."

Tess watched the dogs, who were hanging out in the front yard with a watchful eye on Jaimie. One of them was an Australian shepherd.

"Did George bring his dog over here?"

"All the time. Is she okay?"

"She was taken to Animal Control."

Her mouth flatlined. "*That* figures! It was that stupid bitch, Pat, am I right? Anyone who'd do that to a dog after she lost her human, that's just plain evil! " She crossed her arms and glared at Tess. "I have half a mind to go get her."

"She's already been adopted."

"Well, *that's* good. At least she's got a home." Jaimie looked out at her own pack. "Adele was always welcome. She loved coming here." She nodded to the Australian shepherd. "Bandit and Adele got along great, but that's true of most dogs. Pat should have called me and I would have come and got her. She would have been a happy dog."

Tess asked her again (how many ways could you answer the question? She was about to find out) regarding George Hanley's relationship with the other people on the board of SABEL.

"He got on great with everybody. People loved him."

"Anyone who didn't?" Danny asked.

"Nope. He was just that kind of guy."

"Was there anyone he was really close to?"

"Not really."

"No one he might've rubbed the wrong way?"

"Nope."

Danny said, "Anyone else besides SABEL members who had any interaction with George that you've noticed?"

"Nope." She paused. "Except for my brother Michael—he was his financial advisor. You might want to talk to him." She started down the steps of the house. "Now if you'll excuse me, I've got six stalls to clean."

Tess remembered the notation on George Hanley's calendar. "What's his name?"

Jaimie Wolfe stopped and turned to look at them. "Michael. Michael DeKoven. He lives in Tucson—he's in the book."

~

"So what do you think?" Tess asked Danny as they drove out.

He buzzed down the passenger window of the Tahoe and rested his elbow on the door and watched the scenery fly by. "She's smooth."

"Lying?"

He shrugged. "Could be. But there's nothing I can point to."

"So, your first impression."

Danny turned to look at her, the sun bouncing off his aviator shades. "I don't think she works and plays well with others."

Tess nodded.

"I bet you could figure her out, *guera*. You know, use your X-ray vision."

"Doesn't work that way."

"I bet you remember every word she said. That would drive me nuts."

"I file most stuff away."

"What, like filing cabinets in your head?"

"Memory is selective for everybody. If I don't think about a thing, I don't think about it. Just like everyone else."

Danny said, "My wife remembers everything."

CHAPTER 14

Michael DeKoven's office was twenty-three floors up, the second level from the top of the Dystel Energy Building at One South Church in Tucson.

Tess was on her own—Danny had to testify in court on another case. As she stepped into the elevator, she was joined by a man in bicycle togs and a racing bike.

He noted that she'd hit the button for the twenty-third floor. He didn't reach past her for another.

Tess recognized him as Michael Ross DeKoven himself—the head of DeKoven Financial.

Tess knew he was thirty-five—the oldest of the four DeKoven siblings. He was youthful and athletic, with brown hair and the square jaw of a comic-book hero. Tess knew he had a wife and two children, a boy and a girl. His wife was a little younger but not by much, and she had worked as a financial advisor at DeKoven Financial.

As she stepped in, Tess was aware he was watching her out of the corner of his eye. They both watched the floor numbers change.

Finally, he said, "Are you the lady detective?"

Tess smiled at him. "That's right."

"And remind me, why are we meeting today?"

"I wanted to ask you about George Hanley."

"George Hanley?"

"He worked with your sister, Jaimie Wolfe, on SABEL. An older gentleman."

"Oh, I think I remember him—vaguely. He was the one that was killed? The old man?"

"That's right. Jaimie said he was your client."

"No, actually, he wasn't." He cleared his throat and looked up at the numbers. Tess could feel the tension between them. It was almost as if he were hoping she'd disappear if he ignored her.

Fat chance of that.

The elevator dinged. The door opened onto an opulent office.

Michael DeKoven said, "I need to shower and change. Can you wait?"

"Sure I can."

"Because if you're busy . . ."

"No. This is Number One Hit on my Hit Parade."

He smiled. "See you in two shakes, then."

Tess waited.

And waited.

She knew all about waiting people out. She did it all the time in interviews. Sometimes it psyched people out and sometimes it didn't. She appreciated the man's willingness to try something like this. She guessed he did it a lot—a power play.

Tess didn't plan to ask him anything major. She wanted to know a little about Hanley's finances. But he'd scotched that in the elevator.

She also wanted to find out more about the DeKovens, to get a better handle on Jaimie DeKoven. Their star had faded in recent years, but the family was still important to this part of the country. Tess was new to southern Arizona, but she liked history. She'd been reading up on Tucson and its past, and the DeKovens were a big part of that.

Tess knew these were powerful people, and any place she was, she liked to check in with powerful people.

Because things happened around them.

She noticed a watercolor behind the desk, well lit and beautifully framed. Walked over to get a closer look.

"I see you noticed my new purchase," a voice came from behind her: Michael DeKoven all spiffed up. He spiffed up good. A handsome man.

"Charles Russell?" she said.

"Good eye."

Tess did have a good eye—she'd noted the signature.

"It's an original Russell—I just bought it at the Scottsdale auction. A hundred and twenty thousand dollars. Beautiful, isn't it?"

Tess had to get used to people who not only put a financial value on everything, but stated it outright. Was it insecurity? Or just pride?

"'Counting Coup,'" DeKoven added. "It was quite a battle to get this piece, but I won in the end. Do you like it?"

"Yes."

"I buy a lot of Russell and Remington. They speak to me. I was raised in the Southwest where a lot of these struggles happened—

lots of struggle. The Apache wars, Geronimo . . . my family was a big part of the taming of this area, so historical paintings from that era have always held an attraction for me. My great-great-great-grandfather was the first to operate a cattle ranch in the Rincon Valley. He helped build this state." DeKoven sat down behind his massive desk. "What did you want again?"

"George Hanley?"

He laughed. "Oh, I can't tell you much. I only met him, I think, once or twice."

"Just a few questions," Tess murmured, "and I'll be out of your hair."

"I don't know if I can be helpful at all." His tone diffident. "You know, I meet a lot of people."

"But he came to you for financial advice?"

"As I recall, we had a meeting. I told him what I thought he should do, that I'd be happy to look into his finances in depth if he wanted me to. We talked about how he could make that money work for him instead of letting a lot of it go to Uncle Sam. Although in the general scheme of things, it wasn't much money at all. I was worried that he might not have enough to see him all the way through retirement." He paused. "But I guess that's not an issue now."

Tess didn't like the way he said that. It was just a toss-off remark, but it sounded inappropriate coming from DeKoven's mouth.

"So that's the extent of my involvement with Mr. Hanley." DeKoven stood up and reached out his hand. Manicured nails, expensive watch, and a handsome wedding ring.

His voice was hearty. "Other than talking to him at a few of Jaimie's meet-and-greets, that's about the extent of it. I hope this has been helpful."

Tess read it as, *I hope I haven't been the least bit helpful.*

She was being dismissed. That pissed her off, so she stayed put. "Did Mr. Hanley ever mention problems with his son-in-law?"

He blinked. Tess could tell he was surprised that she was still here. "No . . . not that I can remember. We didn't really talk."

"What about his daughter?"

"No."

DeKoven didn't look so handsome anymore. He looked put out. He'd cued the music and was waiting for her to take the hint and hustle offstage, and so far she'd proved to be dense.

Tess said, "Do you know a man named Steve Barkman?"

She saw something in his eyes. Which was new, because there'd been nothing there during the whole interview.

"Barkman . . . Judge Rees's son? I've heard of him but I don't believe I've had the pleasure. Why?"

"He was in Credo," Tess said. "I got the feeling he was interested in George Hanley's death. He mentioned you." Lying was an important tool in the homicide detective's toolbox.

For an instant, Tess saw something new cross DeKoven's face. She couldn't read it. Then his expression smoothed back to bland. "He mentioned me? I'm flattered."

Tess waited.

"What did he say?"

She shrugged. "Just that he knew you."

Michael DeKoven didn't take the bait. He smiled broadly and held out his hand for her to shake. "This has all been very interesting. I'm sorry I couldn't help you out. Now if you'll excuse me, I have an appointment I'm late for."

The official term for this in the detective's handbook was "the bum's rush."

~

Tess sat in the car in the parking lot with the air running. She felt shopworn and vaguely greasy having just talked to Mr. DeKoven.

She looked the family up on her laptop.

There were four children—two boys and two girls. Their father had died a few years ago in a plane crash, leaving them a massive fortune. (At least that was what she read.) Tess managed to find a photo of the pioneering family in happier times, when the kids were young and the mother, Eloise, was still alive. The photo was of a ribbon-cutting ceremony for a water treatment plant in the desert south of Tucson, to be built by DeKoven Construction. It was a sunny day, everyone shading their eyes and staring into the camera, the whole brood. A big day for DeKoven Construction. The patriarch of the family, Quentin DeKoven, looked both proud and grim, as if he had just finished climbing Mt. Everest and had some time to gloat. He stood apart from his wife and children.

The mother, Eloise, had a bland expression. Tess sensed discontent there. The girls wore shorts and tops. Jaimie looked thin and bored. The younger sister, Brayden, was a little shorter and a little plumper. She had a sweet expression. Her hair was blonde, lightened by the sun. Michael looked like the teenage version of what he was now.

Tess tried to think of a word for it. Disconnected, maybe? As if he were watching a play, but not participating. Removed.

Except when she mentioned Steve Barkman. That had wiped the self-satisfied smirk off his face.

She squinted at the photograph. The fourth child was the younger son: Chad. He looked slightly down and away from the camera. Tess got the impression that the boy didn't want to be there, which would fit with his age—he was just starting his teen years. But the biggest impression she got from him was passivity.

No so with Michael. Michael gave her the impression of smoothness. Smoothness and distance.

Except when she'd mentioned Steve Barkman.

CHAPTER 15

Tucson, Arizona

Irene Contreras had the key to Steve Barkman's house.

His place was on a little patch of desert, which could be reached off Ft. Lowell Road, not far from El Fuerte across Craycroft—the old army post ruins at Fort Lowell Park.

Her granddaughter played soccer there.

The dirt lane off Ft. Lowell Road meandered through creosote desert and ended up at a brick house built in the sixties. Irene knew the house was from the sixties because her father had worked for Beauty Built Homes, building houses just like this one.

Irene once was the secretary for a construction company for over twenty years, but times were tough and she'd lost her job, so now she worked for a cleaning service, Happy Maids. She wasn't all that happy, because she'd loved her old job and this was a lot more work and hard on her back, but the nice thing was, she lived only five minutes away from Mr. Barkman's, and he was on her regular schedule.

She pulled up behind his SUV, got the cleaning caddy from the hatchback of the Happy Maids car, and crunched up the lane to the house.

When she pushed the door open, she caught a whiff of something spoiled. Meat, maybe? Or fruit or vegetables that had turned?

But the stronger smell was alcohol. She was used to that. Mr. Barkman liked his bourbon and his beer. She'd had to put enough of the bottles in the recycle bin.

The room was dark, the blinds drawn.

But even before her eyes adjusted, she knew something was wrong.

It took a moment for Irene to make sense of the scene. Her first thought was that someone had shoved a massive tree stump through the living room coffee table.

Only, tree stumps didn't bleed.

CHAPTER 16

Alec Sheppard pitched headfirst out of the Twin Otter, the wash of the propeller blasting him in the direction of the plane's tail—free-falling in a perfect no-lift dive, spinning away and down like a drill bit. Pure joy in what he could do.

He threw out the pilot chute to deploy the main canopy and started counting down. One thousand one, two thousand one, three thousand one—three seconds to deployment. Kept his eyes forward as he counted. Alec had been trained to look straight ahead, and in all his jumps—he was coming up on a 125—he'd never broken faith with this most important tenet.

There was a reason for this.

Looking at the ground could stop the thinking process cold. It could lock up your brain function and bring home the very real prospect of mortality at the exact moment when you needed all your wits. You never wanted to be mesmerized by ground rush.

When he reached "three thousand one," he looked up.

He already knew what he would see—his main canopy hadn't deployed.

But he had options.

Plan A: Because his legs and arms were spread out, he might have created a "burble," a vacuum pocket flat on his back, which would keep the main canopy from deploying.

So he dipped his right shoulder.

Nothing changed.

He dipped his left shoulder. The canopy still didn't deploy.

Okay: Plan B. Pull the reserve.

He pulled the ripcord on his reserve canopy.

There was no response. He reached back again and felt along the brake cable—he'd have to manually find the pin that would release his reserve chute. He started stripping the cable with both hands, pulling, pulling, pulling—

Something sharp sliced into his index finger.

A thrill went through him. The pain—but also, the first ripple of fear.

He was now at twelve hundred feet.

He had time . . . maybe five seconds.

Alec went back to pulling on the cable, rooting around inside the reserve rig, going deep—and sliced his finger again. Adrenaline shot through him a second time, leaving his extremities momentarily weak.

The cable had been sheared in half.

That was when the image floated before him: the man in the SkyView Café Starbucks.

Pointing the finger gun at him.

Pointing the finger gun.

Don't panic.

No time for troubleshooting. He'd tried Plan A and Plan B. All he could do now was keep on with Plan B.

Once again he reached around with both hands and tried to get to the reserve pin inside the rig. He clawed and dug around in the pouch, stretching his arms to the breaking point, squeezed and pinched and pounded and scrabbled, slicing his fingers on the shorn cable strands, trying like hell to find the damn pin and pull it out. Any minute he'd get to it. Any minute, but all the while he was counting down the seconds, like a news crawl running through his head. One thousand feet, nine hundred feet, eight hundred—

His back was arched. His arms were straining. His neck was tired. His fingers and hands were slippery with blood—cut to ribbons.

He looked down.

The ground rushed up, faster and faster. Ants became people, and then people became people-with-horrified-faces. He was going in undeployed—again.

Six hundred feet.

He forced his eyes back up to level. He wasn't done yet. Pulling, shoving, hitting, grabbing, shaking the reserve rig—he'd go down fighting. But at the same time as he fought to save himself, Alec could feel his mind shift into pure acceptance mode.

I'm going to die.

No way he'd survive something like this twice.

The twenty-third psalm flitted through his mind—"Yea though I walk through the Valley of the Shadow of Death I will fear no evil—"

Because I'm the Craziest SOB on God's Green Earth. That was the saying.

But this time it was different.

Evil was the exact thing he feared.

~

Alec awoke to the ringing of the phone. It took him a moment to swim out of his dream and realize where he was: Tucson, Arizona.

The last thing he'd seen before waking was something dark hurtling from above slamming into him—hard.

But the image that stuck with him when his parachute didn't open wasn't the shattering memory of the disastrous free fall into the slough in Florida, which left him with a fractured pelvis, splintered ribs, a broken collarbone, and a stopped heart.

No. This time when his canopy didn't deploy, Alec Sheppard saw the face of a stranger.

The stranger was a good-looking man, about Alec's age, mid-to-late thirties. He wore a jumpsuit. He was about to jump, or he'd already jumped. He sat at one of the café tables at the SkyView Jump Center, a cup of Starbucks coffee on the round table in front of him. The man appeared to recognize him; his eyes lit up and a smile played on his lips. Alec had never seen him before—at least he didn't think so, but he'd jumped a lot of places and interacted with a host of people he'd never meet again.

What puzzled him was the thing the man did next. He pointed his finger at Alec, like he was shooting a gun.

~

Sun streamed through the sheer outer drapes of the hotel's window.

Alec had beaten the Reaper twice. The second time he'd literally landed on his feet—no injuries at all.

As he reached across the hotel bed for the phone, he thought about the man at the SkyView Café in Houston. The man who shot the finger gun at him right before he jumped three weeks ago in Houston might have been the same guy as the jogger on the roof in Atlanta last September.

Both of them were strangers. Both of them had targeted him. The jogger with the red tag had smacked him on the chest. The other guy had sabotaged his rig or found someone to do it for him. The cables to both the main canopy and the reserve canopy had been cut.

The phone stopped ringing. It was probably Steve, calling to remind him about their breakfast downstairs in the hotel restaurant.

Alec turned on the TV, still thinking about the guy who had plastered the red tape with the number five to his chest. He hadn't been hurt, but it did qualify as an assault.

And the other guy. The Starbucks Guy, as Alec had come to think of him. Sitting there with that strange smile on his face, shooting the finger gun at Alec approximately thirty minutes before he almost fell to his death. If the jump master hadn't been able to pull the ripcord on Alec's reserve canopy at the last possible moment, he would have cratered again. As it was, he'd landed unscathed.

Alec took a shower, dressed, and called Steve, but got his voice mail. Looked at his watch.

A half hour later, he left the room and took the elevator down to the restaurant.

Steve was a no-show.

Alec called Steve again, and once again, got his voice mail. He left another message and ordered breakfast.

He ate alone.

After breakfast, Alec called again. He left another message. He tried not to sound annoyed. A half hour later, just as he was headed for the hotel gym, he got a call from a number he didn't recognize.

Alec answered—he had a bad feeling. "Hello?"

"My name is Detective Sergeant Dave White of the Tucson Police Department. Would you mind telling me why you've been trying to reach Steve Barkman?"

CHAPTER 17

Tess was halfway back to Nogales when she got the news.

By coincidence, she'd been asking a friend of hers, Terry Braithwate, with the Pima County Sheriff's Office, about Steve Barkman.

"Just a minute," Braithwate said. "You won't believe this."

Tess could hear the scanner in the background—Braithwate was monitoring the TPD frequencies.

"Small world—there's a possible 01-01 at 5425A East Ft. Lowell Road."

Possible homicide.

Tess heard it, and knew immediately. "That's Steve Barkman's residence."

"Jesus." A click of computer keys. "I'm looking . . . oh, I didn't know that. The place is officially owned by his mother—Geneva Rees."

"So what's the nature of the 01-01? Do they know?"

"Still trying to figure it out."

"But the deceased is . . ."

"Let me check—hold on." He came back on a moment later. "Shit. It *is* Steve."

"They don't know if it's a homicide?" Tess said.

"Not yet. Ds are at the scene though."

Tess got off the horn with Braithwate and called Danny.

"Barkman? The guy you had to apologize to?"

"Yeah." Tess told him how Barkman had seemed to be obsessed with George Hanley's death.

"There might be something there," Danny said.

Tess said, "I'm going back."

"Hey, *guera*—I'll meet you there."

There he goes with the white girl comment again.

Sometimes it was such a pain in the ass to be Anglo.

Tess parked on Ft. Lowell Road. The dirt road into Barkman's mother's property was jammed with vehicles. She saw four TPD units—one of them a D car and another belonging to a detective sergeant—and a crime scene unit, TV satellite truck, and a regular TPD unit. All of which were parked either in the long driveway or along the side of the semirural stretch of road.

She waited for Danny. When he appeared, they walked toward the property.

The officer guarding the crime scene tape looked like he'd give them trouble, and he did.

Danny badged him. "We have an ongoing investigation involving Mr. Barkman—"

"Nobody can come in here."

Tess glanced at the crowd beyond the tape and spotted a woman with a blonde ponytail in conversation with a crime scene tech and another detective. She wore a long-sleeved blouse, tan slacks, her weapon in plain sight, and most important, a silver shield clipped to her belt.

"Cheryl Tedesco!" Tess called out.

Cheryl Tedesco looked up, shading her eyes against the bright Arizona sun. She detached herself from the group. "Tess! Holy cow, girl! What're you doing here?"

Tess introduced her partner. "We think your case links with ours."

"I'm all ears." Cheryl lifted the tape, and Tess and Danny ducked under. "Tell me what you've got."

Three months ago, Tess and Cheryl had roomed together at an interrogation methods course in Lake Havasu City. Not only did they hit it off right away, but they shared an experience that bonded them. On their way to dinner the first night, they witnessed a car accident that nearly wiped them out and did knock down a pedestrian. Fortunately, the pedestrian survived with cuts and bruises, but the driver had to be cut out of her car. The woman was in a panic, because her dog was in a crate on the backseat. Tess and Cheryl took turns directing traffic and placating the woman as they waited for the paramedics. Between them, they were able to get the small dog carrier out and show the woman her pet was all right. This enabled her to calm down and cooperate, and eventually she was freed of the wreckage. She only went off to the hospital after they promised her the dog would be taken care of. And a day later, the woman and her dog were reunited.

Tess admired the efficient way Cheryl handled triage, the calmness with which she directed traffic and talked the panicked driver down. Maybe because Tess hoped that what she saw in Cheryl, she saw in herself.

"So what's your interest in Barkman?" Cheryl asked.

"He was very curious about a case I'm working." Tess told her about George Hanley, and about Barkman's seeming obsession with the idea Hanley had been shot multiple times.

Cheryl looked mildly skeptical, and Tess didn't blame her. It was a tenuous link. "Tell you what. I have to get back in there, but I'll see who can brief you." She scanned the group behind her. "Manuel—can you come here?"

A detective left the group and approached them. Cheryl introduced them and said, "Catch them up on what we've got, will ya? I'll be back in a bit."

The sun was high in the sky by now and hot, even for April.

Manuel hitched his trousers. "The victim fell through a glass-topped coffee table headfirst. What it looks like, he was in the process of changing a light bulb in the ceiling fan—there was one of those short stepladders like you'd use? He could've slipped and fell and hit the coffee table with his head, which is what it looks like he did. And his head went right through the glass. We think he bled to death."

Tess stared at him, tried to assimilate this.

Danny said, "You saying it was an accident?"

"We don't know. But it looks that way."

"Man, that's a weird one," Danny said. "Talk about a freak accident." He added, "If that's what it is."

Tess asked, "The ceiling fan was close to the coffee table? Close enough—"

"That he could take a header into the coffee table?" Danny finished helpfully.

"We're trying to figure that out now."

"Can we get in to see the scene?"

"I don't know—"

"Hey!" It was Cheryl, walking toward them. "Thanks, Manny. All right, here's the deal. I can slip you in to take a look, but it'll have to be quick, okay?"

She went to the trunk of her car and handed out blue booties and gloves.

They went up to the house. A thick-trunked eucalyptus tree towered above the flat roof of the brick ranch. The desert around here was basically untouched, populated by creosote bushes and a few mesquite. A bank of vertical windows framed by posts from roof to foundation looked out on the carport. The carport was just a pad of concrete with a ramada covering above. Tess recognized the Range Rover parked on the pad.

Cheryl passed around the Vicks VapoRub.

Tess dabbed some in her nostrils. It would help, but if the smell was bad, it wouldn't help a lot.

The door was open and the crime scene techs were already working the scene.

Tess wasn't prepared for the carnage.

Steve Barkman had been driven by his own weight nose-first into the coffee table, shattering the glass. One shard had pierced his eye. His face had stopped five inches from the floor, and blood collected on the slope of his nose and then dripped and spattered on the Saltillo tile below.

His neck and spine had accordioned into the table—part of the force that drove his head through the glass—and the forward momentum of his torso had been stopped instantly in an awkward sprawl. He'd tried to avoid his fate by throwing out his hands, but it was too late.

He wore shorts and a T-shirt, similar to those he'd worn when Tess had met him in Credo.

It seemed like a hundred years ago.

She looked around. There was the aluminum stepladder, three to four feet tall. It had fallen to the floor. Iridescent orange paint circled the broken light bulb lying on the tile. Above, Tess saw the empty socket for the light. Barkman must have set the light globe on the coffee table; now it lay on the floor, one side broken open.

Tess kept her hands under her arms and stared at the body and the environs.

The television was on. She looked at Cheryl.

Cheryl said, "The maid said he always had the television on."

Tess saw the logo on the bottom right-hand corner of the screen. Fox News.

"You seen enough?" Cheryl asked. "We haven't even got a body temp yet. We're gonna have to clear out and let the techs get to work."

Outside, the sun shone down on them, a mockingbird sang in a tree nearby, and the air smelled like fresh laundered clothing on the line—a memory from her childhood. It smelled like spring.

But the death smell lurked underneath. It sat in the membranes of her nose and lay at the back of her soft palate.

It happened at every death scene. Tess carried the residue on her, like a thin film of dust mixed with sweat, just gritty enough to stay on her clothes and her hands. She knew this was her imagination, but it didn't stop the odor from taking up inside her, from clinging to her pores.

Tess thought it was the price she paid to do the work she did. It was something she took from the crime scene, a part of people who had lost their lives. And it resonated for a while.

A physical manifestation of a respect for the dead.

Like a mortuary that knew part of its job was to comfort the survivors, speaking in low, respectful tones, the flowers beautiful but not glamorous, the music lovely but muted.

Just part of her job.

"So what do you think?" she asked.

"Everyone's thinking—not just me—that it looks like an accident. Anything out of place other than what we saw?"

"Let's wait for the techs to finish with the body and then we can go back in."

It took about an hour, and finally Steve Barkman was on his way to the morgue.

Inside, they looked around. The place was pretty neat. There was a plate in the sink that had been rinsed, and a bottle of beer out.

"He drank about half," Cheryl said. "We'll submit it for DNA."

"No other glass, no other beer?"

"No." Cheryl pulled out a plastic tub from below the sink. "There were several bottles of Rolling Rock and an empty of Jack Daniel's. Have no idea what the timeline for that will be. We'll draw blood."

Tess glanced around the place. There was a laptop, which TPD would put into evidence, and a printer.

Danny looked at the printer. "Hey, he's got all the bells and whistles."

Tess came over. The printer was older—a Hewlett-Packard Office Pro L7780.

"Wow, lots of features on this baby."

"What do you mean?" Tess asked.

"Look at this—space for a whole bunch of micro card slots—anything you want. Wonder if he's a photographer."

"We've been all over this place," Cheryl said. "He doesn't have a camera."

"Not even a digital one?"

"Nope."

"Huh." Danny shook his head. "Sure is a lot of space." He shrugged. "Have you checked his phone?"

"They did. I don't remember them saying anything about a micro SD in there, but I'll ask."

"Maybe the laptop will tell the tale."

Cheryl said, "If there's a tale to tell."

～

As Tess and Danny came back outside, someone called out to them. "Excuse me, could I talk to you a minute?"

Tess looked in the direction of the voice and saw a man approaching them from the road.

Danny said, "Hey, man, we're not—"

"A minute's all I ask."

The guy was in his midthirties. By the way he walked, and the expression on his face, Tess discarded the notion that he was just a spectator. She tried to file him somewhere. He could be with another law enforcement agency, or he could be a reporter. He had no credentials that she could see. She glanced at Danny.

The man reached them. He was dressed casually—Docker-type slacks and a short-sleeved shirt. Casual or not, the clothes were several cuts above Macy's. He had brown hair, was tanned and fit. Tess couldn't see his eyes because he wore aviator shades.

"I'm Alec Sheppard," he said, holding out his hand to Tess and then to Danny.

The guy had a way of taking over. It was subtle, but Tess knew it when she saw it. Not overbearing. He was used to starting the conversation and setting the tone—she guessed he was successful in whatever endeavor he pursued.

"Are you with homicide?" he asked.

"We're homicide," Danny said, "But with Santa Cruz County."

Tess thought her partner sounded eager to please.

This guy Sheppard had a way of making you want to talk to him.

"Maybe you could help me anyway. Do you know what happened to Steve Barkman? This *is* a homicide scene?"

Tess said, "What's your interest in this, Mr. Sheppard? Are you related to Mr. Barkman?"

"No. We're friends. He was doing a job for me, and now I'm wondering if it got him killed."

CHAPTER 18

Tess and Danny sat in on the interview at the Tucson Police Department midtown substation. The substation was located near the Reid Park Zoo—Tess thought this was appropriate, considering the many strange people who found themselves under the bank of fluorescent lights and in trouble. Cheryl Tedesco found a room big enough for the four of them. She rounded up sodas, water, and coffee and sat Alec Sheppard down at the postage-stamp table. Tess and Danny were strictly observers.

After her introduction on the tape recorder, Cheryl got down to it. "You told us that Steve Barkman was working for you?"

"Not officially. He was looking into something for me."

"But you paid him?"

"I did, yes. I paid him expenses, and sent him some money for his time."

"What was he looking into?"

"It's a little hard to explain." Sheppard was one of the few people who didn't look washed out like aged cheese under the fluorescent lights. "This is going to sound outlandish. Steve was looking into an incident that happened to me a couple of weeks ago."

"This was a job he was doing for you?"

"He wanted to do it as a favor to me, but I thought he should be paid."

"Why would he do that?"

"We were roommates at the University of Arizona. A long time ago."

"What work did he do?"

"He was looking for someone for me."

"And who was he looking for?"

"He didn't say."

Tess tried not to react. She kept her face bland. Now Barkman was dead and the lead he was following might be dead with him. "Why didn't he say?"

"He told me he wanted to be sure first."

"And that's why you're here?"

"I wanted to see for myself if the person Steve was tracking was the guy I saw last month on a jump."

"On a jump? What do you mean by 'on a jump?'"

"I'm a skydiver."

"And this guy Barkman is tracking, he's also a skydiver?"

"I don't know."

"But you said you met him on a jump."

"It's a long story."

~

It was going on five p.m. and the sun was lowering in the sky when Tess and Danny walked out to the parking lot.

Danny said, "So this guy Sheppard comes here because Steve Barkman has a hot tip on a guy who aimed his finger at him?"

"The guy aimed his finger at him right before he jumped out of a plane and his chute didn't open. I can see why he'd come here."

"You believe the guy."

"What does he have to gain?"

"Hey, *guera*, if you don't know . . ."

Tess knew what Danny was talking about: people who liked to attach themselves to investigations, who got a vicarious thrill from being in on what the police were doing. "He doesn't strike me that way, Dan."

Danny mumbled something.

"What did you say?"

"Guy bothers me, is all. What about this bullshit about a jogger putting a sticker on his chest?"

Tess had to admit that bothered her, as well. What an outlandish claim.

"If this is true," Danny said, "it shoots the hell out of the freak accident theory. It could be the guy who threatened Sheppard—and I use the term 'threatened' loosely—might have objected to Barkman finding him, In a big way."

"I think Cheryl's going to look at Barkman in a whole new light."

"Barkman's death was a homicide staged to look like an accident?"

"Could have been a smart move," Tess said. "The way it looked, we spent a lot of our time concentrating on how freaky it was." She stood by her car, which she'd managed to park near the shade of a eucalyptus tree. "It could have happened like this. Someone was there, hanging out with him, having a beer, and noticed the light was out."

Danny nodded. "Yeah. So. Whoever it was—and now maybe we'll never know—pointed it out to him. Like: hey, your light's out. And while he's up on the ladder, the guy kicked it out from under him. But how'd this guy know falling into the coffee table would kill him?"

"Maybe Barkman hit hard and while he was out—"

"Or at least disoriented."

"They helped him along."

Tess knew they were thinking about the same thing: the shard of glass that went straight through Barkman's eye and into his brain.

～

After Danny drove out, Tess waited a while. She watched some joggers follow the path at Reid Park, enjoying the smell of the sprinklers on the grass at the golf course.

When Alec Sheppard came out of the substation, Tess walked over to see if he'd like to go out for a drink.

They met at a bar called Badwater on Fourth Avenue. It wasn't far from the Marriott where Alec was staying, and he told her it brought back memories of his college days. By now the sun was almost down. They sat outside at a picnic table under the lights, surrounded by a kite-string of moths. There was a lot of babble of beer-drinking patrons, but not so loud they couldn't talk.

Cheryl Tedesco had been thorough, but Tess wanted to go over it again, in case there was a revelation she might be missing.

After some small talk, how he'd liked the U of A, what he did for a living—he'd run a company that had specialized in oil cleanup in the Gulf—Tess said, "You said Steve Barkman worked for you. But he didn't give you a report?"

"No. He'd only been looking into it for a few days."

"How many days?"

"Four? Five. Five days."

"Did you talk to him during that time?"

"I thought we went all over this before."

"Bear with me. What did he say?"

"He said he thought there was a connection."

"What kind of connection?"

"He didn't say. But he recognized him. He wanted to be careful because the guy had money, and he didn't want to get in the middle of a lawsuit. Maybe he was worried about defamation of character."

Tess said, "Could you wait a minute? I'll be back."

"Sure."

Tess left him and headed for her car. She'd put a copy of *Tucson Lifestyle* magazine in the murder book, which now resided in her briefcase under the front seat of the Tahoe. In a perfect world, she'd have other, similar photos of men the same age to go with it. But who was she kidding? It wasn't a perfect world.

Back at the bar, Tess handed Alec the magazine. "Would you mind looking through it?"

There was a question in his eyes, but she just nodded at the magazine. "Just flip through it."

He stopped where she expected him to stop.

Looked up at her, his face grim.

"That's him."

"The man you saw at the jump center?"

"That's him."

"Had you met him before?"

"I don't think so. But I meet a lot of people. I can't say I'm absolutely sure about that. But Steve knows—knew him."

Tess remembered at DeKoven's office, the look on Michael DeKoven's face when she mentioned Steve Barkman. She wondered if Barkman had made contact with him by then. "What did Barkman say about the guy he was investigating?"

"He said something about pulling the surveillance tape at the center." He added, "Wish I'd thought of that."

"But he didn't tell you who it was."

"He wanted to be sure."

"But you were surprised whoever it was lived in Tucson?"

"A little. It's been a few years since I got my degree. Maybe he knew me from a jump. At the time I chalked it up to making an enemy here somewhere along the line, and maybe that's what happened—could have been when I was jumping at SkyDive Arizona in Eloy. Skydivers live in a small world. We're always running into each other."

"Can you think of anything that might have made the guy go off on you like that?"

He stared into space, thinking. Shook his head. "No, I can't. But he looked at me like he knew me. When he pointed the finger gun at me, he acted like it was a big joke. No, that's not right."

"Not a joke?"

"It was a joke, but it was a mean joke. It was . . . I guess the closest thing I can describe it to is celebrating in the end zone."

"Why do you think he did that?"

"If he found a way to sabotage my rig, then I think he did it because he knew he could."

"You mean if you were killed."

"Yeah. No one would ever know."

Tess noticed that he seemed to take the idea of being killed in stride. "If it's true, he really screwed up."

He grinned. "I guess I'm just naturally a survivor."

Tess said, "There's no doubt your rig was sabotaged?"

"None. My reserve rig was up for repacking—I wouldn't be allowed to jump without having it done. Every hundred and twenty days the rigger has to repack the reserve. It's a safety issue."

"You think DeKoven bribed the rigger?"

He sat back. "He didn't have to. Since it's a long wait, the owner of the rig doesn't usually stick around, so all the guy who wants to sabotage the pack has to do is wait until no one's watching, find the rig he's looking for, and cut the cables."

"It's that simple?"

"Oh, yeah. He could pretend the pack is his and he's checking it—all he'd have to do is lift the flap to the cable housing and cut the cables with wire cutters—the cables to the main canopy and the reserve canopy. No one would ever see it. The pack is sealed with a red cord and a lead seal. Extremely doubtful the pack's owner would recheck it. There'd be no reason to. *I* sure didn't."

The band, a local group called the Blasphemers—they were loud and pretty good—struck up, and it was hard to talk for a while. Finally they took a break.

Tess asked him, "Did you ever meet Jaimie DeKoven?" Michael DeKoven went to Stanford, following in the footsteps of his father, but his little sister Jaimie spent a couple of semesters at the U of A.

"Who's that—a sister? No, I don't remember her. I don't remember anyone by that name." He grinned. It was an attractive grin. "I met a lot of girls in college."

"I'm sure."

"Did you go to college? Can you remember every guy you ever met, or even dated?"

"Nope. Not a one of 'em," Tess lied.

Unfortunately, she remembered every single one of them. She'd pushed them to the back of the file cabinet and let the cobwebs grow. She said, "Tell me again about the tagger."

He ran down the facts. His jog on the roof of the Hilton Atlanta. The sinking sun in his eyes, the jogger coming toward him and slapping the tag on him.

"You didn't get a good look at him?"

"He wore a hoodie. And I was looking right into the sunset. It was just a shape, just a jogger—I didn't pay any attention until he smacked me in the chest."

"And you went after him."

"Eventually, but he got a head start."

"Height?"

"Shorter than me."

"Sex?"

"We've been through this. It was dark, hard to tell, what he was wearing—a jogging suit with a hoodie."

"I was hoping the beer goggles would help." She glanced at the half-full beer glass at his elbow. "Quick—height."

"Shorter than me."

"You're six foot one, two?"

"Two. I'd say, *maybe*, five eleven."

"Build?"

"Slight. A jogger, or maybe more like a long-distance runner."

"Do you think the tagging and incident in Houston are related?"

Sheppard hesitated. Then he said, "It had the same kind of feeling."

"What feeling?"

"Like the joke was on me."

Tess asked about the tag.

"I threw it away. I thought it was just some stupid punk playing a prank."

"It had the number five on it?"

"Yeah, but they could have gotten that anywhere. I saw it kind of like tagging, like graffiti. Only I was the surface instead of a wall."

"You were assaulted."

"Yes."

"You said it was like tagging. But you know what it makes me think of? Wilding."

He thought about it. "But those are bands of kids, right? And they don't just stop at assaulting somebody. They've killed people. So you think it was random. Some kid showing off for his friends? That I was just in the wrong place at the wrong time?"

"Could be. Anything else you can remember?"

Sheppard looked inward. She could see him trying to come up with something. When you tried, it usually didn't work. But then he shifted his gaze to her, and if he'd been a slot machine he would have rolled three sevens.

"The shoes," he said. "They were expensive. Athletic shoes."

Tess thought: *So the kid had money.*

If it was a kid.

CHAPTER 19

Michael DeKoven had fallen asleep with the light on. He awoke at midnight beside his lover. Martin had crawled in under the sheets and was kissing his neck.

They made love. First urgently. Then slowly.

Martin was a model for those underwear ads they had in *GQ* and *Esquire*. He had the sleek but muscled tanned body that shimmered under the lights, perfect against the tight white underwear he wore while posing by swimming pools or against the sand, often with an equally disinterested female model.

Michael called Martin his "Tighty-Whitey," in reference to the underwear—and other things.

Martin cradled Michael in his arms and said, "How'd your day go?"

"A man was murdered today."

"Anyone we know?"

"An acquaintance. But I wouldn't be surprised if they're going to question me."

"*You?* Why?"

Michael shrugged. "It's a high-profile case, and I've had dealings with the guy."

"Well. I'm sure you'll pass with flying colors." Michael said nothing.

"Are you worried about this? If the detective is rude, I'll—I'll slit his throat. How about that?"

"That's a little extreme." Martin was always threatening violence against anyone who might hurt Michael. Which was ridiculous. Michael doubted Martin had a violent bone in his body. It was all swagger. But it was cute.

Michael was the one who pushed the limits. Now he said, "Look, I've got everything under control. You can be a little too protective—and we only have until this afternoon."

Martin would be winging his way back to New York for another shoot. They saw each other less and less, and to be honest, Michael preferred it that way. The few times a year they were together, it consumed them both. It left Michael sated but also drained. His thinking was less sharp. And he couldn't afford to make a mistake, not even on a micro level.

Sometimes, too, Michael's dark side took over, and things got . . . out of hand.

He always felt bad afterward. But while Martin would act hurt and betrayed for a while, he always came back for more.

It was as if he hated himself for some reason, and felt he deserved punishment. He'd once said to Michael that he had always wanted to be someone's slave.

They made love and then shared a breakfast out by the pool. Michael's wife was, as usual, nowhere in evidence. She didn't mind his dalliance with Martin, because they weren't really a couple any-more anyway.

She said he kept too many secrets.

Martin bit into a strawberry and stretched his long, tanned legs out on the flags. Instead of the tighty-whities that made him famous as a model, he wore a long black pair of trunks with white laces at the fly. Delicious white laces, if you wanted to know the truth.

"What are you thinking?" Martin asked.

"You don't want to know."

"I know you have a dark side," Martin said. "I know you have secrets. I wish you wouldn't keep secrets from me."

Did he actually pout?

Suddenly, Michael couldn't take it anymore. He had too much on his mind. "I'm calling a car for you," he said. He happened to look up at the shiny windows of Zinderneuf and saw his wife staring down at them. He smiled and waved, and she flipped him the bird.

CHAPTER 20

DAWN PATROL
Laguna Beach, California

Chad DeKoven's mornings started the same way every day. His board clamped under his left arm, he opened the low gate to his pocket yard and took the narrow sidewalk to the steps leading down to the beach.

This morning he'd awakened early—four a.m. Couldn't wait to get out there. Even the slight wine hangover couldn't take away the excitement he felt. His hands tingled and so did his legs, and his stomach pricked with excitement. Every morning, he was always impatient, the only time during the day that he wasn't easygoing. For anything else, he wasn't goal-oriented. He didn't care about jobs or politics or even getting the girl. But pulling on his wetsuit, even after all these years, he couldn't wait to get out there.

He'd passed on his favorite Stewart board for his new fave, Sacrilege—Rolf Baer's latest work of art, shaped for him to perfection and ideal for the day. This would be his first time out with the Sacrilege board, and he *could not wait*.

The fog was dark blue gray and clung to everything. The smell of seaweed tumbled up by the waves permeated his nostrils. He loved the smell of seaweed in the morning! He loved it all. His life was very simple. Surf. Hang with his friends. Find a lady who wanted to sleep with him—no strings.

He might have been born for another decade—the sixties, maybe the seventies. In fact, he even had an original Volkswagen Microbus, which he had painted the color of the sunrise, with the rocks black in the distance and a wave like glass.

At twenty-nine years old, Chad had an associate's degree in business (didn't do jack shit for him, either), a marriage that had lasted seven months, no kids (incredibly fortunate, because he didn't think he'd be much of a father), and the beach house in Laguna. He had enough money for his needs.

And he had his boards—he'd built himself quite a collection, enough so he had to add on a little room off the shed and got into a ton of hot water with the zoning people.

The moisture clung like pearls to the iron railing edging the steps. The neighbor's place was dark—his neighbor was a hippie lady who came from money like he did and just wanted to be left alone to enjoy life and occasional weed. He peered into the darkness and saw the white of the churning surf and the dark shine of the sodium arc lights, way up on poles, shimmering off the hardpacked sand over by the park. The forecast was good but not spectacular—waist high to chest high.

A light rain started up, dimpling the sand.

Chad was debating which beach to hit when he heard something he didn't expect. The scrape of a shoe on the concrete behind him.

Maybe it was Bobbert, a surf bum who lived across the street. He turned halfway, said, "Hey bro, what you—"

Something heavy thudded into his back and pressed into him *hard*, and a meaty arm shot out of nowhere, pulling him backward and off his feet. An elbow crunched his neck like a vise, closing his air passage. He tried to tuck his chin *down*, tried to reach up and pull at the elbow, but he couldn't get a grip. His board hit the walk with an ugly *crack!* and maybe it was broken but it didn't matter because all that mattered was trying to *breathe*, and his vision was swimming—

And that was when full-blown panic set in.

CHAPTER 21

The next morning Tess was up early—first the coyotes and then the birds woke her. While she ran a wash she took her coffee and breakfast out on the porch and took notes on what had happened the day before.

The case was shifting. At first it had looked like a cartel hit—or some unaffiliated bad guy trying to act like one. Someone sending a message. You cross us and you're dead. Not just dead, but we'll torture you first.

But in this case, there was no message. She was pretty sure of that now.

Someone had tried to make it look like a hit.

Which meant someone knew what he was doing.

Steve Barkman had been obsessed with Hanley's death. To be more accurate, Steve Barkman had been obsessed with the way Hanley died.

Multiple gunshots.

Tess had checked out George Hanley's MacBook Pro from evidence. Maybe now she'd get some answers.

She spent an hour going through his files. There were very few. She went through his bookmarks on Firefox and his history. There was very little in history, mostly stuff that didn't mean much. How to fix a leaky faucet. A few cop sites and a gun catalog. Cabela's online.

There were a number of photos of places in southern Arizona. Many of them of buffelgrass and the volunteers. Pictures of Credo, some of the tours he led there. A few homes—maybe because he thought he'd be moving out of his apartment soon. One of them quite nice, up on a hill, with tall trees around it.

And there were photos of Adele.

Tess had a Mac, too. The first view in "Finder" was not of the photos themselves, except for little squares you couldn't see to the right of the print, but letters and numbers: DSC120234.JPG through DSC120240.JPG. So at first Tess didn't know what the photos would be, except for a brief description. But she figured "Adele" was a pretty good signpost.

Tess clicked through the photos of Adele. Pretty dog. One side of her face was colored brown. Her chest and legs were white. The rest of her was that blue-gray color populated with black spots. One of the spots looked a little like a bow tie.

There were times when her memory was a pain in the ass. Times when she didn't want to remember the terrible things she saw. Like George Hanley's desecrated body.

But this time, she was grateful for it. This time it made her job a whole hell of a lot easier.

Jaimie Wolfe stood in the center of the riding ring, shouting instructions to her students. When she saw Tess, she turned her back and ignored her.

That was fine with Tess.

The dogs came up. They milled around her, asking to be petted. Tess patted each one, rubbed their ears, let them sniff her hands, massaged their chests and rumps. Inundated with slavering tongues and wagging tails. She took a knee, the better to pat them, and let them surround her with doggy attention.

Jaimie glanced back at her once, then pointedly ignored her once again.

Tess rubbed her hands in the Australian shepherd's luxurious coat. "Good Bandit," she said. "Nice Bandit." Jaimie Wolfe's boy dog. Tess reached down and around the dog's tummy. Slid her hands back, reveling in the soft, luxurious fur. Reached down and between the dog's legs. She was gentle but thorough. "Good boy," she said.

Jaimie glanced her way.

"Good *boy*!" But by that time, Tess knew Bandit wasn't a boy at all.

It wasn't even Bandit.

~

Back at the sheriff's office, Tess pulled Jaimie Wolfe's DL and put together a photo lineup. She chose five other women of approximately the same age and body type. All of them were photos from driver's licenses. Then she took off for Animal Control and found Sally, the woman who had processed the dog's adoption.

"Do you recognize any of these women?" Tess asked.

Sally pointed to the photograph of Jaimie. "That one. She was the one who adopted the dog you were asking about."

"You're sure?"

"I can look it up. But I'm sure. I remember, because I really like her hair."

Yes, Jaimie Wolfe had glorious hair.

In the car, Tess had the SABEL list printout. One of the members of SABEL was a woman named Bernadette Colvin—the woman who supposedly adopted George Hanley's dog, Adele.

Tess drove to her townhome and rang the bell.

It was the same as last time. The street was empty. The blinds pulled in the window. The garage door closed.

Tess was about to get back into her Tahoe when a car drove up the street and parked across the way. She hailed the woman when she got out.

"Do you know the woman who lives here?" she asked. "Bernadette Colvin?"

The woman saw her badge and her brow knitted. "Something wrong? I thought she was already gone."

"Gone?"

"She's in assisted living. Her family is putting the house up for sale."

Tess said, "Do you know how I can contact her?"

"Her daughter used to come by here with her kids," the woman said. "To see their grandma. But I honestly don't know how you'd get in touch with her."

"Anything you can tell me about her family?"

The woman thought for a minute. "One time they came over and the little girls were dressed to go riding."

"Riding?"

"Boots, breeches. Like you see in the Olympics."

～

The DeKoven family:

Tess started with what she knew: Michael was a financial advisor whose office was at the top of the highest building in the city. Jaimie was divorced and ran a riding school. The youngest, Brayden, was divorced with a little girl. She practiced real estate law and had put up her shingle at her home in Tucson. And the second youngest, Chad, lived in Laguna Beach, California.

Tess spent some time looking for and accessing a *Tucson Lifestyle* article on the DeKoven family from a couple of years ago. There had been stunning photographs of the ancestral home—Zinderneuf—named by the great-great-grandfather after the doomed fortress in P. C. Wren's epic novel, *Beau Geste*. The house was Moorish, built in the 1940s at the height of the architectural style's popularity, on a bench of land overlooking the Rincon Valley not far from the old and now-defunct Rita Ranch. Michael and his wife and two children lived there.

The article profiled the family in all its glory: the four heirs to the DeKoven dynasty.

Instead of bored kids standing out in the sun for a ribbon-cutting ceremony, these were polished adults, posing for the beautifully orchestrated family photo. Inside the exquisite Moorish house, the light from the picture window filtered in, catching them perfectly coifed and handsome.

A beautiful family, the DeKovens.

Tess's gaze fell on Jaimie. Why would Jaimie take George Hanley's dog and pass her off as one of her own?

The woman smiled vacuously into the camera.

Tess knew Jaimie enjoyed the game. And it was a game. She'd bird-dogged her own brother, sending Tess his way by telling her Michael was George Hanley's financial advisor, when in fact he wasn't. Tess got the feeling that Jaimie enjoyed playing people one against the other.

Tess found a few newspaper articles and accessed public records as she tried to put together a picture of the family.

The history of the DeKoven family was similar to other cattle baron/mining magnate/politicians who made a fortune in the state in the early part of the twentieth century: wrangling over land, water and mineral rights, Apache attacks (back in the 1890s), and various ventures in the new era, including aviation and moving pictures. The story was always colorful and sometimes heartbreaking, like the time DeKoven's great-grandfather lost his daughter when she played in a creek during a thunderstorm and was swept away.

A couple of incidents were dramatic. Quentin DeKoven, Michael's father, was the lone survivor of a small single-engine plane crash in northern Arizona. After dragging the dying pilot nearly three miles though rugged country and spending the night in frigid temperatures, DeKoven was found by the search team, nearly dead from exposure.

He subsequently lost two fingers on one hand and a foot to frostbite.

Tess read between the lines. Despite his heroism, Quentin DeKoven was not a nice man. He steamrolled over congressmen and governors, mowing down his opposition with money and lies.

His businesses flourished. His business practices rode roughshod over the competition. He ran for governor and lost.

He and his wife, Eloise, had five children. The eldest, Quentin Jr., died at ten in a freak accident—a baseball hit him in the head during a Little League game.

According to the magazine, life was never the same again in the DeKoven household.

Zinderneuf was a beautiful place—but it was also an unhappy one. After Quentin Jr.'s death, Eloise rarely went out in public and wrote bitter letters to the editor of the local newspaper—screeds. Mostly about politics, but her vitriol regarding just about every subject, no matter how insignificant, was legendary.

She died at a relatively young age—she'd been ill.

Quentin DeKoven died ten years later almost to the day, when his private plane abruptly lost altitude and crashed into a wilderness area in the Pinaleño Mountains. The ensuing fire consumed a couple hundred acres of pristine forest.

Tess called Cheryl Tedesco at TPD. "Have you interviewed Michael DeKoven yet?"

"I'm doing it later today."

"You mind if I come along as an observer?"

"Can you get here in an hour?"

"Make it an hour and twenty minutes, and I'm there."

"See you then."

~

Tess took I-19 to I-10, amazed as usual at the sprawl. Tan-colored houses spread like a circuit board across the desert valley. She'd been to Vail a few years ago, and was surprised by the change in the area.

Once Vail had been a collection of old buildings and a beautiful Catholic church in a rural area. Now it was a sprawling outlet-mall-slash-fast-food jungle. She spotted Cheryl Tedesco's car at a pull-out just off the freeway. Cheryl flashed her lights and pulled out onto Colossal Cave Road. Tess followed.

By the time they reached Old Spanish Trail, the jillions of Monopoly houses had disappeared in favor of more expensive homes on larger lots, and finally to open land. Tess glanced at the wrinkled flanks of the Rincon Mountains, still pristine for the most part, especially the higher you looked. The road curved and dipped in and out of a mesquite bosque. Now they were in ranch country. There was a sprinkle of expensive new homes in the foothills—Thunderhead Ranch. On the right a dirt road headed up into the wilderness. Cheryl turned onto the dirt road.

Tess dropped back to avoid the chalky dust funneling up from Cheryl's vehicle—so dry out here. The road was a washboard. They went several miles. They rounded a curve and Tess spotted a house a couple of miles ahead, looking down at them from a high promontory. Shaded by giant eucalyptus trees and Aleppo pines, the walls in the afternoon sunlight were dull red brown.

Zinderneuf.

Up the hill and into a clearing for parking.

There were two cars in the lot. One was a silver Toyota 4Runner with a rack for bicycles on the back. The other still had the temporary sticker in the window. The car was a dark blue luxury sports sedan Tess didn't recognize— but she knew it was expensive. It was also unusual—sleek and dangerous-looking. She leaned down to read the make and model just behind the front wheel: Fisker Karma. Both cars were parked outside, but there was a four-door garage, painted to match the house, at the edge of the lot. Tess wondered how practical a low-slung car like that was, given the flash floods that inundated Tucson in the summer. There were a few low spots in the dirt road up here.

"This guy really *is* rich," Cheryl said.

"No kidding."

The Moorish building could have been in Tangiers. Royal palms clustered around the entrance. A tall wall surrounded a courtyard. In the wall was a gate inset with a mosaic of peacocks. The house was two stories high and sprawled along the hilltop. Beyond, Tess saw a rectangular swimming pool that must have gone in in the forties, and a smaller, similar house on the other side.

"That must be their Mini-Me," Tess deadpanned. With Danny out of commission, she felt it incumbent upon herself to be the wisecracker.

Cheryl pressed the doorbell. They waited. She pressed it again. "He said he would be here."

Tess glanced back at the parking lot. She assumed the Fisker Karma belonged to Michael. It looked like something he would drive.

Then the door opened. Michael DeKoven greeted them. He was wearing a bathrobe. He said, "Don't tell me. You're here to sell me a magazine subscription."

The inside of the house didn't look as nice as it had in the *Tucson Lifestyle* spread. There seemed to be furniture missing, and some of the beautiful things Tess had noticed—like a Tiffany lamp—were gone.

DeKoven excused himself to change. Tess realized that this was the second time she'd met him when he was half-dressed.

He returned, wearing a Ski Aspen T-shirt, madras shorts, and boat shoes, sans socks. Tess had seen his well-developed cyclist's calves before.

He caught her looking and smiled. "Real men shave their legs." Then he said to Tess, "You get around, don't you?"

Cheryl said, "How about the kitchen table? We might as well sit down."

He led the way to a kitchen that had been remodeled to accommodate industrial-size appliances. They sat around the table. Tess farthest away, hoping to fade into the woodwork and let this be between the two of them. She would watch him for truthfulness, or any tells that might show he was lying.

Cheryl set down the minirecorder and made her introduction—the date, time, who she was interviewing, who was a witness, the case number, and the name of the victim. She started with asking him simple questions—his occupation, who was in his immediate family. Then she asked DeKoven if he knew George Hanley.

"I met him once or twice. He's a friend of my sister's."

"Did you ever work with him professionally?"

"I thought this was about Barkman. You mentioned him on the phone."

"We'll get to that, but would you please answer the question?"

"I'll tell you what I told Ms., uh . . ." He looked at Tess, as if he had forgotten her name. "My sister suggested I take Mr. Hanley on as a client. The old guy came in, we talked, and he left. I never saw him again."

Cheryl asked if he knew Steve Barkman.

DeKoven folded his arms and pressed his index finger to his lips. "Mr. Barkman's mother is a sitting judge in Pima County. I might have met him once or twice—maybe at the symphony. No—a fundraiser. His mother . . . introduced us." He looked from one to the other, all innocence. "What does this all have to do with me? You weren't clear on the phone."

"What would you think if I told you that Steve Barkman was investigating you? Would that surprise you?"

He stared at her. Then he frowned—all innocence. "Investigating me?"

"He seemed to center around April tenth. Were you in town on April tenth?"

He looked bemused. "I'm sure I was."

"You're sure."

He crossed his leg to the other side and rested his hand on his chin. "What are you saying here? Should I have a lawyer present?"

"These are just questions," Cheryl said. "If you like, we could have a more official interview downtown."

He absorbed this, then smiled—*no harm, no foul.* "No, that's okay. I have nothing to hide. April tenth . . . I worked all day at DeKoven Financial—I'm pretty sure of the date because I had a big account that I had to ride herd on—deadlines are a bitch—and after that I came home for dinner here at the ranch. Ask my wife, she'll tell you."

"We'll do that."

"Have at it."

He was sure of himself on this point. Maybe it was because his wife would lie for him, or maybe because he was telling the truth. Any way you looked at it, Tess was pretty sure Michael's wife wouldn't say anything.

Cheryl said, "Is your wife here?"

"No, she's out with friends at the moment." He held Cheryl's gaze.

Tess couldn't tell if he was lying or not. There was a hint of a dare in his eyes, which went well with the self-satisfied smirk.

She had to remind herself that just because she didn't like him, just because he made something recoil inside her, didn't mean he was anything more than a sociopathic financial advisor.

Cheryl said, "What about March twenty-eighth? Were you here in town?"

"I'd have to look. I've gone to Phoenix twice in the last month."

"Could you do that?"

He pulled out his phone and looked at dates. Held it up for her to see. There was nothing marked for those dates, which didn't necessarily prove anything. But it didn't disprove anything either.

"You weren't in Houston?"

"Houston? Why would I go to Houston?"

Cheryl moved on. "Do you know a man named Alec Sheppard?"

He looked mystified. "Who?"

"Alec Sheppard. He lives in Houston."

DeKoven shook his head. "I'm sorry, no."

"Don't be sorry, I'm just asking you about him." She smiled.

He smiled back.

Cheryl Tedesco said, "Alec Sheppard has indicated that he knows you. He claims you were in Houston at the SkyView Center."

Tess and Cheryl both knew that there was no record of Michael DeKoven going to Houston. No flight information, no hotel information. Tess knew that Cheryl had been scrupulous in her search. But that didn't mean he didn't go.

"Mr. Sheppard says he recognized you," Cheryl lied.

All's fair in love and war.

"Then this Mr. Sheppard is either a liar, or needs to get new glasses, or there's something screwy up here." He wound his finger around his ear. "You might want to do more research—especially on this guy. Because I don't know him from Adam."

"He claims you made a gesture."

"What kind of gesture?"

"That's what I'd like to hear from you."

He stared at Cheryl. His eyes were dark glass. You could not see into them. There seemed to be nothing there. Not anger, not worry—nothing. "I haven't been to Houston in years."

He sounded solid. Just the right amount of outrage—not over-the-top. Other than the strange feeling that he was above it all, and better than them, he gave them nothing.

It went on that way for a while longer. Unsatisfying, but Tess thought they got something out of it. At one point her eyes met Cheryl's—and she saw confirmation there. They both knew he was lying. There would be a trail, if they could just find the trailhead. Perhaps a chartered jet. Perhaps another name. Perhaps both.

He escorted them out. Pleased with himself.

Tess said, "What kind of car is that? It's really impressive."

"It should be, for $103,000. It's a Fisker Karma."

He'd quoted the price on his Charles Russell painting, too. As rich as he was, why did he have to prove himself?

"Do you have any trouble on that road?" Tess asked. "Looks like there are places you could bottom out."

"I just take it slow," he said. "The key is to know where the dangerous spots are, and try to avoid them."

Which pretty much described his side of the interview.

～

Half an hour after the two female detectives left empty-handed, Michael's wife, Nicole, who had just driven in from a shopping trip, paid an unexpected visit to his side of the courtyard. She knocked on his door so hard, if it weren't two inches thick, she might have put her fist through it.

When Michael opened the door she pushed past him, her whole body shaking with anger. "You must have really messed up, Michael."

"Always a first time," he murmured. "To what do I owe this great pleasure?"

"Oh, shut up! You could put us *all* in danger."

She was spoiling for a fight. He wished he'd never confided in her, but that was when they were happy, three years ago. Before he finally realized that women just didn't turn him on. Twelve years into a marriage, that was awkward.

"You said this, this *thing* you do wouldn't make any waves. You said you had it all covered, and I would never have to worry about a policeman knocking on my door."

"Not so you'd notice, but the police didn't knock on *your* door."

"Give them time, Michael. I don't want the kids exposed to this. I don't want to be exposed to it myself. I'm thinking of leaving."

Nicole always said that, but she never did. She liked it here. She liked her own house across the pool, the beautiful rich furnishings from his parents' house filling it up nicely. She had a great touch. She appreciated his family, if he didn't. She loved the nice cushy life, didn't want to take the kids out of their elementary school, didn't want to be too far from her horsey friends or the new day spa that had been built in the new subdivision down the mountain. She was happy with the way things were. She knew she wouldn't get much— her lawyers weren't as good as his.

Plus, she had something to hold over his head.

Nicole liked it just this way. She could forget about him most of the time, but funnel her resentment to him whenever she liked.

Make fun of him, make fun of Martin, whom she called "Cabana Boy." As in, "How's Cabana Boy today? Did he get a sunburn on his witto tiny *wienie*?"

This was the level of discourse he had with her. She embarrassed him, and at some point he'd find a way to get rid of her. She was an albatross around his neck.

Don't shit where you eat.

"Just tell me you had nothing to do with that guy Barkman's death."

"I didn't have anything to do with that guy Barkman's death."

She hauled back and slapped him hard across the face.

He shrugged. "It doesn't change anything. I know you're upset. I know you hate it when Martin stays over—"

"Shut *up*! I couldn't care less about your boy toy, as long as you don't have sex in front of the kids. I'm talking about Barkman. If it wasn't you, who was it?"

"Nobody I know."

"Nobody. Right, nobody. That's an intelligent answer! The fact is, you don't know, do you, Michael? You think you're in charge, but you aren't in charge. You think you're so clever. You—"

He grabbed her arms—both of them—and shoved her out the door. She tripped and had to grab the doorjamb to keep from falling. "Fuck you, Michael! You can just . . . burn in hell!"

She stalked toward her own smaller, more tasteful house. Turned back to say, "You are so screwed, Michael, and you know it! They're going to come for you, and if they ask, I'm going to tell them what I know."

"What you know? What you *know*? You don't know jack!"

He slammed the heavy door. Hyperventilating.

The bitch.

He called Jaimie. He'd called her earlier, to warn her that a detective might be coming her way, but she hadn't returned his message. She'd ignored him—again. Jaimie was such a game player, and that was what he wanted to talk to her about.

When his spoiled bitch of a sister answered, he heard a horse blowing loudly through its nostrils. He could barely hear her, but he could sure hear the horse snorting its guts out.

"Jaimie, what do you think you're doing?"

"What? What are you talking about?"

"You told that detective from Nogales I was Hanley's financial advisor."

"So?"

"I told you he decided against going with me. You knew that. Don't you know the police talk to each other? I just had a visit from them, by the way. The police."

"Oh, come on, Michael! Why would I do that? I can't keep track of your clients. For all I knew George *was* your client. What's the big deal? You're the best liar I know, aside from myself. *Quit!*"

A rattle of a chain and a bang of a bucket. She was disciplining one of those big fat horses she couldn't afford.

Michael swallowed his impatience. Jaimie wasn't very intelligent. And she was impulsive. Which was the thing he wanted to talk to her about. He needed to broach it the right way, because Jaimie would just clam up if he pissed her off. The more furious she was, the more likely she'd stonewall him. Jaimie was the type who would go into a sulk for days. Normally he didn't care, because she wasn't really in his circle of friends, sister or not, but in many ways best not gotten into, they were joined at the hip.

"Jaimie," he said. "I know about the dog."

"What dog?"

"How did you think that could possibly work?"

"Michael, I don't know what you're talking about."

"Your new dog. The Aussie mix."

"So? I like dogs. I've got plenty of them."

"You know what I mean."

Silence.

"Why did you do it?"

"I don't have to justify myself to you. Maybe I just want to do something *good* for a change. She's a nice dog. She needed a home— a good home. That was the least I could do."

"What do you mean, the least you could do?"

Silence.

"Jaimie?"

"This is so fucked."

"What's fucked?"

"You know. You know exactly what I mean."

"Are you having regrets, Jaimie? Because as I recall, you didn't seem to mind what happened at Huka Falls. In fact, you had the time of your life."

Silence.

"You do not want to even think about screwing with me, Jaimie. I don't want you messing things up with the games you play."

"The games *I* play? What about you? What about Houston? What about Alec Sheppard? You're the one inviting trouble."

"Why'd you take that man's dog?"

"I wanted to. Okay? I wanted . . . *something* out of it."

"We come to the meat of the conversation at last."

"What? What are you talking about?"

"What did you do, Jaimie?"

"I didn't do *anything*!"

He had to be careful. That's why he used the landline, not his cell. Heaven only knew what they could do with cell phones. He lowered his voice. "You didn't jump the gun?"

"What are you talking about?"

He was ninety-nine percent sure nobody was monitoring this call—he'd done a sweep this morning, but still, you never knew. He said carefully, "Was it you?"

"Was it me *what*?"

"Try to keep up, okay? You took the dog. We all know how impulsive you are—"

She exploded. "*I'm* impulsive? Look what you did in Houston! You know, Michael? Before you lecture me, you'd better take a look at yourself first. You'd better take your own damn advice!"

"What *about* Steve Barkman?"

"What about Steve Barkman?"

He kept his voice steady, even though he was angry. "I want to know how far you've gone off the reservation."

"*Me?* What about *you*?"

"I'm asking you to tell me what else you've done. Did he approach you?" He almost said, "Did he blackmail you?" but stopped himself just in time.

There was a pause. Then Jaimie said, "Fuck you, Michael! Just . . . fuck *you*!"

And she hung up.

Michael sat there, hearing only the dial tone.

His heart thudded in his ears. His mouth went dry. What did Jaimie do?

Whatever it was, however deep she was into this, she wasn't about to tell him. He hit End, planning to call her back, but the phone rang before he could punch in her number.

"Look, Jaimie—"

It wasn't Jaimie. It was Brayden, his little sister. And she was crying.

He asked her what was wrong, but she was sobbing too hard for him to understand what she was saying.

At first.

CHAPTER 22

Tess turned onto Spanish Trail headed for the freeway. Her mind wasn't on Michael DeKoven. It was on Alec Sheppard.

There was a spark there. She didn't like to think about that.

She loved Max.

But the simple fact was, Max lived in California. She could relocate to California, but she couldn't relocate to the world Max lived in. She couldn't fit inside the bubble of his celebrity.

Her life was here. She worked homicide and it was part of the fabric that made her. Her identity as a homicide cop went far back. It went way back to her childhood, when her closest friend was kidnapped and a big, strong, gentle man had helped her through. His name was Detective Joe Clayborn, and he'd promised her he would find her best friend, and after he did—after he found Emily's body—Joe Clayborn promised her he would find her killer and put him away.

He found him.

He found the neighbor kid before he could kill again.

Tess couldn't live inside Max's bubble. He would argue that she could do what she wanted, could pursue her own career. But she knew she'd be caught up in it—all of it, the tabloids and the fanzines and the paparazzi—and she didn't want that kind of life. She wouldn't be able to ply her trade there. Cops were insular and they kept to their own circles, and she wouldn't fit in. She wouldn't be effective. She would be an outsider.

It was hard enough here, with Danny teasing her all the time.

So she didn't know what to do.

She was attracted to Alec Sheppard, but it was only because she wasn't spending every day with Max, day after day, week after week, month after month. Absence didn't make the heart grow fonder. It made you forget.

If she and Max had any shot at all, they needed to be together.

And that was a bridge too far—for both of them.

Sometimes she woke in the middle of the night and a voice screamed inside her head: What are you *doing*?

But she couldn't cut the tie. Couldn't. Not yet—

That was when Tess felt it—a piece falling into place.

Up ahead was the little general store in Rincon Valley. She pulled off the road and parked.

There were two reasons to stop at the store. One, she needed chocolate—dark chocolate, preferably—which she knew helped her think. And two, she might have to make more phone calls, and she didn't want to do that while she was driving.

Inside the store, Tess bought a Dove Bar, her hands fumbling as she pulled the debit card from her purse.

When something happened in a case, she always felt she was on the edge of something big. Tremendous. Sometimes, too big for her to assimilate.

She felt like that now.

The woman at the cash register had long blonde hair and looked like she was a couple of years out of Rodeo Queen range. She said, "Are you okay?"

"I'm good."

She walked out of the store and into the parking lot and out toward the back. There were corrals behind the store, and horses. This was a nice little spot, the Rincon Mountains rising up to the east, their golden flanks shadowed navy blue by clouds that seemed to wander over the mountain like a herd of buffalo.

The air smelled rural, like her place on Harshaw Road. The horses were at their feed tub at the far end of a pasture, their tails swishing. She could hear them stomping and banging their noses against the feed tub—sound traveled out here. It reminded her of Jaimie Wolfe and her equestrian center, and she wondered if Jaimie was part of the narrative she was building, too.

She punched in Alec Sheppard's number and he answered on the first ring.

"You said something I didn't quite get," Tess said without preamble. "What did you mean when you said you were 'getting in shape after the accident?'"

"Oh, that. I got busted up pretty bad in Florida."

He sounded embarrassed.

"What happened?"

"I had what they call a partial malfunction. My reserve canopy tangled with the main canopy, and neither of them inflated. Do you know what terminal velocity means?"

"No." Tess's eye followed an old ranch truck—seventies vintage—pulling into the lot. Sunlight arrowed off the bumper and she shaded her eyes. When the engine shut off she smelled gas.

Sheppard said, "It's an equation. People fall at different rates. If you weigh more, you fall faster. There are a lot of conditions that can change your velocity. In my case, the canopy was a mess but it did slow me down. Because the two of them were wadded up together, they created even more drag—that got me down to sixty or seventy miles per hour. I got lucky. Really lucky. I thought I was dead."

"What did you do?"

"Nothing much I could do. I tried to make like a flying squirrel and hope for the best. That was probably what saved me—pure luck I landed the way I wanted to. When I hit, my entire body absorbed the impact. If I'd gone in headfirst or hit with my feet, I would have accordioned, and that could have killed me. At the very least I'd have serious internal injuries."

"That's a dangerous sport."

He actually laughed. "I made one hell of an impression—literally—went in six, seven inches down in the bog. Just smushed into it—the mud got into my eyes, my nose, my mouth, I was this close to drowning. Thank God someone got to me in time to pull me out. Even so, the wind was knocked out of me and my heart stopped. I broke my ribs, collarbone, fractured my pelvis—"

"You survived all that?"

"I was lucky someone was there to give me CPR."

"You could have been killed."

"I *was* dead, for a very short period of time."

Tess felt the tingle low in her abdomen. She had always—literally—felt with her gut. When she was getting close, when everything came together or was about to . . .

"You should go with me sometime," Alec Sheppard said. Tess barely heard him. There was a buzzing in her ears. She saw the burned and crushed frame of the Spokane Indians' bus—a photograph that had accompanied the article.

"Lucky Lohrke," she said.

"Who?"

"Just a guy. Look, I've got to go. Can we talk later?"

"Sure."

Tess knew he sounded a little put off, but that didn't matter. She loved Max.

Scratch that. She was in love with Max.

She walked back to her car.

~

Tess turned onto the freeway going west. Thinking about DeKoven.

Not Michael DeKoven.

Quentin DeKoven.

She could see it on the page, as she had a few days ago.

"In 1999, Quentin DeKoven was the lone survivor of a single-engine plane crash in northern Arizona. After dragging the dying pilot nearly three miles through rugged country and spending the night in frigid temperatures, DeKoven was found by the search team, nearly dead from exposure.

"He lost two fingers on one hand and a foot to frostbite."

She saw the words. She remembered the sun beaming down on the page. She knew what she was wearing, knew the side street she'd pulled into, knew the time of day.

"In a cruel twist of fate, Quentin DeKoven died in 2005 when his private plane abruptly lost altitude and crashed into a wilderness area in the Pinaleño Mountains, six years after he survived a similar incident in 1999."

Quentin DeKoven had survived a private plane crash that should have killed him.

Six years later, he'd died in another.

He wasn't the only one who'd dodged the Reaper.

Tess flashed on Steve Barkman's self-satisfied grin. The cat-that-ate-the-canary grin when he asked her about George Hanley's death.

How many times was he shot?

The question hadn't made any sense when he'd asked it. Why was he obsessed with the number of shots?

Now she knew: George Hanley was shot six times the first time he died. Yes—died. His daughter Pat had told her he "died on the operating table." He'd died and been revived.

There were similarities.

That first morning, waking up, Tess had thought of that base-ball player in the magazine, Lucky Lohrke. Lucky Lohrke, who was bumped off a flight back to the States at the end of World War II. Lucky Lohrke, who was traded to another team and got off the bus before it crashed and burned on a snowy mountain.

Lucky.

George Hanley had been lucky. He'd survived death on the operating table.

Later, he won the lottery.

But after that, all these years later, his luck had run out.

She called Danny. "Remember the DVD George Hanley had in his apartment? You found it, the second pass through?"

"*The Ultimate Survivor* show."

"That's it. The show he was featured on."

"Yeah, the one that's on the History Channel."

"Have you watched it yet?"

"Yeah, I watched it the other day. It was kind of hokey. You know how they have to catch people up with the story after the commercials, just in case somebody new is watching?"

"Repetitive, I know," Tess said. "When did the show air?"

"I'll have to go look at my notes. Call you back."

Ten minutes later, he did.

"It was last season."

"What month?"

"November. Why?"

"I've got a theory, but that's all it is."

"Care to share?"

"I will after I look into it some more. Right now it's just a wild hare."

"Hey. Shoot it, skin it, put it in the pot with some *mole* and let's have a feast."

Tess saw Steve Barkman again, his head through the coffee table. The man who had blazed the trail for her.

He'd been investigating Michael DeKoven.

She had three men here: George Hanley, Alec Sheppard, and the patriarch of the DeKoven family, Quentin DeKoven.

Quentin DeKoven survived a plane crash in 1999.

Quentin DeKoven died in another plane crash in 2005.

Alec Sheppard's parachute failed in Florida a year and a half ago.

Alec Sheppard's parachute failed in Houston in March 2013.

George Hanley was shot in Phoenix in 1991.

George Hanley was shot to death in Credo in April 2013.

Only Alec Sheppard survived, and that was because he had help.

In all of these cases, there was one common denominator.

Michael DeKoven.

CHAPTER 23

Jaimie Wolfe's place was buttoned up. There were no little girls on big horses prancing around the ring. Jaimie's Dodge Ram was gone. The only vehicle on the property was the old ranch truck.

Tess heard a vehicle slow down on the road and turn in, rumbling over the cattle guard but hidden by a copse of trees near the entrance. Tess watched as the truck appeared, shadows from the trees scrolling over the hood.

A Ford—not Jaimie's Dodge Ram—a recent-model Ford F-350. If it wasn't covered up past the wheel-wells in mud, the truck would be white—typical for working trucks in Arizona.

White deflected the heat.

The driver was thick-bodied but not fat and looked to be in his early fifties. He wore jeans, boots, and a snap-button long-sleeved shirt. Pink face, sun-peeled nose, aviator sunglasses, straw Stetson.

Rancher.

"Hey," the man called out, slamming the door of his truck and walking toward her. "You a friend of Jaimie's?"

Tess introduced herself and asked who he was. He hitched his thumbs in the belt loops of his jeans, framing his rodeo belt buckle, and breathed in the spring air. Taking stock of the place with a country smile. "Names's Barnes," he said, "Dave Barnes." He shook her hand with his big mitt. He wore a Super Bowl–type ring that would have dwarfed another man's hand. "Jaimie asked me to look after her livestock while she was gone."

"Gone? Do you know where?"

He screwed up his face. "Didn't say. Just took off—I gather she was in a hurry and she wanted me to feed the livestock. So you're with Santa Cruz County?" He added, spotting the shield on her belt. "Nobody broke in here, did they?"

"Not that I know of."

He strolled over to Jaimie's porch. "Jaimie's a little slack on security. I told her that. She leaves her key right here." He lifted a plant in a pot on the porch and picked up a set of keys in the saucer underneath. Opened the door to wagging tails and slavering tongues. "Hey there!" he said as the dogs funneled out of the house.

Adele was among them.

"You want to come in?"

"No, thanks," Tess said. She would need a warrant if she did—and who knew what might happen down the road. She didn't want to hurt a potential criminal case because of the "fruit of the poisoned tree." But she did peer around him at the inside. It looked the same as it did the last time she was here.

"Jaimie has business with the law?" the man asked.

"I wanted to talk to her. Are you a member of SABEL by any chance?"

"SABEL? Nah. That's a little too environmentalist for me." He scratched his neck. "You think that they're doin' any good? Seems like a hopeless cause to me. There's just too damn much of that g.d. grass."

"Did you ever meet a friend of hers named George Hanley?"

He thought about it. "Nope, don't believe I had the pleasure. Who's George Hanley?"

"He also belonged to SABEL. Did you hear about the man killed down Credo?"

"Old guy got himself shot up?"

"That's the one."

He looked down and kicked at a clod of dirt. "A real shame. Heard it was illegals or cartels—damn, it's getting so bad. Shooting people up and cutting heads off and burning folks . . . I sure do hope he rests in peace."

"How would you describe Jaimie Wolfe?"

"Let's see . . . one hot babe." He grinned. "Not that she'd notice me. Good on a horse. Like a horse whisperer, you heard of them? She's always been nice to me."

"Would you mind giving me your contact information, just in case I can think of anything else to ask?"

He said, "This Hanley guy who died in Credo, you think *Jaimie* had anything to do with that?"

"Doubtful," Tess lied. "I'm just talking to anyone who knew him."

"Tell you what. Give me your card, and if I hear somethin', I'll give you a call."

She did so, scrawling her home phone number as well.

∽

Tess drove up by the road and parked. She'd turned on her laptop, and looked for tire treads that matched what she'd seen—just in case Jaimie had been to Barkman's house. Then she started up the Tahoe and put it in gear, turning east on 82. A glance in her rear-view mirror showed the white Ford belonging to Jaimie's friend driving off the ranch and turning in the opposite direction.

Her mobile rang. It was Cheryl Tedesco.

"One of our techs found something interesting at Barkman's place," she said. "You remember that printer he had with all those slots for micro cards?"

Tess listened while Cheryl explained that Steve Barkman had hidden a micro SD card in plain sight.

"I remember a tech mentioning something about it at the scene. What exactly *is* a micro SD card?"

"A storage device. It's tiny, but apparently, it packs a lot of gigabytes on it—actually terabytes. My tech tells me that one terabyte holds one thousand gigabytes."

Tess would be impressed if she knew precisely what a gigabyte was. "Computer memory."

"Uh-huh. He told me, no wonder they didn't find anything on his laptop except a bunch of bookmarked web pages, Facebook, and other crap. He must have kept it all on the card."

"Where did your tech find it?"

"First, you gotta understand how close it came to being thrown out. It was in that jar of pens and pencils on his bookcase. But fortunately, our guys are scrupulous in looking for and bagging evidence. You know how big a micro SD is?"

"Small?" Tess guessed.

"Try a little black rectangle you can put on the tip of your finger."

"You think there will be a lot of info on Michael DeKoven?"

"That's the hope."

"How far along are you?"

"Well, it's on the tip of my finger right now. I'll keep you posted."

CHAPTER 24

Michael, Jaimie, and Brayden said little on the flight over. Michael rented a Town Car at LAX and drove down to Laguna Beach.

No one talked.

Michael sat still, staring at the traffic but not seeing it. Stunned.

Chad.

His *brother*.

His little brother.

Chad was kind of a nonentity. He'd never progressed in any way—not in school, not in a career, not even in his social life. He was an overgrown, carefree child. Their mother used to call him an innocent.

Not that he was dumb. He wasn't. Maybe all the pot he smoked and the beer and the fast food he consumed contributed to his . . . haziness, but he'd carved out his own little life in the Laguna beach house and he wasn't a bother to anybody. They could just forget about him and go on with their lives.

Michael felt guilty. He should have paid more attention. They just left him out there on his own, thinking he was fine. Happy. But he must have run across some bad people. As head of the family, Michael felt responsible.

They checked into the Retreat at Laguna, then drove to the Laguna Police Department on Loma. It took Michael a while to find a parking space and they were late. They waited in the outside office until a detective came to meet with them. He was tall and Hispanic, with a pitted face and bad breath. His name was Pete Morales. He took them back to his office.

He didn't talk long. They would have to go identify the body at the hospital morgue, and there was very little he could tell them.

"It looks like he was going surfing. His neighbor says he usually goes out between four and five-thirty in the morning. He was found just below the steps down to the beach by a couple of surfers—" he read their names. "They must have found him shortly after he was killed."

Michael absorbed this. "Do you have any leads? Who do you think would do something like this?" Aware of Brayden sitting beside him, her hand on his arm, stroking over and over, as if she were in a trance.

Jaimie asked, "How was he killed?"

"He was choked."

"Strangled?" asked Brayden.

Morales shifted in his seat. Michael noticed his pants were polyester. You'd think cops in Laguna Beach would dress better. "Yes."

Brayden continued to paw at Michael's arm. "Why would someone do that?"

"There could be a few reasons. An argument, maybe. Or a robbery, although no one took his board."

Michael reflected that while Chad had few needs or even wants, he spent his money on surfboards. "So it wasn't robbery then?"

"It doesn't look that way, but I can't be sure. We're looking at everything."

Michael disengaged his arm from Brayden's grooming efforts and held the detective's gaze. "So . . . what? You think it was for the hell of it?"

"We're trying to find out who did this and why, but there aren't any obvious pointers to anyone. I'm sorry I can't tell you more." He shifted in his seat again. "Did Chad have any enemies?"

"Enemies?" Michael thought Chad was the least offensive person he knew. Easygoing, friendly, willing to go along to get along. "No. At least none that we would know about."

"We have interviewed the two young men who found him. They said the same thing."

~

Cheryl Tedesco called just as Tess was pulling into her driveway.

"There's some great stuff on the micro card. I can't send you anything official. This is FYI only. With your memory, you'll probably be able to say this back to me verbatim."

When Tess got off the phone a half hour later, she thought: Steve Barkman was a damn good investigator.

Tess saw in her mind George Hanley's calendar—the three-day trip to LA written there. She'd found the ticket he'd paid for but never got a chance to use—the round-trip ticket to John Wayne Airport in Orange County.

Now she clicked on the link Cheryl had sent her. An AP article came up, no more than a few paragraphs—about a man whose remains were found near a mountain bike trail in Orange County.

The story was two years old.

Peter Farley was a systems analyst for a tech company in Orange County, an avid mountain biker who tackled the trails into Asteroid Canyon on the weekends. Asteroid was a canyon running through a relatively remote section of the Cleveland National Forest.

Farley had parked his vehicle in the wildcat parking lot at the entrance to the canyon. When he did not return to work after the weekend, a search ensued. His bike was found at the base of a short but steep hiking trail leading to a waterfall. Farley was found near the pool at the waterfall's base, partially eaten and dragged into a hollow under the oak trees, buried under leaves and underbrush, his bloodstained wallet still in the pocket of his shorts.

The wounds appeared to come from a mountain lion. Hunters searched for the lion, but never found any sign of one. Not surprising, since a rainstorm had come through between Farley's disappearance and the day he was found.

And then the kicker.

"In a cruel twist of fate, Mr. Farley was attacked previously at his home in Los Angeles by a pack of javelinas while walking his small dog."

He'd saved the dog but was seriously injured in the attack when one of the javelinas bit into his femoral artery.

Tess thought of that day at Credo. Steve Barkman leaning into her space, too close. An obnoxious character with a creepy smile.

Still.

What Steve Barkman lacked in appropriate behavior, he made up for in brain cells. He had figured out what happened to Peter Farley. And he had linked it to George Hanley's killer.

CHAPTER 25

Walking back to the car from the police department, Michael was silent. They each dealt with Chad's death in their own way. Jaimie looked mad at the world. Her silence was icy. Brayden's tearstained face was crumpled up and every once in a while she hiccuped.

Michael was the man of the family. The leader. But he didn't know what to do. He thought about the enemies he'd made. The cops were sniffing around. He wasn't worried about that—he was too smart for them. But maybe he'd crossed the line with someone. Could they have gone after Chad for revenge, since Michael himself was too strong? He went over every expedition they'd made, every kill.

His only mistake was Alec Sheppard.

~

Later, Michael lay on the bed in his room at the resort, staring at the ceiling fan. The women were in the kitchen—he could hear them talking in low voices, occasional sobs from Brayden.

He was stunned. He felt as if he'd gone into shock. His extremities were cold. He rarely experienced fear, but he felt it now, deep in his chest. A tingling feeling. He was a clear thinker, a logical thinker, and so he identified the tingling in his chest and the cold in his extremities and the way his legs shook as a sixth sense for danger from outside.

Something evil.

Stalking them.

Chad was the baby of the family. Chad was the kid. A sweet, shy boy who never really grew up, whose whole life revolved around his quiver of surfboards and the water in Laguna Beach. There was no reason for anyone to kill him. Maybe it was random, but the detective didn't leave that impression. He'd said Chad was strangled, but Michael could read between the lines. He could often tell when a person wasn't telling the whole truth. He guessed there was more to the "strangling" than the detective had let on.

He'd also said: *Did Chad have any enemies?*

Maybe Chaddy did. But it was doubtful. Michael knew that he himself had an enemy—Alec Sheppard. Those two women cops were no real threat. He wasn't worried about them. But Sheppard came all the way from Houston. He'd hired Barkman to spy on him.

Barkman's house would be locked up tight behind the crime scene tape, but maybe . . .

His chest tightened again. The beginning of a heart attack? No, that was stupid. Panic attack, maybe. His heart was great. He was an athlete. He needed to go home, get away, go for a bike ride. Clear out the cobwebs. Try to get rid of the sight of Chad lying on the slab with a sheet over his head.

He needed Martin.

~

The next morning Tess showed Danny what she had. She gave him her theory about Michael DeKoven.

It sounded ridiculous even when she laid it out for him.

Danny was distracted. His wife was finally going into the hospital the next day so they could induce labor. But the bottom line was he thought it wasn't going to fly with Bonny.

"But I'm going on leave, so don't ask me."

Tess knew Bonny well. He'd brought her with him from Bajada County because he trusted her. He relied on her. Some of it was due to the fact that in Albuquerque she had been in homicide for four years and had dealt with some of the ugliest crimes imaginable. Some of it was due to her superautobiographical memory, which Bonny considered a big edge. Their secret weapon. But most of all, he liked her. He liked her and he trusted her judgment.

Tess realized she'd have to lay it out for Bonny in the right way. The first thing she had to do was print up the information on Hanley's trip to the OC. If she could make that link to Bonny . . .

Tess printed up what she needed and went down the hallway to the undersheriff's office. She nodded to Luke Grayson, one of the deputies, who was just going in.

Bonny looked up and saw Tess. "I have to talk to Luke," he said. "Can you wait a minute?"

Tess nodded. She leaned against the wall in the hallway. Aware that her heart was beating hard.

Electricity seemed to branch out through her veins.
I'm right about this.
Still, it would be a hard sell.
She had what she had.
She hoped it would be enough.

CHAPTER 26

Bonny looked down at the pages Tess had printed up and back up at her. He looked skeptical. "You're saying you think Hanley was going out to LA as part of his, uh, 'investigation?'"

"Orange County. He did go out there. He and Barkman were on the same trail."

He clasped his hands over his stomach. "It sounds far-fetched to me."

Tess said, "Look at his itinerary. He planned to fly into John Wayne Airport. He had a reservation at the Starbrite Motel in Sylvan."

The old mining town was at the edge of the Santa Anas, not five miles from the entrance to Asteroid Canyon.

Peter Farley lived there and commuted to his job in Irvine.

Bonny sighed. "You honestly think you can find a link to Michael DeKoven? He's got a lot of money, and his family has never been afraid of lawsuits."

"I think George Hanley thought DeKoven was after him."

Bonny sighed. "If he was, he got him." He swiveled on his chair. He'd brought the office chair from the Bajada County Sheriff's Office, beat up as it was. He said his butt was used to it. The chair squeaked when he swiveled, and Tess liked the sound of the squeaking—which usually meant Bonny was thinking—and she liked the smell of tobacco on him, even though she didn't smoke.

There was a bond between them. She'd asked him to let her do ridiculous, sometimes impossible, things.

"All right. You go. I'll put in for one day."

Tess had been ready for this. "Overnight? That will give me two full days if I get there on an early flight."

"I don't know. I'm going to get flak just for the plane fare. We're going to be shorthanded as it is."

"I can pay for the motel."

"That's not the point."

Tess said, "What if I find what I'm looking for and don't have time to pursue it? I'd have to fly back."

Bonny swiveled. Finally he said, "Okay. I'll see if we can pay for the overnight. But if it doesn't look like it's gonna pan out, you come back pronto."

∿

Chad DeKoven had wanted to be cremated and his ashes scattered over the waves in Laguna, so they made arrangements for Chad's best friend, Dave, to pick them up. Michael didn't know about his sisters, but he didn't plan to return for the ceremony.

On the way back to LAX, he was silent. Twice Brayden had tried to engage him—wanting comfort—but he just said nothing. He was thinking of the Commandments.

There were only four.

First Commandment: Player must have survived a previous encounter.

That was the whole point.

Second Commandment: No expedition shall take place within the Kingdom. (In other words, don't shit where you eat.)

That was why they had waited on George Hanley.

Why *he'd* waited. He still didn't know if Jaimie or Brayden had jumped the gun.

Third Commandment: For all expeditions, new equipment must be purchased. Any unused equipment must be disposed of, i.e., destroyed.

Fourth Commandment: There could be no connection between the Player and the Gamer.

None.

Simple enough to memorize. Harder to implement.

He didn't think he'd broken any of the commandments. He only knew Barkman through Barkman's mother, Geneva Rees— and even then, he'd only met him once. Michael couldn't even remember the circumstances, although he thought it might have been at the symphony. They were not even acquaintances.

Still . . . it was what it was.

Shit, meet fan.

Jaimie, pulling that crap with Hanley's dog. That was what bothered him. Did she take the dog out of guilt, or was it something else? If she took the dog as a trophy . . .

What *else* did she do?

Michael knew that there was plenty of room for improvisation—and this was where the danger lay. It was only human nature that the written commandments would only be part of the game.

The other things they made up as they went along. Because they could. Because it was fun to create a world and add to it.

As time went by and they were successful in staying under the radar, Michael realized he'd taken too much for granted. They'd become too improvisational.

Cocky.

Like what he did in Houston—no excuse for that.

It didn't start out that way. Improvising had been discouraged from the outset. He'd made a big deal of it. Go off script, and you could blow the whole deal. But Michael admitted he was as guilty as Jaimie was. The game was . . . well, it was exhilarating. It made him feel like God, and that kind of thinking led to carelessness.

He realized he should have added another rule. "No celebrating in the end zone."

One reason he'd chosen Sheppard—he himself understood what it was like to dive out of an airplane. He'd been on a toot for some time, but lost interest in it when he realized that the odds were thinner with every jump, that his number might come up.

The whole idea of it fascinated him. Having jumped himself, he tried to imagine what that would feel like—the panic. The fear. It must be like being on speed. It must be exhilarating and scary at the same time, a whole lifetime of fear in a few seconds.

But there was something about the man . . .

Maybe Sheppard wanted revenge. Maybe he had it in him to be like Michael, himself.

Michael knew Sheppard was a shark in business. He'd started from scratch with a petroleum cleanup method he'd patented after the oil spill, and it was only three years before his startup had gone public, and now he was rolling in it.

Which made him so attractive in the first place. His death would have made a big splash.

Michael had been extremely careful. He'd covered his tracks. Used an assumed name, chartered a jet. Every step of the way he'd been careful, thought it through. Once, twice, three times he'd gone through it. He made sure the whole plan was fail-safe.

And then, at the penultimate moment, to make a mistake like that? To telegraph his knockout punch?

What had driven him to do it? Did he *want* to fail? Did he *want* to get caught?

Like his sister and that stupid dog!

Now he wondered if Sheppard was coming after *him*.

Coming for him through the weakest link—his poor, simple, pathetic younger brother.

Once the thought crossed Michael's mind, it ate at him. Scratched behind his eyelids. Sheppard was in great shape. He was strong. The guy was mentally and physically tough.

Was he the type to seek revenge?

Would he really go after Michael's brother? The slowest, most vulnerable beast in the herd?

CHAPTER 27

Tess arrived at John Wayne airport at 7:38 a.m. and picked up her rental car. She took the 405 to Irvine, and from there she made her way to the gated entrance to Asteroid Canyon in the Santa Ana Mountains.

A detective had been briefly assigned to the Farley case, but it was soon classified as an unnatural death due to misadventure. Barry Zudowsky of the Orange County Sheriff's Office North Operations was in his mid-to-late twenties. Tall and skinny as a string bean, he had freckles and a crew cut. His posture was erect, and he struck her as serious, if maybe humorless.

He'd e-mailed her reports on the case and she'd read up on them. There was little evidence, but the conclusion was that Peter Farley had gone up to a canyon pool, maybe to cool off, when he was attacked.

Tess had also read up on mountain lions as part of her homework. "I heard attacks like this are rare."

"They are."

"So the thinking here is that the lion had a cache of food, something it had killed, and somehow Mr. Farley came too close?"

"Either that or it could have been a female with a cub. Farley wasn't located for three days and there'd been at least one big rainstorm. There was no sign of a mountain lion."

"No evidence at all?"

"No tracks, no scat. Not even a sighting. The only evidence was Mr. Farley himself. The ranger and the subsequent mountain lion expert I talked with were skeptical."

Tess looked up the gate barring the forest road. The asphalt ended just before the gate and turned to graded dirt.

Zudowsky nodded to the padlock and chain. "The Mullets."

He opened the trunk to his unit and took out a lock cutter, then went to the gate and removed the padlock and chain.

"The Mullets?"

"It's a clan of hillbillies, that's what we call 'em, they have a homestead about a mile up this road. This is Forest Service land, but as you can see from the signs, there's access for people who want to drive up in the canyon to the first place where the creek comes in. Dave Mullet thinks this whole canyon is his property and he's been known to threaten people. He and his wife are always yelling at folks that it's a private road, and if you heard what they were screaming your ears would turn blue. So get ready."

They got into Zudowsky's unit and drove through the open gate.

"Be ready," Zudowsky said. "I heard one time Mullet's wife pelted a ranger with cantaloupe rinds."

The canyon was beautiful. Sycamore trees filtered the sunlight, and it was beautiful and quiet in late afternoon.

They came around a curve and there was the Mullet homestead. It looked like every squatter's camp Tess had ever seen. Shotgun shack with a green asphalt roof. Corn patch. Falling-down corrals. Goat staked to what passed for a lawn. Kids' toys scattered everywhere.

Tess asked if an asteroid had hit the canyon, if that was how it got its name.

"That's the legend, but the locals think it was made up. The Manson family lived out here for a while. People who've lived out here a long time think it was them that came up with it. Used to be called Sycamore Canyon."

"The Mansons?"

"Amazing, huh? Some official decided to change the name to Asteroid, and now that's what it says on our maps."

As they drove up canyon, he told her that mountain bikers loved the thirteen miles of road they had access to, as well as trails up into the hills. One of the trails led to the small waterfall and pool where Peter Farley's remains were found. "Not much of a waterfall, except when it rains. It's not year-round. Farley parked his vehicle outside the gate back there, so he could ride all the way up."

"When was his car discovered?"

"After the weekend. It had been a couple of days—Monday was a holiday. He lived alone and it wasn't until after the long weekend that a ranger called it in."

They reached the bike and hiking trail to the waterfall, parked on the verge, and started up.

When they arrived, Tess glanced around. A pretty spot. Oaks and a willow leaning over the lower pool.

"He was up there." Zudowsky pointed up at the rocks above. They followed the path and came to another pool with a small beach, but most of it was wild. Oaks, tall grass, underbrush, and a mat of wild grapevines. Tess recognized it from the scene photos and diagrams. A wire stuck up through the leaves—an orange flag. Someone had left candles at the base of the oak tree, plastic flowers and the fender of an old bike.

"So that's it."

He folded his arms and rocked on his heels. "Yup."

"No mountain lion sightings?"

"No legitimate ones. People around here just say stuff. Anything brown they might call a mountain lion. But no confirmed sighting in this part of the mountains."

"But they're shy. You wouldn't see them."

"No, you wouldn't. A mountain lion's range is about a hundred miles. So there would probably only be one."

Tess had read the report. She also had read up on mountain lions. They did not stalk people, unless that person was a threat to whatever cache of food they had, or if the victim came too close and threatened a female's cubs. "And no cat tracks."

"Yeah, but you have to remember—"

"That there was a rainstorm between the time he went missing and was found. That was over the three-day weekend?"

"Can't remember which day. The vehicle wasn't ticketed until Tuesday at the earliest, and towed later."

"So no one was looking for him. They assumed he was out there somewhere camping?"

"Yeah." He scratched his neck. "But bottom line, he was mauled by a mountain lion. The claw marks, the teeth marks, the measurement of the jaw. That's all in the report. It bit into his neck and face, and ate a little of his heart. A chunk was taken out of his lung. Then it buried him under all this stuff for later."

~

On the way back, a dirty Dodge Ram parked outside General Mullet's place.

A man came out onto the front porch and stared at them.

"Here goes nothing," Zudowsky said, turning in.

They got out.

"Hey, you here about the trespassers?" the man yelled.

On the way in, Tess had noticed the property was plastered with No Trespassing signs.

Barry Zudowsky yelled. "We wanted to ask you about the guy who died up by the waterfall."

"That's old news." Dave Mullet remained on the porch. He had a massive white handlebar mustache like a Civil War general, if a Civil War general wore dungarees and a biker T-shirt. He obviously used the weight bench and barbells on the porch, because his arms looked like balloon animals.

Even from where Tess stood, she could smell his cologne. It wasn't the good stuff.

"What I want to know is why you keep opening that gate! This is private property."

Zudowsky kept his hands on his belt, close to his weapon, but looked casual enough. "Now, Dave, you know that's not true. This is Forest land."

"You tell people to stay off my land. I have grandkids here. People are racing up and down that road at night. Maybe that's what happened to that bike guy."

"We lock the gate at night farther up."

"Yeah, but what about down here?"

They stayed where they were, in the threadbare yard, and he stayed on the porch.

"This is Detective Tess McCrae from Arizona Sheriff's," Zudowsky said. "She'd like to ask you a couple of questions about what you remember."

"Go ahead, don't mean I'll answer, though."

Lots of yelling. No one moving.

So Tess yelled too. She asked him if he knew of any mountain lion around here, or had heard of one.

"No mountain lions around here. That's bullshit. I'd bet my bottom dollar on it."

Then he paused. "Except for the one that's up at the animal sanctuary."

∽

"Animal sanctuary?" Tess said, as they drove out of the yard. Dave Mullet had yelled, but he'd turned out to be helpful, and they had returned to the car with all body parts intact. "He gave directions, but do you know exactly where?"

"Near Black Star Canyon. On one of those back roads. I don't know that area."

"I'll find it," Tess said.

∽

It was going on noon when she drove into the old mining town of Sylvan. She stopped at the first coffee shop she came to. As she waited for her lunch, she called the expert on mountain lions, June Hackler.

Hackler was in and happy to talk to her. Tess sketched out the story she had so far.

"There could be a mountain lion in Asteroid Canyon," Hackler said. "As part of its range, it has running water, woody areas, and plenty of game. But it's highly unlikely it would attack an adult human being. The only reason would be to protect its food source."

She explained that after eating, a mountain lion buried the rest of its prey and would come back to it later.

"So you think it's unlikely."

"Very unlikely."

"Peter Farley was partially eaten—most of his heart, some of his lung, and bone marrow. And it was a mountain lion."

There was a pause. Hackler said at last, "That is unusual. The animal would have to be starving, and there's plenty of prey in that canyon."

Tess paid her check and walked out into the sunshine. A beautiful Southern California day. She drove up canyon looking for the motel.

A low hum seemed to start up in her stomach when she saw the sign up ahead on the curve, tucked into the hillside.

The low hum spread up through her chest and into her ears.

The Starbrite Motel. She'd chosen it specifically, after googling motels in Sylvan. It had its own website, had been described as a "hideaway off the beaten path."

The Starbrite Motel had been built in the early sixties. The rooms levered out into the wedge-shaped parking lot like a fan. Glass and frame and old wood.

Tess loved old movies. Especially the old noir movies, like *The Postman Always Rings Twice* and *Double Indemnity*. She had them on DVD.

There was something sexy about them. Not just sexy, but forbidden. The people in those stories set one foot on the road, the wrong road, and things went to hell from there.

Tess went back and forth about what she was doing.

She knew she was skating at the edge. She knew she was flouting an unwritten rule.

The motel was anchored by a coffee shop. The coffee shop wall was faced with rocks, a mosaic of colored rocks taken from the mines.

Narrow cursive spelled out STARBRITE COFFEE SHOP in turquoise.

Tess parked and got out.

The shade was cool but the sun was warm, and the enormous cottonwood tree split the difference. The sky was an aching blue. It ached and she ached. She could feel it building.

One foot on the road.

Tess had always prided herself on being a straight shooter. In Albuquerque, her nickname was "By the Book McCrae."

A breeze funneled through. The bright green cottonwood leaves shifted, catching the sun and shining silver.

She felt like one of those women in the old movies. Where were the scarf and the dark glasses? For a moment she felt playful, thought about signing in under a fake name.

But this was the age of credit cards, and she had no cash on her.

The man who accepted her credit card didn't look at her. Didn't smile. Hardly said a word.

Her room was cool despite the floor-to-ceiling expanse of window.

She set her suitcase on the floor. Felt exhilaration but also guilt, mixed equally.

She'd paid for the room herself.

Bonny had given her a voucher. What would she do now? Give it back to him? Already she was screwing up.

She was no femme fatale. If she'd had a scarf and dark glasses, she would have had to turn them in on the spot.

Tess didn't think Bonny suspected. He was a straightforward man and he expected his people to be straightforward.

But Tess knew what she was doing was unprofessional. It might even get her in hot water, if it was found out. Ethically: Did she really need to stay here overnight? Could she have concluded her business in one day? If she'd put her case first?

But there was the animal sanctuary. She had to follow that path and see where it led. The idea of the place lodged in the back of her mind, part savior, part mystery.

She'd go looking for the animal sanctuary later this afternoon. And if she found anything, if there was anything to find—she'd follow it to the end of the trail.

But first, she made her phone call, and settled down to wait.

~

A motorcycle pulled in to the parking lot. Tess looked out the window. A man swung off and removed his helmet.

The man's hair was short and looked like it had been cut by one of those places you just walk in to, like Supercuts—the cut was simple and kind of dorky. He wore faded jeans that somehow made him look chunky (how did he do that?) and the jeans were boot-cut over scuffed desert boots. His knit polo shirt, untucked, was horizontally striped. He hooked the helmet on the motorcycle and headed her way, elbows slightly out from his body, as if he was used to lifting grain sacks all day—just kind of stumped along. She noted a clunky turquoise-loaded sandcast Navajo bracelet and a watch that looked cheap even from here. His wallet made a huge square in his back pocket, and a cheap duffel bag, old and used, was slung over his shoulder. He could have been a construction worker on his day off.

She opened the door. Max Conroy leaned against the doorjamb and gave her a cute blue-collar grin and said, "Hello, sweetness."

≈

The first time it was two people tearing off each other's clothes, urgent—no, more than that, lunatic *crazy*, two lovers caught up in some fevered hallucination, desperate to rid themselves of the boundaries between them.

As if they could not be apart for one more moment. Nothing mattered but the need to join together, to try as people had for centuries to somehow become one.

The sweetness was painful. A starburst that took a long way to burn down.

≈

They lay tangled, legs wound together, hips touching, and Tess felt the beating of his heart.

At that moment, she wanted so much to never leave. Never be apart. Never ever pull away.

Maybe on an island somewhere. Alone together. Castaways.

The yearning was so deep at that moment that she discounted everything else about her life. Who she was, what she was, where she was going.

His chin rubbed against her face.

Five o'clock shadow.

His voice against her neck. "I miss you."

They lay there, sated. Until they weren't.

Slowly, the urge came back.

She tilted her head up toward him and looked into his eyes. They were the color of the ocean at sunrise—teal green.

She felt his strength, in the broad wings of his chest, in the crook of his neck.

Moving. Tingling warmth. She melted like an ice cream cone on a hot summer's day.

Love for him seemed to grow under her solar plexus and spread out all over.

It was great.

~

Tess's mind drifted. Max was asleep. She looked at him, feeling the smile inside. Max was good at disguise. He could melt into any crowd.

They had stolen this moment.

He was in the middle of shooting the TV series. He was off for the week, but shooting of the next episode would start back again in Tustin on Saturday. It had worked out perfectly—this tiny window of opportunity.

She tried to tell herself that the tiny window was enough.

CHAPTER 28

They were getting ready to go out for dinner—there was a steak house that looked pretty good—when Max's phone sounded. His ringtone was "Gangnam Style," no lyrics.

He put the phone to his ear and turned away.

Tess had a bad feeling.

Max sat down on the bed, bending forward, listening. He said, "I canceled that."

Tess watched him. Out of the blue she had the feeling he would be leaving soon. Which she could understand—he was busy; he was both the co-producer and star of the show—but she'd hoped they could spend some more time together.

She'd certainly made her own life more complicated by meeting him here.

"I thought we'd worked this out." Max looked at her. His look said everything. "I can be there in," he checked his watch. "Forty minutes, if the traffic isn't too bad. Yes, I know how they are. All right, yeah, okay. I'll see you then." He looked at Tess. "Shit."

"You have to go."

"It's unavoidable. So much going on with this production, and something . . ." He looked in her eyes. "Fell through the cracks. I have to do an appearance. I don't know if I can make it back. Maybe late tonight."

"A late dinner?"

God, she hated the way she said that.

"It's too far, I'd never make it back here—unless you want to eat at eleven o'clock at night."

Tess realized that he was used to eating at eleven o'clock at night.

She also realized that she didn't really know what his lifestyle entailed. That she didn't know much about his life in California as she should.

"I can wait that long," she said. Inwardly wincing as she said it.

She'd compromised herself by meeting him when she should be on the clock, and this was the result.

He ran a hand through his badly styled hair.

"There's so much crap going on. I don't even know if we're gonna get another season. There's just so much that's undecided—the nature of the game. You're all in until the next roadblock. It isn't fair to you." He came up behind her and held her in his arms. "I shouldn't have wasted your time."

"It's not a waste of time." But even when she said it, she thought of the last time she'd come out. It had been the same way. It was his job. He was busy, she was busy. She had her own life and he had his.

But it seemed that she was always the one to make accommodations.

The joy she'd felt—the *rightness* of the day—evaporated.

"I have to make this appearance tonight. I thought I'd gotten out of it, but they're holding me to it, and I don't think they're all that thrilled with how things are going." He broke away from her, sat down on the bed, and rubbed his eyes.

Stressed. Maybe he'd dressed to look chunky, but Tess noticed that he had gained a little weight.

This in itself could be disastrous for a leading man.

The thought crept in, catching her unawares. Maybe he was drinking and using again . . . but the one thing the madman who ran the Desert Oasis Healing Center had done was break Max's habit in two.

There was no evidence at all that this was the case, and she sensed that he was all right, at least in that regard. But even that momentary distrust . . . what was that all about?

He looked up at her as if he'd read her mind, and grinned. The patented trademark Max Conroy grin. "I'm sorry. I'm glad you have something you can do."

"It's okay, really."

Liar.

Just when had she lost her honesty?

~

He called her late at night. Apologized again.

"It's okay," Tess said. Not feeling it was okay and hating herself for saying it. Max was not to blame. She knew that. "You're busy. I'm busy. Which reminds me, I'm going to try and wrap this thing up quickly and get an earlier flight."

Wondering why she said it. Did she think it would hurt him?

"That's probably good. I won't be able to shake loose tomorrow."

"I didn't ask you to."

There was a pause. "Look, I'm sorry that it didn't work out. I tried."

"I know you did."

"If you lived out here—"

"We've discussed this. I just started up with Santa Cruz County. It's my career we're talking about here."

He didn't say anything.

"Look," she said, hating herself while she said it. "We'll work it out. Maybe you can come out when . . ." *When* was the issue. He was constantly working.

Tess heard voices in the background.

Max said, "Hey, I've got to go. I'll call you soon."

Disconnected.

Tess sat on the bed, looking at the mirror opposite.

Stared at her reflection for a long moment.

"Dumb-ass," she said.

CHAPTER 29

When Jaimie landed back in Tucson she didn't drive straight home from the airport—she was too unsettled for that.

Everything was going south. It was like she was in the back of a car going faster and faster on a narrow road, and the driver wouldn't stop no matter how much she begged. She was in that car to the end of the road.

She saw her ex-lover's chopper parked in front of the Buckboard Saloon. She turned into the parking lot. She'd taken a miserable trip down memory lane at the beach house in Laguna—Chad had really messed the place up, it smelled like a goat pen—and now all she wanted was to forget. Maybe her ex would help her to do that.

Gloomy as she felt, when she opened the door to the dark saloon, she suddenly felt beautiful and sexy. Every man in the place—and most of them knew her—still marveled at her good looks. Many men tried with her, but few had the goods. She had her favorites, the guys she'd sleep with once in a while if the mood took her, but the rest could just hang out their tongues like slavering out-of-luck dogs. Today, though, her first goal was to get so drunk she could forget about her little brother.

Joe—the bartender, his name really was Joe, and she always called him "Set 'em Up Joe," was her boyfriend in high school. Now he was a part-time welder and part-time bartender and full-time husband.

"How you doin' today, darlin'?" He polished off the bar with a towel and set down a glass and poured a liberal supply of whiskey in it. She knocked it back like she always did, and said, "Fine." The first one was always free. His daughter, Kayla, rode free at Jaimie's place in return for cleaning the stalls, so really, it was an exchange. He kept her old ranch truck running and had done some nice ironwork around her place, beautiful stuff that she could put on her business cards and brochures. If she ever got around to it.

He repeated the question. "How's it goin'?"

"You don't know?"

"Know what?" He had hazel eyes and they were sexy, but damn he was actually one of those men who were faithful to their wives, plus, she already had her eye on the one she wanted to pick out of the herd—Harley Cawdle. He was playing pool and watching her like a dog watches a can of Alpo on the counter.

She held out her glass for another shot. Joe poured another.

"You don't know about what happened? To my brother?"

"Michael?"

"No, the one in Laguna Beach."

"So what about him?"

"He's dead."

"Oh."

"Yeah, oh."

"You don't seem that upset."

"He was a dumb-ass."

"I don't know as I ever met him."

"You wouldn't. He hasn't lived out here in, like, ten years."

"I'm sorry."

"Wanna know what happened to him?"

Joe Shively looked troubled. She knew he didn't want to hear it, but she said it anyway. She slammed the shot glass down on the counter and said, "Somebody choked him to death, that's what happened."

Joe just stared at her. Opened his mouth. Almost said something. Closed it again.

She started to cry. She didn't want to cry because it would mess up her makeup, and she really did want to get laid by Harley, but all of a sudden she wasn't just crying, she was braying. Braying like a fucking donkey! And she couldn't stop.

Through her tears she looked over at Harley. He was watching. His pool cue standing next to him, his hand frozen on it. Then he looked away.

Like she was embarrassing herself.

"What are you looking at, Harley?" she yelled.

He shook his head and turned away, tried to make a shot, and the pool cue shot over the ball and the ball jumped a little. His back was to her.

"Hey, Harley, you know you want it!" she yelled at him.

He studiously avoided her gaze, lining up his shot.

"You're gonna blow it, Harley. You're going to screw the fuck up."

And he did. His pool cue rammed into the felt and banged against the side of the table.

Likely be the only satisfaction she'd get tonight.

She paid for two more shots and got the hell out of there.

~

Jaimie turned under the sign and drove down to the stables to check on the horses. Her eyes were red and she knew she didn't look good. She'd repaired her makeup in the little cubicle they called a bathroom at the Buckboard. Coming out had run right smack into Harley. The bathroom was in a narrow hallway that led out past the kitchen—the back way out, and he'd been headed that way. She said again, "What are you lookin' at?"

He'd mumbled something. She thought it was about her brother, but she was so angry, so embarrassed—humiliated by the weakness she'd shown—that she stomped hard on his instep. He banged against the cheap veneered wood paneling of the hallway, and she charged past him out into the night.

It was a nice night, and the stars had turned the sky blue roan, the color of her first pony a thousand years ago. The horses were all in good shape. It was sweater weather at night, and she was wearing a slinky tank top, so she rubbed her arms.

She was pretty bad off. All the crying and all the whiskey. So she let herself in, and followed by a crowd of dogs, went off to bed.

CHAPTER 30

The following morning, Tess was on the road early.

Turned out that there were two wildlife sanctuaries in the Santa Anas. The first was well-run, and it was clear the people there cared. There were several birds in rehab, including a golden eagle. Many animals had been injured—shot or poisoned or rescued from some backyard hell. Most of them would stay there forever. Others were being prepared to go back into the wild. There was a veterinarian on site, and tours to educate the public about the importance of wildlife.

Some animals—antelope, mostly, were allowed acreage to roam in.

Tess asked the wildlife biologist, a tall Swedish beauty with an earnest way about her, about the possibility of a mountain lion in Asteroid Canyon. She confirmed June Hackler's theory.

"There probably *is* a mountain lion who goes into that canyon. They have a big range, but that would be a good source of food. But it's also possible that no one would ever see it."

She, too, thought it highly unlikely that a mountain lion would attack Peter Farley.

~

The second place, Desert Winds Animal Sanctuary, was more like a circus that had pulled up stakes in the middle of the night. It wasn't really a sanctuary at all, but a minizoo. The place sat at the end of a dirt road in open country not far from Black Star. No one was around when she went to look at the animals. There weren't very many. Tess peered into the window of one of the modular units and saw a bear inside a smallish cage. The bear looked depressed.

Outside, there were several empty cages, none of them cleaned out. The animals that were there looked as if they had just given up. There were faded index cards stuck into plates. Tess saw a tiger, a lion, an ibex, and a deer. Two of the enclosures were empty, the gates open. The index card for one said "Cougar."

She waited around for an hour, but nobody appeared. The house, not that much better than General Mullet's in the canyon, was buttoned up tight.

Occasionally a wind blew through and the rank smell assaulted her nostrils.

Tess looked at the animals drowsing in the sun. At least they had ramada shelters.

She should report this facility. No way should this place have something as dangerous as a tiger here. Tess couldn't imagine how the tiger had not found a way into the ibex's pen. Crazy.

Tess left feeling depressed.

What she was thinking was beyond logical. It was insane.

But it made sense in the larger scheme of things.

Driving out, she looked back at the animals. Most of them appeared to be underweight.

One thing June Hackler had told her stood out: *the animal would have to be starving.*

~

As Tess opened the door to the room—it was cool and smelled stale and no longer held the magic of her tryst with Max—her mobile sounded.

For a second she thought of Max.

That's right, it's rope-a-dope. And you're the dope.

The number on the readout wasn't his. The name was Frieda Nussman. Tess answered. Nussman ran the Desert Winds Animal Sanctuary.

She had a voice like a goose honk. Tess thought uncharitably that it might account for the nervousness of the animals at the "sanctuary."

"I had a lion but someone bought it."

"People can do that?"

"Sure. I checked them out, made sure the lion would go to a good home—a zoo in Palm Springs."

"You checked their accreditation?"

"Oh, yeah. The guy was a wildlife biologist."

"How long ago was this?"

"Goldie's been gone a couple of years now."

"Can you remember when you sold him?"

"No, I can't. It could have been spring, but I'm not sure. I'd have to look at my records, and I'm outside right now."

Why did Tess somehow doubt she had any records?

"Can you describe him?"

"It was a long time ago. I can't describe what I had for dinner last night."

"Try."

"He was good-looking, I remember that, because he flirted with me."

"How old was he?"

"I don't know—midthirties?"

"Did the man have a cage?"

"Of course he had a cage. That went pretty well. I'm away from my desk right now. I'll look up the paperwork when I get in and give you a call."

She hung up.

Tess had a feeling she wouldn't call back. The woman had made a quick buck off an old mountain lion, and that was that.

Tess looked at her watch—she had time.

She called Barry Zudowsky, and he agreed to meet her there.

He sounded like he wanted to get it over with. Professional courtesy, that was all.

Tess had something specific she wanted from him. He might do it, he might not, he might argue about it. She's learned always to ask, even if it made her uncomfortable. That was part of the job description, getting into peoples' faces and asking them to do something they didn't feel comfortable doing, something that didn't fit with their agenda. She did it every day, but today she felt foolish about it. So she said it right away—*another* favor.

"I'm going to send a photo to you of a man I suspect could be involved in Peter Farley's death. Frieda Nussman might recognize him. Could you make up a photo lineup with this photo in it?"

He agreed that he could. The he asked, "You think he killed Farley?"

"Yes."

"How? Farley was killed by an animal. That's indisputable."

"I know that."

Just saying it emboldened him. "He was killed by a mountain lion. The jaw size, the tooth marks. This was a death by misadventure, just as we pegged it."

"That's what it looks like."

"You think someone faked it?" He was incredulous. "How could they do that?"

"I'm not sure if they could."

He said nothing. She knew he was thinking: *Wild goose chase.*

He was thinking: *Wasted day.*

Tess said, "I'll see you there. You'll bring the photo lineup?"

"Will do."

~

She put her bag in the car and drove back out to Desert Winds Animal Sanctuary, this time pulling off the road outside the gate to the property and waiting for Detective Zudowksy.

He pulled up behind her.

As she got out she saw that he was still sitting in his car. It looked like he was writing something down. Defending himself, maybe, for spending the day with a madwoman? She saw him shift in the car and unlatch his shoulder harness. She couldn't see much past the windshield except for his shape. Finally, he levered his tall beanpole of a body out of the car. Reluctance in every line. *A waste of time.*

He approached. He said hello and then after that he said nothing. She knew he was trying to figure out what her game was. She hadn't been completely forthcoming about her theory because it sounded outlandish and she wanted to keep him on her side.

He hadn't pushed.

But now she could see he was getting fed up.

A waste of a day. Nothing in it for him.

"I brought the photos."

"Good."

She followed him to his car and went around and opened up the passenger's side. He gave her the lineup. He'd used driver's licenses to match the photo of Michael DeKoven's DL.

"Good job," she said.

He didn't reply. Just looked straight ahead.

Tess just had to deal with it. She needed Zudowsky. Having him there in his official capacity might make Frieda Nussman more cooperative.

They bumped up the road and got out.

Nussman wore a flannel shirt and jeans. Her hair was long, down to the small of her back. She had an angular face, and was thin, almost skeletal. Tess wondered if she might have an eating disorder.

Nussman was prepared. She had the bill of sale in her hand. She described the man, who'd paid her one thousand dollars in cash for the mountain lion and a large cage she'd had rusting around the place. Tess shivered when the woman described it—she'd purchased it at a swap meet, the cage had been used in a circus that had gone out of business. "Paid a pretty penny for it, too," she said. "I thought it would draw people, but . . ." She glanced around the yard.

The name on the bill of sale was a Dom Derring.

"He paid you in cash."

"I told you that."

"Just great."

"He called me from out of town," Nussman said. "He wanted to put a hold on the cat until he could get here, so I charged him a hundred dollars on his credit card."

"You have the credit card number?"

"I'm pretty sure I still have it in my records. I'm not one to throw anything away."

"Please look for it."

She went inside and was gone a long time. Tess could picturing her rummaging around. She didn't think the chances were too good of seeing that credit card number—but she was wrong. The woman came back out with the name and the credit card number.

Zudowsky walked away and called it in. They waited. Tess continued to talk to Nussman, trying to get on her good side, if she had one. Asking about the animals. The woman answered her questions but wasn't forthcoming. She seemed to have her mind on something else. Zudowsky ended the call and came their way.

"Excuse me," Tess said to Nussman. She walked out to meet Barry Zudowsky.

"There was a Dom Derring listed," Barry Zudowsky said, his voice low. "But the credit card was canceled almost two years ago. You think it's your guy? DeKoven?"

"Sounds like a made-up name. He applied for it and used it for that one purpose," Tess said.

"Unless there were others."

Tess nodded. Time to show Nussman the photo lineup.

She had a good feeling.

Dom Derring—a made-up name.

Michael DeKoven acting cute.

Obvious.

Zudowsky produced the photos.

"Do you recognize any of these men? Could one of them be the man who bought the mountain lion?"

The woman stared at the pictures for a long time. "No, the guy who came here was blond."

"Just look at their faces. Hair can be dyed. Do you recognize any of them?"

She shook her head. "Nope. Sorry."

Driving back, Detective Zudowsky said, "I guess that's that. He's not your man."

"Maybe, maybe not. He could have paid someone to buy the mountain lion."

"You really think that happened?"

"I do."

"Why would anyone do *that*?"

"He wanted a mountain lion kill."

"*Why?*"

Tess said, "He wanted it to look like Farley was killed by an animal. He had his reasons—it was a game."

"A game." He looked straight ahead.

She knew what he was thinking.

She'd tell him what she suspected. Might as well. He'd have something to yuk it up with, with his buddies. And so she ran it down for him, that DeKoven had likely killed an ex-cop named

George Hanley, Peter Farley, and his own father, Quentin DeKoven. She told him about Hanley's investigation.

"So this, uh, *Hanley,* wrote all this down? He called it an investigation? You said he was retired."

"He was a homicide cop for twenty years."

"He was how old?"

"Sixty-eight."

"Uh-huh." He did not look at her. "So you're saying this was a game he played, finding people who survived accidents, then killing them?"

"That's the theory we're working under. He got the jump on Mr. Farley, maybe knocked him out in some way, and put him in with the lion."

Zudowsky kept his eyes on the road. "The lion probably wouldn't attack him even then, from what I've heard."

"He would if he'd been starved."

Silence. It hung there like the dust over the graded dirt road.

Finally Zudowsky said, "I just don't see how your theory hangs together. I can't see someone doing something like this. It's much more likely that Farley was attacked by a mountain lion. It could happen, if Farley was bent over his bike. That's what happened north of here. We've had two attacks of mountain bikers, and they're both fairly recent."

Tess said, "Did anyone do a tox on Peter Farley?"

"I don't remember seeing anything about one. His cause of death was pretty obvious."

"Also, I wonder if there were any marks on the body from the cage."

"DNA wasn't at front of mind when you're dealing with an obvious mountain lion attack. Plus, there wasn't enough of Farley to identify him except for his wallet, bike, and his vehicle parked at the entrance."

Tess said, "I would like to find that cage."

He said nothing.

Tess realized that his respect for her had run out, along with professional courtesy.

∾

Just before they split up she said to Barry Zudowsky, "I'm going to ask you to do me one favor."

To his credit, he didn't roll his eyes. But he said nothing.

"I'd like to pair Ms. Nussman with a sketch artist. The person who bought the lion is key."

Zudowsky said, "I'll see what I can do."

When he got back in his car and drove away, she thought she'd never hear from him again.

CHAPTER 31

It wasn't until Jaimie was up drinking tomato juice (she swore by it for a hangover if there wasn't any *menudo* around) and squinting at the car coming down the hill—Marisue Jennrette's Armada—that she realized she hadn't canceled lessons for today.

Shit.

Felt like a crushed box in the road. But she went out anyway, squinting against the harsh sunlight, and met Marisue and her daughter as they were getting out.

Shielding her eyes against the glare, her brain throbbing in her skull, Jaimie said, "I can't teach today. I'm sorry."

"What?" said Marisue. Like she'd been told the sky was falling. She always was a bitch.

"I'm sorry, but my brother died. I'm just getting ready to go to his funeral," she lied.

"Michael?"

"No, Chad."

"Chad? Why didn't you call me? It's fifteen miles to get here, and I've got a lot to do today. I'm working on the flower committee at the Chamber of Commerce!"

God, her head! Jaimie pressed a thumb into her left temple. "I'm sorry. But it's just this once. My brother, you know? My brother is dead."

"Fine."

The woman said it the way Jaimie always said it, the way women said it to men. If that's the way it's going to be, fine. Just fine. And by the way, fuck you.

Well fuck you, too, she thought.

After Marisue and her chunky untalented daughter drove off the property, Jaimie walked back toward the house.

Her dogs followed her up onto the steps. They milled around while she opened the door. They stood there, chastened, while she told them to stay outside.

She went to bed. She slept. When she woke up, it was early afternoon. She heard rocks pop off car tires—someone *else* coming. She hoped it wasn't Michael. Or Brayden. She wasn't up to that today. She just wanted everything about what happened in Laguna Beach to just fricking go away.

She got up, not bothering about her wrinkled clothes, her tank top and jeans. It was a truck like any other around here, a white Ford. But she didn't know this particular one.

She opened the door and the dogs milled around.

The two little terriers, the black lab. The two mutts, one of them spotted. The coon hound.

The truck bumped along the road toward her.

Six dogs, not seven. Jaimie was missing the familiar blue-gray, white, and black—her prize.

Her consolation prize.

Adele was missing.

~

The guy was just a guy, looking at various pieces of land around here. He asked her if she knew of any. "Just a couple of acres, kind of like a homestead," he said. He had an open, friendly face. Straw cowboy hat. Jeans, denim shirt. Your average middle-aged guy who maybe grew up rural and now wanted a small place of his own in God's country. She'd met a million like him. He was way too old for her. But she wasn't thinking about sex right now. Just get rid of him. Adele was missing. She had to be around here somewhere. But she could be hurt. Not like her not to come when she was called.

Jaimie scanned the yard as he talked, bending her ear with useless babble. On and on and on, as if he enjoyed boring her to death. When all she wanted to do was find Adele. She tuned him out, her eyes searching the grassland, hoping to see some light blue and black and white. Looking for Adele. Maybe she was in the barn. Maybe . . .

She wished the guy would just get in his fucking truck and go.

He didn't seem to get the hint. She told him about a place up the road where she'd seen a FOR SALE sign. Just *go*, already.

Finally he did. In the truck, he honked the horn once and gave her a salute.

Jaimie barely noticed. She was too busy looking for her dog.

~

Tess was now certain that the lion was purchased to kill Farley. The name on the credit card was made up, but DeKoven had been too

cute about it. She looked up the word "Dom" in an online diction-
ary. "Dominus" meant "lord." And Derring. She knew that "derring" was part of the term "derring-do." Her mother had used that
term all the time. It meant, basically, doing something that was dar-
ing. So it could be that Michael was saying he was superior to others—a lord—and he was, at least in terms of wealth and privilege.
Michael was the scion of a wealthy and important family. And he
would certainly think of himself as having plenty of "derring-do."

Old-fashioned term for a young guy.

Derring-do—maybe it was an expression he learned from his
mother or father. It took a whole hell of a lot of derring-do to go
around the country killing people because you thought you could
get away with it.

She wondered where the animal was now. If he had been in the
cage with Farley, if he had been driven out of hunger to eat Farley,
then there could be evidence somewhere.

The cage was the most likely piece of evidence left.

But how to find it? Michael DeKoven had money and means to
do pretty much whatever he wanted to do.

He could have killed the mountain lion and buried him. He
could have destroyed the lion cage. Break it up for kindling. Burn it.
Melt down the bars. Leave it in a landfill, or push it down a mountain. Plenty of places to do that. There were infinite ways he could
dispose of the evidence.

Trying to find the cage, trying to find the mountain lion—that
would be like looking for the needle in the haystack. There was so
much open county. Forest land. Canyons and washes out in the
boonies. Junkyards. Trash heaps.

The lion was gone. The cage was gone. Tess knew it.

She was convinced now that DeKoven was killing people who had previously escaped death. People who should have died, but lived instead.

If it was a game, it was a rich kid's game. Michael was in his midthirties, but Tess thought of him as a kid. Look at his toys. Look at that car, the Fisker Karma. Look at those expensive paintings. She thought of Jaimie as a kid, too. The two of them in it together?

That left the second-youngest, the girl. Brayden.

And Chad in Laguna.

Could all four of them be involved?

What were the odds of that?

Four siblings, in it together? She grouped them by age. Michael and Jaimie were closest, at thirty-five and thirty-four. Then came Chad at thirty-two—two years' difference between Jaimie and Chad, and three years' difference between Michael and Chad. From Chad to Brayden, the youngest, it was three years. Which made Brayden five years younger than Jaimie and six years younger than Michael.

Six years' difference in age might make a difference. Michael might not have included Brayden in this.

Tess hadn't met Brayden. She hadn't met Chad, either.

She wondered which one of the family had tagged Alec Sheppard on top of the Hilton Atlanta.

CHAPTER 32

Tess collected her bag at the Tucson International Airport carousel and walked out to her car. She saw she had a message from Alec Sheppard. She punched in his number as she walked.

"Mr. Sheppard? I thought when people sat across from each other at a picnic table and listened to a band called the Blasphemers, we could at least call each other by our first names."

"I'm ever the professional."

"No doubt in my mind. I haven't heard from anybody and wanted to know if there was a—what do you call it in cop lingo? Break in the case? Anything on Steve Barkman?"

"Nothing yet." She wasn't about to tell him about the micro disc. "I plan to talk to Detective Tedesco later today. Are you still in town?"

"As a matter of fact I am. I'm looking at houses."

"Houses?"

"I'm thinking of relocating."

"Relocating?"

"You know, as in moving here. To Tucson."

"Why?"

"I like it here, and I don't need to live in Houston . . . you have a problem with that? Me being in your jurisdiction?"

"Technically, you'd be in Cheryl Tedesco's jurisdiction. So what kind of place are you looking for?"

"When I was a college student, I thought it would be pretty cool to live in one of those neighborhoods with the old houses, like the ones in Encanto. So I'm standing in front of this pink adobe pueblo-style monstrosity and I was wondering if you'd give me advice, since you're a local. Wait, let me send you a picture of it."

Tess's heart sped up. She cleared her throat. "That's not necessary. I'm here in Tucson. I could meet you there."

~

Tess drove north on Palo Verde and ended up twenty minutes later outside a very pink house surrounded by desert on a street in a neighborhood called Colonia Solana.

Alec Sheppard was waiting by his rental car.

He looked good.

He was a good-looking man.

She liked Alec Sheppard. In fact, she liked him a lot.

~

They toured that house and two others. One was in the foothills. The sun was starting to get low. "We could have dinner," Alec said.

Tess opened her mouth to say she had to get back. Instead, she excused herself and went outside to call Bonny's extension. It was late and he was already gone. She left a long message detailing what had transpired in California. She sent photos from her phone of the area where Peter Farley had been buried by the mountain pool. She sent photos of the animal sanctuary.

Then she went to dinner with Alec Sheppard. The food was good. The conversation, better. However much she liked him the first time they went out together, she liked him even more now.

She went up to his room for a nightcap.

Not advisable. She knew she was letting herself in for big trouble. He was too attractive, too decent, too nice, too smart, too good a man for it not to cause a major wrinkle in her life, but it was all operations go from the moment they stepped inside. She wanted him and he obviously wanted her. It started to get warm and then hot, and Tess realized she was equal parts attracted to Alec Sheppard and angry with Max.

It was hard to stop. Like a pilot trying to pull a plane out of a dive. He wasn't just a good kisser, but a good toucher, a good hugger, a good feeler, and she was getting to the point—quickly—where she would not be able to stop.

She might be there now.

They were more urgent now, lips, mouths, tongues, hands, hips, molding each other into an approximation of the act but with clothing between them—it was impossible.

They tangled on the bed. She unbuttoned his shirt. She ran her fingers down his chest and then below that. He was doing plenty of research on his own. It seemed physically impossible to break away.

Too late . . . too late.

But there was Max.

Maybe she and Max were over, but she couldn't do it this way.

She managed to pull away. It was one of the hardest things she'd ever done.

She said, "I'm in a relationship."

Alec looked at her. His face was a mirror of hers. Not shock exactly. He wasn't bereft, or brokenhearted, or disappointed. More like the rug had been pulled out from under him and he'd hit the ground flat on his chin.

She felt the same way.

He sat up, rubbed his neck. Looked away.

"I'm in a relationship," Tess said. "It's . . . problematic." Then she added in a rush of words, "I can't add to that, to our troubles. I have to . . . I have to think about it and I have to figure out if I want to stay with him."

She was aware that she sounded like she was pleading.

He sat still beside her. He blew air out of his lips. Looked into the middle distance and then down at his hands.

A good-looking man.

A man she liked being around.

A man she could maybe, possibly, fall in love with.

But she wasn't going to do it this way. "I'm sorry, Alec."

"I know."

She managed to pull herself together. Uncrimp and straighten her clothes. Tell her body to stop screaming at the top of its horny little lungs.

She heard herself say, "I want to keep in touch."

Then she bolted out into the chilly spring night.

Wondering just how much more she could screw up her life.

~

As Tess headed for her car, her phone chimed. It was Barry Zudowsky.

"I got a sketch artist with Frieda Nussman today. I'm going to send you a photo of her sketch."

"Do you have a name?"

"No. Let me send it to you."

He disconnected. Tess knew he was done.

A few moments later she was staring into the face of the man who had purchased the mountain lion.

She'd seen the face before—twice. In the first picture she'd seen of him, he'd been thirteen years old, standing at the ribbon-cutting ceremony for a water treatment plant. He'd lost the baby fat he'd had as a child but had retained the passivity in his expression. She recalled the more recent version of him from the family portrait in *Tucson Lifestyle*.

As a young man, his mane of blond hair was streaked with white from hours, days, months, and years of the surfing life in California. His face had become more angular and was deeply tanned. Chad DeKoven was a true boy of summer.

He was also a gamer like his brother, Michael, and his sister Jaimie.

He was part of it.

Tess looked for an address for DeKoven. He lived in Laguna Beach. She was able to access the DMV files, and this in turn yielded his phone number.

She sat in the car and considered how she would approach him. If he was a killer as she suspected, he would stonewall her. She knew she would only tip him off if she approached him head-on. She knew she'd need to do an end run around his defenses, run a game on him, but right now she couldn't think of anything. So she decided to call and see if he was there. She used her home phone to punch in his number.

A canned message sounded. Chad DeKoven's phone had been disconnected.

There was one person she hadn't yet talked to, other than Chad—Brayden DeKoven McConnell.

CHAPTER 33

Brayden McConnell lived in a very nice townhouse in Ventana Canyon at the foot of the Santa Catalina Mountains.

The first thing Tess noticed was a wood gilt-edged sign beside the door said, "Brayden McConnell, Real Estate Law."

She rang the lighted bell.

No answer. She tried again. Nothing. She was walking back to the car when Brayden answered.

Brayden's hair was pulled up messily in a clip. She wore a sweatshirt and purple drawstring velveteen sweatpants, none too clean. But she was pretty in a plain, sweet way. She looked nothing like the whippet-thin Jaimie or comic-book-hero-handsome Michael.

She kept the door between them, her pale eyes wide, sad, and frightened at the same time.

"Oh, I thought you were the babysitter." She started to close the heavy door. Tess was practiced at putting her foot between the door and the jamb. Thinking: you're going out like that? "Just a couple of questions, I'm a detective with Santa Cruz County." She nodded to the shield clipped to her belt.

"This is Pima County."

"I'd like to talk to you anyway. I can come back with a TPD detective if you'd like, or we can go to TPD midtown."

"Might as well. " She opened the door and led the way inside.

Tess pulled the door shut behind her.

Nice place, expensive furnishings, but sparse. Tess knew Brayden was divorced. It looked like someone had taken half of everything.

Her little girl, Aurora, was shy at first. They sat on a couple of sofas, and Aurora warmed up quickly, showing her dance steps and eventually building up to running around them shrieking, and alternately crawling onto Tess's lap.

"I'd like to ask you about your brother, Chad."

"Isn't that a little soon?"

"Soon?"

Brayden played with her hair clip, kept poking stray strands of hair into her chignon or whatever it was. "My brother Chad was a really good guy. A sweetheart. That's all you need to know."

Something off, here. Brayden sounded defiant. She'd said "was" a good guy. Tess summoned up the photo of the artist sketch on her phone. "Do you recognize him?"

Brayden stared open-mouthed at the sketch. Then she started to whimper. "He just *died*," Brayden said. "Can't you leave it alone for a *little* while?"

Then Aurora chimed in. She clung to her mother and started to wail.

Tess was shocked. That was why Chad's phone was disconnected. "When did this happen?"

"I don't think I should talk to you—it's personal."

"Brayden, the sketch I showed you links him to a homicide in Orange County," Tess lied. It merely linked him to an animal that might have been used in one. But Tess needed the upper hand now.

"What do you *want* from me? I don't care and I think you should go and leave us alone. We just had a long airplane ride and Aurora's having nightmares and she's breaking out! She has pimples! She's sick to her stomach and it isn't fair, so *why are you here?* You're harassing us and it's just plain mean and I'm sorry, I'm really really sorry, *excuse* me, but you should come back tomorrow or maybe go harass Michael because I don't know anything and my daughter's stomach needs to be settled!"

The kid was shrieking. Brayden kept on talking, none of it making sense. Just a barrage of words, throwing them at Tess like weapons. At first Tess thought the woman really was in shock, but it soon occurred to her that Brayden was able to avoid specifics by babbling. Her voice was so low even as she said paranoid and angry things, and Aurora's voice was so loud. It was like trying to listen to a babbling stream under a band saw.

It occurred to Tess that they were a good team. Brayden was stonewalling her. Brayden babbling and Aurora crying: a one-two punch.

Fracturing Tess's concentration. "Can you tell me how Chad died?"

"Why are you such a *ghoul*? Why do you care? He's dead, not that you or anyone else cares anything about him." She paused. "All right, Miss Ghoul. You want to know? Somebody murdered him! Someone *killed my brother.*"

"Can you tell me—"

She looked into Tess's eyes. "I don't know anything, except that somebody killed him. He was just going surfing, he was just a harmless adult *kid*, and somebody just throttled him and left him out there like they'd throw away a Dixie cup—like so much *trash*!"

Tess waited for the crying to subside. Either Brayden was suffering from histrionic personality disorder, or she was using the drama to stave off questions. And the daughter took her cues from the mother.

Tess held out the sketch again. "Is this Chad?"

Brayden stopped sobbing and looked. "It doesn't even *look* like him. But he wouldn't do anything to hurt anyone. If you think he's involved in anything bad like that, you're barking up the wrong tree, and I'm not saying anything more."

"Bad like what?"

She didn't miss a beat. "You're with the police. You wouldn't be showing me his picture if you were planning to give him the Surfer Dude of the Year Award."

"Do you know Steve Barkman?"

"*Who?*"

Tess showed her a photo of Steve Barkman.

"No. Who's he?"

"You don't know who he is?"

"I might have heard the name. But I don't know where. Why are you torturing me like this? I just lost my brother."

"So you never met this man?"

"No."

Tess reminded herself Brayden was a lawyer. And apparently a damn good one.

"Do you know a man named Alec Sheppard?"

"*Another* one? Who *are* all these people? No I don't know him!"

"Alec Sheppard. Are you sure you've never heard that name? Maybe when you were in Atlanta?"

211

Brayden McConnell looked at her as if she were nuts. "Atlanta. Next I suppose you're going to say I live on the North Pole. You come in here asking me all this crap when I don't have the slightest idea what you're talking about. Well here's something *I* want to know. If you're going to keep asking me stuff, why don't you tell me what it's all about? And why don't you use your pull with Laguna Beach PD to get some *answers*?" Brayden pulled her daughter onto her lap and held her as if she were afraid Tess would grab her any minute.

Tess knew when she was being sandbagged.

Time to give up—for now. Tess stood. "Thank you for your time."

"No problem."

Seriously?

Tess was relieved when the door closed behind her—and glad to get out from under.

Score one for Brayden DeKoven McConnell and her daughter, Aurora.

Lawyers of the year.

~

Tess positioned herself about seven homes up the street, backing the SUV into a driveway and killing her lights. A large palo verde tree partially screened her. There was only one way out of the neighborhood.

She waited.

A half hour went by. She did not hear a garage door roll up. She did not see taillights back out. No car came by. Another hour. Same thing. She waited another half hour. Nobody drove into the neighborhood.

Brayden wasn't going anywhere. She had not been spooked.

Tess started up the engine, put the car in gear, and headed down out of Tucson to the freeway toward home.

She felt as if she'd been put through the wringer. She had a bad feeling about Brayden. Not just that she was good at barrage tactics, but because there was one moment when Tess sensed something besides just good tactics.

Tess had kept her eyes on Brayden's face every moment. She was distracted by the little girl, she had a hard time following the line of bullshit Brayden was handing her, but she never once took her eyes away from that sweet face and those big little-girl eyes.

And there was one moment when the mask slipped.

Some well-turned phrase, maybe. She'd seen it—raw triumph.

As if Brayden, behind her sweet little-girl exterior, behind the shocked and grieving sister, was playing her.

CHAPTER 34

Lying prone—in the same position he'd taken on the hill above George Hanley's final resting place on the day of his funeral—the watcher conducted his surveillance from a knoll above Wolfe Manor Performance Horses. His Bushnell 10X42 Fusion 1600 ARC laser rangefinder binoculars were as good as they come.

It was still early in the day—not six a.m. yet. But horse people got up early.

His binocs followed Jaimie Wolfe as she fed the horses. Her movements were agitated and disjointed. She was shaken. She was worried and harried and scared and angry. He could hear it in the banging buckets and the yelled "Quit!" and the way she dumped flakes of hay so that some of it got tangled in her hair and in her face and she had to sneeze.

He thought she was crying. It was hard to tell from here. She sped through the feeding and went to the house and came out a few minutes later with a stack of papers, probably from her printer. She pulled the truck door open with force and hopped in and whammed the door shut. There was a moment where the truck didn't move. He could see her, bent over the steering wheel, bent forward over the dash, her loose hair falling forward. He didn't see her shoulders shaking, but he thought she might be crying.

Right now, she was thinking her dog was lost. And she wanted it back. She was desperate to get it back, and at this point, as much as she was in despair, she still had hope.

Hope could be dashed. But first things first. Let her experience hope and then get let down by it. It would be the first in a series of disappointments for her.

This was only Round One.

CHAPTER 35

The next morning, Tess tracked down the detective working the Chad DeKoven case in Laguna Beach. It was a short phone conversation, mainly because Detective Pete Morales had so little to go by.

"I didn't tell the family, but it looked like a professional killing." He described the chokehold that had been used. "Quick and efficient. Nothing was stolen. The kid had an expensive board—a limited edition called a 'Sacrilege,' It wasn't taken. I find that significant."

"Any thoughts on a possible motive?"

"It's a puzzle. Offhand, it seems there was no reason. He didn't have any enemies, was an easygoing kid, kind of did his own thing. More than one friend used the term "harmless." My thinking is that whoever killed him was either in law enforcement, maybe military or former military, or someone who studied martial arts. They knew what they were doing."

"Male?"

"Probably."

"Nothing stolen from his house?"

"His place is a mess. I don't know where they'd begin. The cottage was unlocked and undisturbed, as far as we could tell. We had a crime scene tech go through it—nothing remarkable except for his quiver."

"Quiver?"

"His collection of boards. Massive—and all of them expensive, some of them one of a kind."

"None missing?"

"Can't be sure of that, but it doesn't appear to be. *That* room was locked. It was an add-on, especially to keep his boards. The lock was intact."

"How did the family react?" Thinking of Brayden last night.

A pause. "They were an oddball lot. Prickly with each other over little things. The youngest, Brayden uh . . ." He checked his notes. "McConnell, cried nonstop. People get strange, as you know, when they are grieving, or shocked by something like this. So it's hard to judge."

Tess asked him to keep her updated, and he agreed to send her a copy of the report.

Her phone rang again almost immediately. It was Detective Cheryl Tedesco.

~

Another drive to Tucson. This time to meet an assistant prosecutor who had called Tedesco about her meeting with Steve Barkman.

Tess met Cheryl at Barista, a coffee place downtown that catered to the people going in and out of the courthouse.

Cheryl ran it down for her, that an assistant prosecutor named Melinda Bayless had witnessed an altercation between her friend Brayden McConnell and Steve Barkman.

Melinda Bayless looked like a young lawyer on her way up. She wore a black pantsuit and black shoes with medium heels. Her hair was blonde and blunt cut down to her shoulders. She carried a briefcase. She might be twenty-seven, she might be thirty, she might be thirty-two. The deep salmon lipstick matched her blouse. She saw them and knew immediately who they were. They all introduced one another, three professional women, and lined up to get coffee at the counter. They sat in tall chairs at a table in the corner, the quietest spot in a roomful of babble.

As usual, Tess played the role of an observer.

For a lawyer, Melinda Bayless was pretty straightforward. She used her hands a lot, long tapered fingers, beautifully manicured nails painted the same color as her blouse.

Melinda said, "He came on to Brayden. At first Daffy—that's our friend, Daphne Morales, she's also an attorney—at first she and I were envious." Brushed a strand of hair back. "Well, not envious, exactly. But he was good-looking. When I was younger, that was the main criteria, but we're all older now and good looks are great but they're certainly not enough."

Cheryl led her through the incident. Melinda described the first meeting with Barkman in great detail. "He was only interested in Brae."

"What was his manner?"

"Other than that he zeroed in on her? He was confident. Overconfident, really. I've known a few colleagues like that—they think they're the Young Guns. Cocky. But not over-the-top."

She told them that Steve Barkman looked good but that he leaned in way too close to Brayden. "He violated her personal space. I noticed that right away. I hate that! It made me think of a cat playing with a mouse. And Brayden's no mouse, believe me. A little mousey." She added, "I know that sounds bitchy."

"He was after her, big-time. I thought he was thinking he'd get laid. But we kind of joined ranks and after a while he got the message and left. It was like we all breathed a sigh of relief. It was that intense." Then she described the second occasion, the next day. This time Barkman showed up early. "I saw him coming our way, and I thought, oh, no. We told him Brayden wasn't coming, which was a lie."

She described how Brayden spotted Barkman and took off.

"What did he do?"

"He went after her."

"Brayden didn't come back?"

"No. But she called twenty minutes later. She was freaked. She said he came up to her in the parking lot—said he basically accosted her. She said he tried to keep her from leaving."

~

Outside on the street, Cheryl said to Tess, "She didn't like Steve Barkman putting the moves on her, but I don't see any *there*, there." Cheryl shaded her eyes against the sun and squinted in the direction of the Dystel building, where Michael DeKoven worked. "I dunno, It seems too elaborate to me—even if someone kicked the stool out from under him and he crashed headfirst into the table—and believe me, he could have bounced off or landed in another way—then how did that piece of glass go right through one eye?"

Tess had no answer for that. But she did wonder: Why would Brayden lie about knowing Steve Barkman?

CHAPTER 36

Michael didn't want to see anyone—except Martin. He called Martin first thing.

"So you want me to fly back?" Martin said. "*Now?*"

"Yes. I'll pay for it."

"I have a gig."

"A gig? Or an audition?"

Michael knew that Martin was taking fewer and fewer modeling jobs, that he was trying to break into TV and the movies. In fact, he'd made noises about moving to LA.

"An audition," Martin said.

"You can go to the audition, Martin, or you can come here and stay with me. I need comfort right now."

"But I just got back."

"Martin, I need to be able to depend on you."

"But this part might be—"

"My goddamn *brother* died. I need you. I need a friend, Martin, I need my lover. If it isn't you, it'll be someone else. If you can't do this for me now, when I'm in need, you won't ever be coming back. Think about what that means."

There was silence on the other end of the line. Michael knew that Martin was thinking about all the clothes, the shoes, the renovations to his apartment—hell, the apartment itself. He was thinking of all the trips they'd made together—Milan, Florence, Paris, Berlin, Sydney.

Martin said, "Okay. Book me a flight, though, will you? It has to be first class."

"You're already booked." Michael gave him the information.

After that Michael sat in the solarium and listened to music, mostly jazz. Jazz felt just disorderly enough. The music was all over the place, and so were his feelings. His mind ranged over his memories of Chad. But try as he might to summon up a picture of his little brother, he couldn't quite see his face. Over the years, Chad had kind of . . . disappeared. Chad had always seemed to be swallowed up by this house. By the presence of their father, who dominated over everything and everyone.

Michael had changed out every piece of furniture, relaid the floors, even expanded the room, but his father still dominated this place.

He could move. But the truth was, if he moved, his father would win.

He wasn't going to be driven off his land, he wasn't going to give up the DeKoven homestead.

Maybe it was the music. His father liked jazz. He put on something frenetic—AC/DC.

Sang along with "Highway to Hell."

221

Finally, his mind began to skip to other things.

Flying back from LA, he'd looked down at the Santa Anas, remembering his kill. Farley's death was a triumph of logistics and planning. Elaborate, yes, but also rewarding. Michael had pitted his brainpower and his physical strength against a knotty problem. It had taken athletic prowess and toughness to carry out the mission. Dragging Farley up to the pool was no easy feat.

His sadness was beginning to creep away, replaced by satisfaction of the game he'd played with Peter Farley.

Chad had a good life. They'd let him live his lifestyle out there, never bothered him. Supported him.

The more he thought about it, the more likely it was that Chad's death had been a random killing. Probably by an acquaintance. Someone on crystal meth or bath salts—something like that. They were all pretty doped up around there. Michael thought that a hippie or surfer dude could just as easily be former military, or could learn the chokehold he used from a book. There were all sorts of bad people in the world, and they had their obsessions. They had their own way of doing things. Michael had met a lot of them.

In fact, he *was* one of them.

CHAPTER 37

Danny was now the proud father of a baby girl. Elena was the most beautiful little girl in the world. He knew he was biased, but that didn't alter the facts. Everything had changed, and really it had changed overnight. Now there was another human being here, with a personality he thought he could already see.

He felt as if his heart encompassed the whole world, and yet his gaze was brought down to a tiny little girl with tiny little fists and eyes squeezed shut. He knew he would fight to the death for her. This new little person he already loved beyond himself.

He tried to concentrate on his work—paperwork, which was endless in a sheriff's detective's job. He tried, but it was hard. Theresa was asleep, and although he wanted to wake her and share with her this great feeling, he knew she needed rest.

So when his phone buzzed, he got up quietly from her bedside and walked out into the hallway, where the sun threw down squares of brightness in the hospital corridor.

The readout said Pat Scofield, George Hanley's daughter.

He wondered why she was calling now. Neither she nor her husband had made a peep since the day Danny and Tess had delivered the news. Not one phone call. Pat Scofield had answered his questions dutifully over the phone, as if she didn't care.

He answered.

He heard the edge to her voice right away.

She talked quickly—scared. "I'm sure I just saw my brother-in-law drive by the house," she whispered.

"Your brother-in-law?"

"He was married to my sister. He . . . I thought I'd never see him again. I thought he went to California."

She was blurting out things that made little sense.

"Slow down," Danny said. "Take a deep breath."

He didn't like her. From the moment he'd met her he didn't like her, and now she was taking precious time away from his time with his new daughter. But this was his job, and he had to listen. It was important that he do the job right. For the victim, if not for the people left behind. He had met countless people like Pat Scofield. They sucked up all the energy in the room into themselves, and returned nothing.

"He was married to my sister. He moved to California after my sister died. I thought I'd never see him again but I think he was here."

Danny leaned closer into the phone, spoke softly. "You're afraid of him?"

"I shouldn't be, I know, but . . . I don't like him. He's never had anything to do with us but I think it was him. I was cleaning the front window and I saw him drive by. He slowed down."

"Why would you be afraid of him?"

"I'm not sure."

"You're not sure?"

"I just saw him drive by and slow down, and I remembered some of the things he did."

"What kind of things?"

"I don't know. Maybe it was my imagination. I shouldn't have called." But she didn't hang up.

Danny said, "Can you describe him?"

"I haven't seen or heard from him in eleven years. Maybe longer than that. Right after we buried Karen, he moved to California. Just upped and left, like he was footloose and fancy-free."

Danny was sensing there were old wounds here, possibly imaginary, but you could never count on that. "You want me to come by?"

"No, no. I don't think that's necessary."

"Look, I'm not far away. My wife is sleeping. She just had a baby."

"Maybe you *should* come by."

No congratulations. Not even a "That's nice."

He said, "I'll be there shortly. There are a couple more questions I want to ask you, anyway."

There was silence on the other end of the line. Neither she nor her husband had ever asked about the status of the case. He'd thought that was strange at the time, but he was busy with his own work and, of course, the coming birth of Elena. But after the initial shock, the crying and the desperation to see her father Pat exhibited, he'd been surprised that there hadn't been a flurry of calls afterward.

People reacted to tragedy in wildly different ways. Nothing surprised him anymore. Theresa needed her sleep. And he needed to work.

He left word with the nurse, went by to take another look at his beautiful, precious daughter, and drove down to Rio Rico.

~

When he arrived, Pat was back to her vague, flustered, disjointed self. She was sorry she'd bothered him. She was fine now. Bert would be coming home soon, and anyway, it was just her imagination. Her brother-in-law wouldn't be here. He'd been living in California, and although she'd heard he might have moved back to Arizona, she'd assumed it would be up north, to Phoenix, where he was from.

"You think he moved back to Arizona?"

"I'm not sure. Maybe it was just a visit. Dad mentioned seeing him, but I can't really remember what he said. Dad knew I didn't want to hear about him. He made Karen so unhappy. You should have seen the way he treated her. Like she didn't matter. That's a terrible thing to do to a woman. Especially one who was five months pregnant when she died."

"Your father? They were friends?"

"They were partners. For years."

"You mean your brother-in-law was a cop?"

"Yes, he was a homicide detective, just like my father was."

He said, "Karen died during a robbery? Is that right?"

"Yes."

He asked her to describe it.

She told him Karen had been at a convenience store—a Pit Stop—the night someone came in and robbed the store, killing both the clerk and Karen. "They were the only people in the store," Pat said.

"Where was this?"

"Phoenix."

"Do you know the name of the detective who investigated the shooting?"

"It was . . . Detective . . ." She closed her eyes. "Detective Clarence Sinkwich. I remember that because I've always used word associations to remember peoples' names, and so I pictured a tiny little witch sitting in a sink. He was a very kind man. I don't know how we would have gotten through it without him. He was like a rock. My dad was like that, too. Although I never saw him in action, that's what I heard."

"Do you remember when this was?"

"It was October fourteenth, 2001." She added, "I'll never forget that night."

"What about your brother-in-law?"

"Wade?" She practically spat his name. "He was around. You know, at the funeral. He came by once. He didn't care. He didn't care about her and he didn't give a damn about the baby she was carrying."

CHAPTER 38

Brayden came over with Aurora. Michael and his little sister sat out by the pool, watching Brayden's kid swim with Michael's two children. His wife, thank God, had gone off to "lunch" with her friends. It would be a long lunch, with plenty of alcohol. He knew she drank mostly because she couldn't stand him. She suspected what he was doing but she didn't know for sure. She thought they were playing a game, but she didn't know the extent. She'd suspected he'd had something to do with Steve Barkman's death—one of the few he'd had nothing to do with.

Now it was time for Michael to find out if Brayden was involved in Barkman's death.

Brayden hung tough. She was a hard-nosed bitch. He was getting impatient.

"Brae," he said, using the name he'd had for her when she was a kid, "what do you think is happening here?"

She kept her eyes on her kid. Looking at her, you'd think she was just a sweet little housewife, plain but attractive in a homey way. The kind you'd set up playdates with, the kind who'd go to PTA meetings. "Brae?"

She looked at him. "I think that cop from Nogales thinks she's on to something."

"And why is that, do you suppose?"

She squeezed out some sunscreen and lathered her face with it. "I think she's put it together. The guy who was killed down in that ghost town." She looked at him, her eyes startling. Big round eyes, like the women from the turn of the last century. She had their mother's eyes, but not her sweetness.

"George Hanley?"

"Uh-huh. I think she's on to that."

"On to it?"

Brayden said, "I thought we were gonna wait on him."

"We were."

Of course they were going to wait on him. The show he was on, *The Ultimate Survivor*, had only aired last year. He was too close. Too close in his notoriety, too close in geography. They'd decided early on that George Hanley was a project down the road. Maybe a year from now. But Jaimie . . . "You think Jaimie did this?"

Brayden shrugged.

"Seriously. Would she be capable of it? That was pretty rough stuff."

But he thought she was capable of it. For one thing, she had an AR-15. She loved her assault weapon. It was her passion. She voted NRA exclusively. When she wasn't giving riding lessons or picking up men at the Buckboard Saloon, she spent most of her time at the firing range.

229

Of course there had been few details that had come out about the Hanley killing, except that it was overkill. One account hinted at a cartel. Imagine, a cartel coming up into the US and killing some old man. It didn't make sense. But it could be made to *look* like a cartel killing.

But who would do that?

Michael said, "You think Jaimie'd be capable of something like that? Just shooting the shit out of someone?"

Brayden shrugged. Brayden was the champion shrugger of the world. She never committed to anything. As a lawyer, she could tie you in knots. She was, in many ways, the closest you could get to their father. Their patriarch. She didn't have his mean streak, but she had the confounding part right down.

Michael said, "She took the dog."

"What dog?"

"Hanley's dog. She took it as a prize."

"You mean, like the spoils of war?"

"Exactly. She's trying to pass it off as a dog she just found."

He let that lie out there. Jaimie had always been the weakest link. She was really not to be trusted. But Michael wondered if Brayden was to be trusted, either.

Suddenly, he wondered if she was seeing someone. He didn't care about her love life, but he didn't want any complications. "You know not to tell anyone."

Brayden stared at her daughter playing in the pool, then turned her round face to him, the sweet little housewife face. "Michael, you can be a real asshole, do you know that?"

She put on her sunglasses again. Brayden looked better with them on. Her face was such a dumpling, but sunglasses made her look richer. Richer and more attractive.

"They're still investigating his death," he said. "I get the impression they don't think it was an accident."

She shrugged.

"Brayden, you didn't have anything to do with that, did you? His death?"

"Me? No. Why would you say that, Michael?"

He had no reason, except that she was the most secretive, the most unreadable of all of them. "You never met him?"

"Not that I'm aware of."

He'd have to take her word for it. She was such a good liar you could never really tell, never get a baseline with her.

Brayden kept her eyes on the pool. "You think Jaimie killed that old man?"

"I wouldn't put it past her. The question is, what do we do about it?"

~

Brayden left soon afterward.

Michael stared at the pool. Was everything going to hell, or was it just his imagination? He'd heard nothing more about Alec Sheppard. Maybe Sheppard had already flown back to Houston. It had been close, very close, but he was pretty sure there was little to link him to Houston except that one moment where he'd pointed the finger gun at Sheppard.

But he went back through it anyway.

He'd laid the trap for Sheppard beautifully. A word to the girl at the computer in the rigger's loft at SkyDive Arizona, where he himself used to jump. "My friend Alec Sheppard's supposed to meet me here, but I'm worried that the expiration date on his reserve pack is coming up and I really hope he can make the jump with me. I'd hate to miss him."

Every 120 days the reserve had to be repacked—it was a safety issue.

The gum-chewing girl at the computer looked at the manifest and confirmed that Sheppard had to have his reserve chute repacked before the end of March.

"Damn it! I wanted to surprise him. You know where he's going?"

She looked again. "Looks like he's jumping in Houston next week."

"He hasn't repacked?"

"Nope, not yet."

Michael gave her his best crestfallen look. "Guess he's not meeting me here."

"Guess not."

And so Michael flew out to Houston the week before Sheppard was due to jump. He knew what kind of rig Sheppard had—he'd chatted up his friends and learned he had a red and blue-green Javelin. He was almost certain of the date Sheppard would have it repacked—the same day he'd jump.

Michael stayed in Houston. He kept tabs on Sheppard, *surveilled* him, and on the day he followed Sheppard to the jump center, he'd even confirmed the rig as he watched Sheppard walk it out to the car. Blue-green Javelin with red patches.

He brought in his own reserve to be repacked, then hung around the loft where the riggers were. Parachutes were laid out all over the floor.

It was the perfect setup, because the repacked reserve chutes were all lined up against the wall near the door—the only place for them. Nobody wanted jumpers traipsing on the chutes stretched out all over the floor. Casually Michael asked the rigger if anyone would mind if he looked at that Javelin over there while his rig was repacked. He pointed in the general direction of the packs stacked against the wall.

No problema.

As luck would have it, there was only one red and blue-green Javelin. He'd had a half hour to forty-five minutes for his rig to be repacked, but he didn't need more than ten—if that.

It was a done deal.

There had been only one mistake.

He should never have shot that finger gun at Sheppard.

Sheppard had jumped with a friend, a jumpmaster at the center. When the jumpmaster saw Sheppard going down fast, he'd cut loose from his own parachute and gone down after him, tackling him to slow his descent. He'd been able to reach where Sheppard couldn't, digging into Sheppard's rig and managing to release the pin to the reserve canopy. Michael saw it all, saw the jumpmaster roll out into a backflip and away, before pulling his own reserve.

They'd both drifted down, tragedy averted.

Like a cat, Alec Sheppard landed on his feet.

Seven lives left.

And then there was Steve Barkman, Sheppard's buddy. Michael vaguely remembered making small talk with him and his mother, the judge, at a fund-raiser—they'd shared a table.

Barkman had left a voice message for him weeks ago. Michael had no idea why Barkman would contact him, and at the time he was heading out for a trip and didn't bother to return the call.

The message had been strange enough that Michael had made some inquiries about Barkman through a third party, some people with Pima County Sheriff's. While Barkman's job wasn't important in the scheme of things, the people Michael talked to thought he'd make a good cop. One of them even called him savvy and smart. He couldn't understand why Barkman didn't just apply to the academy. He'd wondered aloud if Barkman might have been a licensed investigator.

In light of what Michael had learned about Barkman's friendship with Alec Sheppard, the call made sense. Barkman had left a message to the effect that he had "something important to discuss, of a personal nature."

Maybe Barkman wanted to shake him down.

But Barkman was dead. The only thing that mattered now: What did Barkman tell *Sheppard*?

His phone sounded. It was Jaimie.

She was crying so hard at first he couldn't understand her. "Someone took Adele!"

His first thought was Alec Sheppard. "Tell me what happened."

She told him how she'd come back from the airport and gone to bed early, how she woke up and Adele was gone. "I've been looking for her everywhere. Maybe she's trapped somewhere. I just went into town and put up posters."

Michael closed his eyes and pinched the bridge of his nose. "What name did you use?"

"Bandit."

"Does she come to 'Bandit?'"

"I don't know. She hasn't been here that long."

Michael could feel the dread building up inside him. Could it really be Sheppard? He was the only one he could think of who would be capable. You just looked into his eyes and you could see the toughness there. One of the reasons Michael had wanted him.

Wanted to notch his belt with him, make the kill. The reason he went.

Face it: the reason he had shot the finger gun at him. It was a visceral thing, almost atavistic. He wanted to dominate him. He wanted to see him die.

Maybe it was because they were about the same age. Men who had done well in business. There was a . . . parity there.

". . . took her?"

"What?" Michael held the phone closer to his ear. "What did you say?"

Jaimie said, "What's going on? Chad's dead, and now Adele's gone? What if someone killed her? I'm afraid to go look around, I'm afraid of what I might find."

He thought, *You wouldn't be so freaked if you saw the people we've already killed, though.* But he said nothing.

"I love her, Michael. I want her back!" Her voice plaintive.

"You should have left her where she was."

"They would have gassed her."

Michael thought about Chad and thought about whoever was out there. Alec Sheppard? Or someone else he didn't know about?

CHAPTER 39

After meeting the guy who would be doing some minor repairs on her house, Tess drove into town for lunch. She spotted Jaimie Wolfe's truck near the post office. Couldn't miss it because of the silhouette of the horse and rider clearing a jump, and the name of her stable on it. Jaimie was stapling a poster to a telephone pole. Tess walked over. "Your dog missing?"

Jaimie had been crying. She was disheveled and her clothes looked slept-in. She swiped at her nose. "Yes. My dog is missing."

"Bandit?"

Jaimie's eyes narrowed. "How'd you know?"

Tess nodded to the poster. "That's the only Australian shepherd you've got. Right?"

Jaimie said, "That's right." She added, "If you see her, let me know."

She got into her truck and drove off.

Jaimie had called Bandit a "her."

~

After a nap, the watcher woke up hungry. He had a blinding head-
ache and needed to eat something. The diner in Patagonia was pretty
good, and he was thinking biscuits and gravy.

He drove into Patagonia and parked across from the post office.

Surprise surprise, Jaimie Wolfe was stapling posters to the telephone poles.

He became aware that someone else was watching her.

He had a well-developed sixth sense. He could feel it when there
was, for want of a better term, involvement from another party.
Even if he didn't expect it, and in this situation he did. He could feel
it as if someone had taken a comb and gently rippled the hair on his
arms.

The other watcher had turned in a few minutes ago and parked
near the old railroad depot.

He squinched his eyes against the light, which at this time of
day was so bright it hurt to see.

The other watcher was a woman cop.

He'd seen her before, at George Hanley's funeral.

He'd even talked to her.

Now he watched her watch Jaimie Wolfe stapling flyers to telephone poles.

The cop walked over and had a short conversation with her,
then went back to her vehicle.

Jaimie got into her truck and drove off.

He followed her at a discreet distance as she roamed the two or
three streets that made up the south side of Patagonia, and the two
or three streets that made up the north side of Patagonia. That's

what he assumed. Today was Poster-Put-Up Day. It was the day when a grieving Jaimie Wolfe would obsess on something smaller than the death of her brother in California.

Her little brother, Chad.

He knew that it was easier to focus on something smaller—bite-size. Easier to do something than just stay home and mourn.

She should thank him. Losing the dog was akin to therapy.

~

Tess had lunch, but she wasn't very hungry. She was thinking about the DeKoven family and how to crack them.

Go for the most vulnerable. That would be Jaimie. While she drank coffee she tried to figure out the best way to approach her.

Walking back to her vehicle, she called Danny to see how Theresa and Elena were doing.

"Great on all counts. I can't believe she's here."

Tess smiled at the sound of his voice. He was trying to sound normal, but he seemed to be bursting at the seams with good feeling.

"So they're both doing great?"

"Better than great! You need to come over here and see her."

"Tell me when and I'll be there."

"Maybe later this afternoon? Wait till you see her. She's the most beautiful baby girl in the world."

"I expected as much," Tess said.

Danny said, "Pat Scofield called me."

"She did? I thought she dropped off the planet."

"I had some downtime while Theresa was sleeping, so I went over there earlier."

He told her about the son-in-law driving by, how Pat had been rattled by it.

"She's afraid of this man?"

"Oh, yeah. She's terrified. Why don't we meet over there and talk to her?"

~

Tess met Danny outside the Scofield house. Their car was parked out front, not yet garaged.

Bert Scofield answered the door. He didn't look happy to see them. His expression said plainly, "Again?"

"We'd like to talk to you about your father-in-law," Danny said.

Bert stepped back—reluctantly. "Come out on the back terrace. Pat's knitting and she likes being out there."

They walked through the small house. Tess noted several framed photos on the fireplace mantel—one might have been Pat's sister. Pat's hair was faded blonde, but this woman's hair was dark. The studio picture was many years old—a portrait of the young bride with her bridesmaids.

Tess noticed there was no photo of the bride and groom.

They followed him out to the patio. It was tiny, with a high wall. Pat sat near a round glass table, her knitting bag at her feet. When she saw Tess she said, "Have you found out who killed Dad?"

"Not yet. You mind if we sit down?"

"Sure. Please." She sat forward, her knitting forgotten. She looked at Danny. "First he drove down this street . . ."

Bert blew air through his pursed lips, did everything to show his exasperation but roll his eyes.

"Bert, you know I saw him!" she turned back to Tess. "He thinks I'm being silly. But it was like a goose walked over my grave. And after what we've been through with Dad . . ." She started to tear up.

Tess said, "Why are you afraid of your brother-in-law?"

"He's a bad person."

"He's not a bad person, Pat," Bert said. "You just got off on the wrong foot with him. He's a good guy."

Tess kept her concentration on Pat. "Why is he a bad person?"

"He was cruel to my sister, Karen. Mean. He'd *do* things, mean little things, like undermine her in front of other people. It was just the way he acted. But when he talked to us, he was nice as pie. Friendly, you know? Butter wouldn't melt in his mouth. I only saw that side of him with Karen."

"Pat, you're painting a pretty ugly picture here. Besides, he lives in California and we haven't seen him in over ten years."

"I saw him, Bert! I saw him slow down and drive by. Maybe he found out that Dad was dead and it brought him here."

Tess asked, "Did they not get along?"

"Oh, they got along great! Even though I think Wade was using him. My dad had a soft spot for him, I guess because they worked together for so long. But Karen said he has a mean temper. And once I saw it. Just for a minute. They were at a party at our house and he was holding her hand. Just leaning over her. She'd gone in to get something—a drink, maybe—from the fridge, and I was coming in with some dirty plates, and he was holding onto her hand and it looked like he was crushing it. She looked up and called my name. And he just relaxed his hand and smiled at me without a by-your-leave. But I know he hated me. And you, too, Bert. He didn't think much of you, either."

Bert shook his head and wandered away.

Tess said, "He was good friends with your dad, though?"

"Yes. But I got the feeling Dad cut him off after what happened to Karen. Like he didn't think Wade cared enough. And that was true. Wade got married not six months later."

"You think he victimized her?"

Pat wiped at a tear. "I *know* he victimized her."

Tess asked her how Karen died. She told her about the convenience store, the robber in the ski mask. How she was shot. "Poor Karen. She was such a great sister. I can't stand to think of it. And I know *he* didn't make her life any better." She added bitterly, "And I don't think he mourned the loss of her child either. She was five months pregnant."

Tess held Pat's hands in hers. "I'm so sorry."

"You know, maybe I'm being silly. Wade Poole wouldn't come by here. He doesn't care about us. We're old business. He lives in California. That's what Dad said."

She asked again about the progress they were making, and Tess had to tell her it wasn't much. "But we're working on it. We'll do our best to find whoever killed him and bring that person to justice."

The words sounded empty in her mouth. Because she was no closer to finding his killer, and neither was Danny.

"I thought it was a Mexican cartel—that's what a friend of Bert's thinks. The . . . way he was . . ." She put her hand to her mouth. "I can't think about that."

Tess said, "He died quickly."

"How do you know that?"

"I know. I've seen lots of people killed."

She saw the recognition in Pat's eyes.

"You're sure?"

Tess nodded. "I'm sure."

He'd been dead before he hit the ground.

As Tess and Danny left the house, Tess said, "I wonder what was going on between George Hanley and Wade Poole."

"You think he's in the area then?" Danny said.

"You heard her. She was sure it was him. Remember what was written on his calendar? Wading Pool. Maybe that was his nickname for Wade Poole."

"Weird, but possible."

CHAPTER 40

The next morning was Michael's regular bike riding day. It was a beautiful spring day, and shaken as he was, he did not deviate from his routine. Lately, his favorite ride was up the mountain to Kitt Peak Observatory west of Tucson, out on the Indian reservation. He thought of it as the Indian reservation, because that's what his father called them. The Indians there now called themselves Tohono O'odham, which meant something positive (he couldn't remember what), but Michael liked the old name Papago. That was the name he'd grown up with. Papago meant bean eaters. In his opinion, the Papago people were like every other minority: overly sensitive. Like they thought they were owed something just because they were called racial epithets and got handouts from the federal government.

It was a perfect day. Clear and bright, with deep blue skies. Michael needed to think, and he did his best thinking alone on his bike. He liked the twelve-mile trip up the mountain from the valley floor for a number of reasons. One was the lack of car traffic.

Hardly anyone drove up there from late morning on, especially at this time of year, unless there were tours. Most of the observatory's visitors drove up at night, when they could take the tours and look through the telescopes at the stars. The road was steep and winding and he liked to push himself. His personal best was forty-eight minutes, but he always strove to beat it. Riding cleared his mind. Every time he reached the top, he felt triumphant. And the ride down was like a video game—pure speed in places, places where he could corner like a Porsche. Thrills and chills.

He took the 4Runner, fitted with a top-of-the-line bike rack. He brought a change of clothes and wore his bike togs—wearing the same jersey he always wore, the orange jersey with a Beechcraft Baron 58 twin-engine plane silhouetted against a yellow sun he'd had designed specially for himself and his brother and sisters. Even though they didn't ride, Chad, Jaimie, and Brayden all had jerseys with the Beechcraft on it.

Above the plane were the words "The Survivors Club."

Because that was what they were. Survivors.

Every time he pulled it on, he thought of Dad and his last moments in the Beechcraft Baron.

He thought: Got you back, you fucking bastard.

~

He took 86 west toward Ajo, the mountain ahead of him. Hardly any traffic after he got past the town of Three Points on the res. He was waved through a checkpoint by the Border Patrol. In his rearview mirror, he noticed how the traffic had thinned out, just one vehicle way back. Probably a Papago's ranch truck, like the white one behind him at the last traffic light out of town. He turned left onto State Route 386 and took an immediate right into the dirt parking area where cyclists left their cars. Two other cars with bike racks had been parked there ahead of him; he'd probably see cyclists coming down. The cars were both older than his and cheap. He parked far enough away that they wouldn't ding him coming out, and changed into his Sidi bike shoes before unloading his most recent purchase, a Pinarello FP Team Carbon—one gorgeous bike. He filled up his jersey pockets with gel packs and Clif bars and a hero sandwich from Santaria Mike's—plenty of carbs.

He locked up just as a white truck turned off 86 and took 386 toward the mountain. Could be the same one. A work truck—certainly not top-of-the-line. Maybe it wasn't a Papago's truck—could belong to somebody working up at the observatory. He sped to catch up with it, hoping he could draft on the truck for fun. Almost got to him, but then the truck spurted away.

Fuck him.

Oh, well—it was a perfect day. There were no other cars.

Riding was pure application and striving for a personal best. But Michael soon realized that his mind was wandering. Wandering back to their family cottage in Laguna Beach, to Chad.

Hard to believe Chad was dead.

As he rode, as he pushed himself up the steep hills—hard—up out of the saddle, pounding out the rhythm on the pedals, he could feel something solid and small walling itself off inside his chest. Like a tiny nut.

He recognized it, because he'd lived with it as a kid. He'd lived with it every time his father turned his evil eye on him. As a kid, he'd read the Lord of the Rings trilogy, and he could picture his father's avid eye turned on him now, could almost see the laser ray, what he called the Eye of Mordor.

His father had done unspeakable things to him—and worse, made him like it.

Made him crave it.

No wonder he was bi. You gravitated to what you were used to.

But the feeling he had wasn't about his father. He'd fixed his father. His father wasn't around to fuck with him now. He'd burned to death in the plane crash in the Pinaleños.

But Michael was still afraid. He still felt that hard little nut of worry.

There was no reason for anyone to kill Chad.

As he pushed up the steepest part, getting into the rhythm, his lungs burning, his calves and thighs straining, the tiny nut in his heart gripped hard:

Dread.

The words formed in his head, as he pushed one pedal down and the other pedal came up, back and forth, back and forth.

Alec Sheppard.

Maybe he was paranoid. Sheppard might be long gone, back to Houston. But who else knew about Michael's trip there? He'd shot the finger gun at him.

Sheppard hadn't forgotten that. He'd hired Barkman to look into it, and he probably had whatever information Barkman had given him. Probably.

One thing, though—the two female detectives had nothing, if you went by their fishing expedition of the other day. He was pretty sure of that. He could read people well, and they were floundering. The two of them.

But Sheppard was different. Michael had read up on him, targeted him, and one reason he'd gone after Sheppard was because Sheppard was a star. He was a worthy foe. Michael had assigned

Brayden to slap the tag on Sheppard, but at the last minute, Michael had decided to do it himself. He'd wanted to see what the man was like. And Alec Sheppard was impressive.

Impressive enough to kill? Few people could do it. Few people had the resolve when it came right down to it. But he had felt it when he slapped the tag on. It had resonated like a tuning fork—the power in this man. He knew about powerful people. He was a powerful person. He'd loved and hated power all this life.

Did Sheppard have it in him to kill Chad? Did he have the ability, the knowledge, to kill him with a chokehold?

Michael didn't know for sure, but he thought that it was entirely possible that Sheppard had come here to even the score.

~

He made it to the top, winded but happy. Shaved off ten seconds—a new personal best. He liked it up here.

Today, though, there were a lot of tourists milling around the gift shop and walking on the winding road that went up to the telescopes. They'd come off a tour bus.

Usually, the place was almost spooky in a quaint way. Michael had always loved the reruns of the scary movies of the fifties. His father kept a video library of them, and later, upgraded to DVDs. This place was right out of *The Day the Earth Stood Still*. *Klaatu barado nikto.* Red brick buildings, all dating to the fifties and sixties. The large white domes of the telescopes like mushrooms popping up on a hill. At any minute he expected to hear an air raid siren. Any minute he expected to see giant crickets coming up over the hill waving twelve-foot-high antennae.

It was a nice spot on top of a mountain.

He found a place under an oak tree and ate his lunch.

The tour bus engine started up. People funneled through the gates in the bus's direction. People were mostly herd animals. Michael respected the cyclists who came up here, but tourists rubbed him the wrong way.

He ate slowly, soaking in the sunshine. He wanted to give the bus some time to clear before he headed down. A couple of vehicles came by. A truck and a Jeep Cherokee, both white. He balled up the sandwich paper and found a garbage can. The bus lumbered out. Time to ride down. *The best part.* And yet he couldn't stop thinking about Sheppard.

The guy was in his head.

He knew it was most likely he was imagining things. Sheppard had sold a thriving business. He had started another one and it was doing well—Michael had read up him. Sheppard might have come down here to see Barkman, but what did he know, really?

Maybe someone had just rolled Chad and killed him in doing so.

But Michael knew that Chad hadn't been rolled. He didn't carry money when he surfed. No one had taken his board.

He got on the bike and started down.

Behind him he heard the start of an engine—probably a truck. Glad at least he'd gotten in front of him so he didn't have to follow him all the way down the mountain.

CHAPTER 41

Tess was working at her desk when Jill, the operator, put a call through. Tess identified herself. "Who may I ask is calling?"

She heard only a rushing sound. Or a cross between a rushing and a whizzing sound. Traffic, going fast. A freeway.

"Hello? Can you hear me? This is Tess McCrae of the Santa Cruz County Sheriff's Office."

Disconnect.

She stared at the phone. Maybe it was a wrong number, or maybe it was an informant who realized he couldn't talk then. She had been given one other outstanding case, one of Danny's—a drug deal that had ended in a shooting, and before the Hanley case she had been trying to round up witnesses.

She went back to compiling what she had on the Hanley case. The phone rang again. Again, she heard traffic whizzing by on the Interstate.

But this time, a voice said, "Sheriff Tess?"

It was the squatter out near Credo—the old hippie—Peter Deuteronomy. "Is this phone bugged?"

Tess said, "No. It's clean."

"I don't trust it. I think I'm being watched. Law enforcement is on my tail. They want to trump up charges that I stole stuff, and I never did. I gotta get off."

"Why did you call?"

"I really need to get off. I know you guys have satellites."

"How about I meet you somewhere and we talk? You called me for something."

"I don't know . . ."

"You called for some reason," Tess said. "I'm guessing it's important, or you wouldn't have."

A pause, and then: "Right. Okay, meet me up at my camp. I got something for you. Come alone."

"Can you tell me what it is?"

"And park a mile down and walk, all right? So no one sees us together."

"Why?"

"I don't want you messing things up."

"What things?"

A pause. "You know."

He acted as if she did know.

"A man's got to live his life. God says we have a right to the pursuit of happiness."

He got things mixed up, but he might be of help. "Okay, I'll be there within the hour."

He hung up.

Tess knew what Peter Deuteronomy was thinking about. He probably had some kind of deal with one of the drug runners—one of them could be his pot connection. As she drove out on Ruby Road, Tess decided she didn't give a damn.

～

About a half mile past the road to Peter Deuteronomy's trailer, Tess pulled off the road and parked. She walked back to the turnoff, rounded the short curve in the lane, and there was his camp. The mint-green former Game & Fish truck. The old camper shell on top. The ancient trailer. And this time, a chained-up dog. The dog threw itself at its collar, barking. But his tail was wagging and there was something in his eyes, a kind of embarrassment, like he knew he was all hat and no cattle.

She heard the door squeak open, and there was Peter D., looking like a string of beef jerky, naked except for a pair of running shorts—the tiny ones.

And his huaraches.

And he had the rifle.

When he saw it was her, he lowered it. "You didn't park a mile down the road. I looked for you."

"I parked a half mile up the road."

He looked confused. She pointed in the direction of her Tahoe, which was way around the bend in the road. "I drove past and parked a mile up that way."

"That's not what I asked."

"I'm sorry, but you weren't clear."

"You had to know what I meant. I have half a mind not to give you what George gave me. I don't even know why I called you."

"Maybe because you know I'm trying to find out who killed him?"

He said nothing, just stared at her. His eyes were a bright, mad blue.

Suddenly, Tess felt uneasiness. It crept up her back. It jelled in her belly. Was this a trap? Deuteronomy lived near where Hanley had been shot. He might have done it himself. *Maybe over the pot connection.* Tess said, "I'd hate to come all this way for nothing. You wanted to give me something. Is that still the case?"

"I don't know." He sounded like a girl at a dance who didn't get many takers and decided to play hard to get.

"I drove all the way out here. Can you at least tell me what it is you want to give me?"

He tilted his head sideways and regarded her. "You're washed in the blood of the Lamb?"

"Yes." She had been baptized. Or christened, since she was raised Catholic. She wondered if Catholics fit into Peter Deuteronomy's worldview. Decided not to ask.

"He was a nice guy," Deuteronomy said. "I liked his dog."

"I liked his dog, too."

"You met his dog?"

"Yes. She's got a new home now."

He nodded thoughtfully. "I only chain Bullet here up when someone's coming. He looks scary, but he's friendly. Just a mutt, you know."

"I like dogs."

"You want to pet him?"

"Sure."

"Okay." He let the dog loose and it launched at her. But Tess could tell he was friendly. He slavered all over her, jumping at her chin, wriggling his hind end, gyrating with happiness. She rubbed him all over and was rewarded with slobber on her arm.

"Bullet, get back here!"

The dog bounced away and jumped at his owner.

"Okay," Deuteronomy said. "You don't know it, but you passed the test."

Tess smiled.

"Wait right here, okay?"

He went into the trailer and she heard him rummaging around in a drawer. He stepped outside. "Stay where you are, okay? I don't like people to get too close to me."

"Sure."

He crept out into the dirt between them. Tess couldn't see what was in his hand. If she hadn't seen genuine appreciation over her friendliness with his dog, she would have kept her hand close to her weapon.

He dropped something daintily in the dirt and backed away.

It was blue, plastic, and small.

CHAPTER 42

In the desperate moments that followed, Michael didn't have a chance to think about the hints he'd gotten, gratis, from the universe. He didn't think about the generic white truck that had tracked him through Tucson traffic until it dwindled far back in his rearview. He didn't think about the truck that turned onto 386, how he'd tried to draft behind it just for fun, and he certainly didn't notice that there was a temporary sticker on the rear window. (He remembered *now*, though.) He didn't think about the truck cruising along the single-lane blacktop at the Kitt Peak Observatory center. No logo on the door, but it looked like a generic work truck, so he took it as such.

But he knew immediately when, only one curve down from the observatory, the white truck came up behind him.

Fast.

There were no other cars. Not one to see them. He was alone.

Even before it became clear the guy was trying to run him off the road, Michael felt an atavistic shiver run up through his body like a power line. He sensed, even then, what was about to happen. And then the truck's grille loomed close and Michael was desperately looking for a place to get off the narrow road and away from the truck.

He hugged the edge of the road. Knew there were two or three curves, and each one of them stopped at the edge of space—hundreds of feet down. But he couldn't think right now how far down he could go if he went over. He was too busy trying to save himself.

Think!

He could feel the heat of the engine behind him. He could hear the diesel rumble. He glanced back and each time thought he saw the menacing grille coming forward.

He would be squashed like a bug.

Michael took off diagonally for the other side. The truck was on him. His tires skittered over rocks and dirt and grass as the truck's rumble filled his ears. In his panic, he could not see—everything was shaking and moving and the truck was pinned to his ass. He feinted right, he feinted left, aware that there might be a car coming up the mountain, around the next curve.

The truck stayed on him.

He pedaled hard, faster—and got up a head of speed. Arrowed down the middle of the road. The truck seemed to falter, than came back, clinging to his back wheel like it was trying to get a draft.

Another curve. Had to stay away from the edge, had to stay in the road . . .

They came around the next bend.

Terror wiring through him. Adrenaline spiking. Heart bursting with fear.

The truck relentless.

He was being driven to the right, his tires jittering on the dirt verge. Down below the valley stretched like a sleeping golden lion—beautiful. It might be the last thing he'd ever see. Thinking, couldn't help the thoughts that crossed through his mind, thinking about his broken body hitting boulder after boulder, smashed flat like a bug on a windshield.

The truck's rough grumble.

Go faster. He had to pick it up. Out of the saddle, speeding up, even though the veering road scared him as it never had before.

He was terrified.

Around the next curve. The Pinarello held the line but the wheels almost slipped out from under him. He was going so fast. *Too fast.*

The next curve loomed. This was one of the cliffs. He could go right off. Oh shit—

His bike shimmied. The tires bit into the rocks, the dirt. He almost went over. The truck was on him like a dog on a little animal, ready to savage him. He saw it hit him, saw his broken body flying—

But the tires held. The bike stayed up. Suddenly encouraged, knowing that there would be fewer places to go off—he knew this road so well—he pushed forward.

"I'm gonna beat you, motherfucker!"

Around the next curve.

And right in front of him: the tour bus.

Too late to stop.

~

Michael was airborne. Cartwheeling. He'd managed to turn at the last moment. His bike rammed into a rock at the edge. He hit and he thought he slid. Grass, dirt, rocks, scrapes.

Came to rest facedown in the dirt. Alive. Whole.

The last thing he'd seen was the back of the tour bus. He'd swerved, headed right for the cliff. And hit the guardrail. He thought he hit the guardrail.

Shaking, he stood up and looked up at the road.

The truck had accelerated past the tour bus and was gone. All there was around him was the wind and emptiness. Blood on his knee, blood on his shin. Road rash from his hip down his thigh, his shorts on that side in tatters.

He staggered up to the guardrail and stepped over gingerly. He could see the next curve in the road below. He saw the bus disappear around the curve as if nothing happened.

Could it be the driver didn't even *see* him?

The white truck was gone.

He tasted blood in his mouth where he'd bit his tongue. Tasted dirt and bits of grass. He dropped to all fours and threw up. Could smell himself. He smelled like fear.

The Pinarello's superior frame geometry had saved his life. He checked the bike, spun the wheels, turned the cranks, and ran it through the gears.

A couple of dings.

He could ride it down.

And he did ride it down. Shaken. Scared. Looking back to see if the truck was coming. Scared of cars. Scared of other cyclists.

Scared.

He rode like a little old man. His neck was torqued. His wrist hurt him. He'd banged it against the guardrail.

Yeah, but you could have broken your neck.

This close to going over.

He rode slowly, a light hold on the brakes, pumping them.

Just get down.

He couldn't think very well but what he did think was this: *Sheppard.*

Sheppard, out for revenge.

At one point he reached the bus. He thought about asking the driver to stop. He wanted to ask about the guy in the white truck. What he looked like.

But he guessed that the bus driver might not have even seen it.

Besides, he would settle it himself. He would take care of Sheppard himself. He didn't want to draw attention to this.

~

Michael's cleats clacked over the hardpan ground as he walked his bike to the 4Runner. He put it back on the rack. He got into the SUV and sat there. Now he could absorb it.

Someone tried to kill me.

He was shaking. Couldn't stop.

He stared bleakly out the windshield—

And saw a sheet of paper stuck under the wipers. Facing him. Written in pencil in block letters.

I KNOW WHAT YOU DID.

CHAPTER 43

Tess didn't have long to wait before Hanley's USB flash drive came back from evidence.

It was pretty straightforward. There was only one document on the thumb drive, entitled "Diary." The opening page looked like a form that had been scanned in. An older form she recognized, even though there were differences: the front page of a homicide detective's murder book.

The victim in the report was a man named Felix Sosa. He'd died five years ago, the victim of a sniper. Sosa lived in the Phoenix metropolitan area where George Hanley once worked homicide.

Only Hanley had long been retired by the time Sosa was killed.

Tess looked at the graphic photos. Read the stats, and what had been done. A detective named Manuel Alvarado was the primary on the case. Tess wondered if Alvarado was a friend of Hanley's, and just exactly how Hanley had managed to get a copy of the murder book.

Tess scrolled down the file until she found Hanley's notes.

Danny picked up on the second ring. Today he and Theresa and their baby girl were going home, but Tess wasn't sure if they were still at the hospital. He sounded like he was on cloud nine.

"How are things?"

"*¡Que bonita!* Beautiful, to you Anglos."

"Are you home?"

"Just got in." She heard him muffle the phone and call out to someone. "My brother just got here. What's up?"

Tess told him about the Felix Sosa case—a man shot by a sniper at a campground in Payson, Arizona. "What do you think of that?"

"So he made up his own murder book, is that what you're saying?"

"That's what it looks like."

"Of a homicide in Payson. The guy was shot by a sniper?"

"Yes."

A pause. "Then he probably was shot by a sniper before."

"You know a guy up there, don't you? Jimmy somebody?"

"Jimmy Tune."

"Jimmy Tune? Really?"

"Yeah. We met at an interrogation course in Phoenix. I still talk to him—I'll give him a call and give him a heads-up to talk to you. I've got his e-mail somewhere. Wish I could do more, but um, I'm a little busy right now."

"You only have your first child once," Tess said.

"You got that right. I'm sending you his e-mail now."

~

Tess finished reading Hanley's makeshift murder book on Felix Sosa. There was no mention of the man having been shot before. But there were more murder books. Tess counted three. One for

Quentin DeKoven, the father of Michael DeKoven. One for Peter Farley.

And one for himself.

He knew they were coming for him.

Tess looked at the murder books. There were holes you could drive a truck through in them—his access had been severely limited. He made up for this lack by scanning photos and articles from newspapers or collected from websites.

Tess had seen the murder book for Peter Farley—briefly, but due to her memory, thoroughly. This one was similar, but different. It had been written by a different detective, one who did not have the same kind of access. More gaps, and more supposition. Tess was beginning to recognize Hanley's way of writing—courtly and old-fashioned. Just the facts, but with an occasional reference to literature or an old-fashioned word. He did not have access to the official murder book photos, but had inserted reams of expert articles on mountain lions and the Santa Anas. He had a picture of a smiling Farley with his wife and college-age daughter, taken several years before—Tess thought he'd gotten it from the newspaper.

There were photos of Quentin DeKoven's plane, scattered across a meadow, and a burned swath through pines and fir trees on the top of a mountain in the Pinaleños. He'd typed in his own theory—something to do with the wrong fuel mixture. He'd included photos of the senior DeKoven, his wife, and his children. He'd found and used the photo Tess herself had seen of the kids and their parents at the water treatment plant opening. And there was an old black-and-white newspaper photo of a similar aviation accident, the one DeKoven had survived. He'd scanned in an article in *Outdoor Digest* of DeKoven's survival. A story of a wealthy man who carried his pilot three miles.

His own murder book was equally sketchy. He had scanned in a photo of himself. He'd scanned in a photo of the DVD of *The Ultimate Survivor* show. He'd scanned in a photo of himself in the hospital, after being shot six times, and the newspaper articles on the shootout he'd survived.

He'd made his case, once piece at a time. Carefully laid it out.

After the murder book came a diary of sorts. It was hard to read. He'd scanned in pages from a notebook—painstaking work. The handwriting was hard to read, and faint, but Tess got the gist.

George Hanley had been wooed by the DeKoven family—by Jaimie in particular. She wanted him to join SABEL. She'd somehow run into him at the Safeway in Continental, and his well-honed homicide cop instincts had told him she had targeted him. She'd struck up a conversation. Flirted. Jaimie was a beautiful woman and he was flattered, but he also could tell that she desperately wanted to know *him*. Him, of all people. A sixty-eight-year-old man. He said in the diary that she'd tried too hard. With instincts about people honed over many years as a homicide cop, he could see through the pretense.

He had wondered why.

And so he'd researched *her*. He'd researched the family.

Tess didn't know how Hanley had made the link. He didn't elaborate. Maybe it was the Phoenix connection. He'd lived in Phoenix. He might have known the homicide cop who had investigated Sosa's death, or he might have looked him up and asked.

She kept reading. The day stretched. And the more she read, the more it dawned on her that there was much more to this story. She could feel it. There was a hint of desperation as he went along, as if he was racing time. How would he know that? Sure, he knew he was targeted, but . . .

It was palpable. His race against time, his race to get it all down. And on the next to last page—his last entry—Tess found the answer. His words:

"What the hell was I thinking? I never should have told him about it because now he wants in. I wish I'd never gone out there, I don't know what got into me. He was always good at getting things out of people, I saw him do it often enough. We called him the snake charmer. He of all people knows I'm not a drinker; one drink and I let out all the state secrets. Now he wants to take over.

"Great homicide det. I was—I shouldn't have let my emotions color my thinking. He played me and deep down, I knew he was playing me. He played everybody all the time.

"I should have done something if I'd known what to do. I'll regret that, should have stood up to him, but I had blinders on because he was my best friend, we worked together all those years, we were almost like an old married couple even though he was so much younger, and when he and Karen fell in love it felt natural, he was already like family. Anyone would think it was a homo thing, but it's not a homo thing, it's a cop thing. I was closer to him than I was to Amy and closer than I was to God, but I should have seen what that son of a bitch was doing, I should have been the one person she could rely on. I wonder if I could have stopped it if I just used my gray cells, but it went right past me. Amy was right, it was a boys' club."

"I was stupid. A stupid fool, not just once, but twice! He charmed me just like I saw him do with people so many interviews over the years. One stupid moment, and it was like the old days, and you know the saying that there's no fool like an old fool. It was always that way with us, he was my partner and had my back and I had his, and so I just put any doubts I had aside.

"*I'm* the one who's accountable. It's up to me to find a way to stop this."

That was the last line.

George Hanley had written down his suspicions, but he had been cryptic. He had been reluctant to tell all. For self-protection?

It was clear he suspected Michael DeKoven and Jaimie Wolfe of the killings. He knew that Jaimie Wolfe had gone out of her way to meet him. To woo him.

George Hanley knew it was a game. And he knew that sooner or later they would be coming for him.

He was going to try to beat them at their game.

But he hadn't figured on one thing.

He hadn't figured on Wade Poole—until it was too late.

～

Tess reached Jimmy Tune and took notes over the phone. He sent her a summary of the case and suggested she come up. Tess wasn't sure if this case had any relation to the others, but Hanley'd thought so, so she hit the road and hours later parked in the lot of the Payson Police Department. Jimmy Tune met her in the lobby and led her to the detective room. He introduced her to Manuel Alvarado, the detective who'd worked Sosa.

Thin with a receding hairline, Alvarado had hypnotic eyes. When he talked, you listened. He was in his midforties, a natty dresser. He flipped through his filing cabinet and placed a file on his desk. "We're converting to electronic," he said, "but it's taking a while. And this is an older case." He pushed it across the desk, those dark eyes like shiny beetles. "I can't let you photocopy it."

"That's okay," Tess said. She could look at each page and it would be as good as any photocopy.

He remained standing, watching her, as if he didn't trust her not to take off with it. His eyes never left her.

Tess compared what she had here with what Hanley had put together on his own. He'd done a pretty good job. Once a homicide cop always a homicide cop.

"So the case remains unsolved?"

"That's the status. It's headed to our cold case division."

"But you worked it."

"Yes, I did."

"One thing I don't see here," Tess said. "The autopsy report says he had a previous wound. Did you look into that?"

He straightened a little. "He was in the service. He was shot in the chest in the opening days of the Iraq War. Fortunately, he survived, although it was touch and go for a while. He recovered, but had PTSD and some related mental health problems."

"What kind?"

"He took drugs, was arrested twice for domestic situations with his wife and once for being under the influence. That led to a divorce, and he was out of work—threatened his boss, got into bar fights.

"He was on a family camping trip with his family when he was shot. They went to the same place every year."

"What do you think happened?"

"We were never able to clear the case—there just was no evidence. The trail went cold—all we he had was the bullet."

$\sim$

He showed her on Google Earth where the campground was. He couldn't go with her. He gave her distinct instructions as to where the table was, and of course she saw not only the autopsy photos but photos of the picnic area, the blood spatter, and diagrams. Tess didn't think she needed to drive out there, but she did, anyway. There had been a rain up here recently, and the small creek near the picnic table had plenty of runoff. It was churning. Tess had the place to herself—it was a weekday—and she looked at the spot where she believed he had been shot.

Just out with his family, celebrating his life. A man who had survived a sniper attack once.

That someone could do this for fun.

That they could do this to this soldier. Who, by all accounts, was troubled and suffered deeply from what he'd experienced in Iraq.

Tess thought about Michael DeKoven.

She wondered if he had a sniper rifle. She wondered where he practiced. She wondered who she could talk to who would tell her.

Finally she got back into her Tahoe and drove south.

Next stop: Phoenix.

~

By the time Michael got back home, he had gone through several stages: fear, despair, and now anger. He parked the 4Runner in the garage and walked to the house. He went to the bathroom off the kitchen, not wanting to create a mess in the master bathroom. Since it was right near the back door it would be easier for cleanup.

Gingerly, he stripped off his jersey and shorts, wincing with pain and ready for a hot shower where he could just stand there and let the water pour over him and he could just . . . think.

He did. But the water pounded him like needles, and he couldn't stand to remain under the spray very long. Just get the dirt and dried blood off, pick out a little of the gravel and twigs.

He'd been unable to think too well up to now. But now he was at DeKoven Central, his power base. A man's home was his castle, and this place *was* a castle.

He patted himself dry and thought about what he could wear— a silk robe would probably be the best. As he walked into the bedroom he glanced in the large mirror and saw two things. How pale and scared his face looked—

And Martin, on his stomach, sprawled on the bed behind him. Tanned and beautiful.

Asleep.

When he first came into the room it had scared him to see someone here. The first thing he'd felt was fear.

As if fear had been sown into him. He could almost smell it on himself. He looked at Martin, felt the usual appreciation for his lover's beauty.

He felt it despite the stinging road rash, the bruises. He was raw to the air. Knew that he'd be stiff and in terrible pain tomorrow, his muscles torqued around in all sorts of ways.

If he was going to do anything of a sexual nature, it had to be now.

And there lay Martin. So perfect.

Just what the doctor ordered.

He padded quietly to the walk-in closet. The birchwood dowel, four feet long and a quarter inch in diameter, stood in the corner of the closet, the price sticker still affixed. On the floor beneath was a nylon cord in a loop. Already cut.

He'd stashed it all here for a moment just like this.

The fucker in the truck ran him off the *road*.

He left that note. I KNOW WHAT YOU DID.

"The fuck you don't," Michael muttered. "You don't know the *half* I did." He grabbed the rope. *Martin still sleeping.* Jet lag? Michael had always been quick as a snake, and he had rehearsed it so many times and done it more than a few, it went fast. Knee into Martin's back. Wrap the rope tight around his two wrists, then secure the two ends to the headboard posts.

Martin squeaked.

Bucked.

Cried out.

"It's okay, Martin," Michael said, gently running his hand down Martin's gleaming flank as if quieting a horse. "It's okay."

But it wasn't okay, not yet.

I KNOW WHAT YOU DID.

"Michael, please!"

"I'm feeling my dark side," Michael said in way of explanation.

"Please!"

"You have a choice."

"No!"

"A choice, Martin." He reached under the bed and groped around for the book. He'd marked the pages with Post-it Notes.

He held up the first page. The Chelsea grin.

"Oh, God, Michael, don't even joke about that—"

Michael felt the dark tide rising in his chest. It all but obliterated the terror he'd felt as the truck bore down on him. But the dread remained.

I KNOW WHAT YOU DID.

That fueled his anger. His anger was always silent, but effective. He said, "You don't like the Chelsea grin? I admit, it would ruin you for acting jobs. Or modeling. Look at the picture."

Obediently, Martin craned his neck to look again. He'd seen it before. The Chelsea grin was what happened when someone took a knife to the corners of a man's mouth and cut to make the grin wider.

"Michael, you wouldn't—"

"Martin, you don't know what I'm capable of."

Martin stared at him.

"You have a choice. Like last time." Michael reached out and touched a black curl of Martin's hair, hooked it behind his lover's ear. "You know you'll be all right. A little bit of pain, and then pleasure beyond your wildest dreams. You just have to choose. The Chelsea grin or—"

"Please! *Please!*"

"Shhhhhhhh." Michael put his finger to his lover's lips. Martin was shaking uncontrollably. It reminded him of his wife's worthless Chihuahua, always trembling. "You don't want that, it's okay," Michael crooned. "There's always another option."

"What? *What?*"

"The bastinado. Some pain, but on the good side, no marks. No *marks*, Martin. Nothing to mar your beauty. Easy peasy. Just something for you to get through, to prove how much you love me."

"Michael, I *love* you. Let's make love and—"

"Shhhhhhh. A couple of whacks, that's all. No more than two to each foot."

"No! Please, Michael! Let's make love! Please, I want you so much—"

"The Chelsea grin or the bastinado? You have to choose."

Martin was crying now. Sobbing. His fear kited up out of his soul and Michael felt that if he opened his mouth right now he could swallow it whole. "You have to say it, Martin."

Martin whimpered, "The bas—the bastinado."

"Legs in the air. Soles of the feet facing me."

Martin raised them slowly.

"Keep them up. No fair cheating. I want my two whacks. I won't be cheated."

Martin's legs were trembling. His beautiful, muscular, tanned legs. He would keep them up. He was completely in submission mode.

Michael took a couple of practice swings. The dowel whipped back and forth, making a satisfying *whooshing* sound as it cleaved the air.

"You know something, Martin?" Michael said as he stood at the foot of the bed and assumed the stance of a Samurai.

Thwack!

"I'm feeling better already."

CHAPTER 44

By the time Tess reached Phoenix, it was getting late. She'd called ahead and the cold case detective, a tall rawboned woman named Jenny Searles, came out to greet her. She led the way down the hallway to the office she shared with two other detectives, both immersed in their own cases at their desks.

Searles had a file on her desk, marked Karen Poole.

Karen Poole's murder book.

Searles said, "Couple of things, so you won't get pissed off at me. This is a cold case, and as often happens, it looks like a few things are either missing or incomplete. There was a big reorganization of the file room seven or eight years ago, and a lot of stuff ended up being misplaced."

Tess nodded. She'd worked in a cold case unit years ago in Albuquerque, and sometimes a cold case was like a piece of paper torn to bits. You had to paste together the story as best you could. "Thanks for the warning."

"No problem."

The first page carried the details of the shooting. Karen Poole, along with the clerk, was killed. Karen had been standing by the counter of the Pit Stop convenience store, talking to the young man behind the counter. It was just before shift change at twelve midnight. She was shot at point-blank range. The young man, a kid with dishwater-blond hair and a stud through his eyebrow, had fallen behind the counter, shot through the eye. The killer had managed to get him to open the cash register and took what little money was there.

Tess watched and rewatched the surveillance tape. The man who entered the store wore a black ski mask and a hoodie. The sweatshirt he wore either made him look bulky or he was heavyset. Under the ski mask his head looked substantial, and from the way he moved, Tess thought he was older—pushing forty. Definitely not a kid.

Tess asked Searles, "Have you made any progress on this case?"

"Unfortunately, no. The only witnesses are dead. And the guy must have run off to a car parked nearby."

"Anything unusual?"

"No. Except usually the robberies are committed by younger males."

She saw no nervousness. No panic. No hesitation.

He was good with a weapon. Just from the trajectory, just from the way he killed.

"How much money was there in the drawer?"

"Twenty dollars."

Tess went back and forth through the report. It looked an awful lot like Karen Poole had been in the wrong place at the wrong time.

There was just too much evidence that this was a convenience store holdup.

But she didn't believe that.

Tess had already formed an opinion, already thought the shooter was Wade Poole. Everything she'd learned about him pointed to that. But the evidence just wasn't there. There didn't seem to be a way to orchestrate it. No way to make it happen. Too many variables.

Tess said, "So what do you think?"

"The guy's a good shot."

The image was grainy and dark. The man had walked out the door to the right, money stuffed into the pocket of his hoodie. To the right along the walkway and out of view. Gone.

"Can we look at it again?"

"Sure."

Tess watched it three times.

"Can we go back?"

"Sure."

"There."

Detective Searles stopped the tape. There was a lot of static, everything frozen, gray and black, blurry image, the greenish light of a car going by, headlights hitting the wall.

"What does that look like to you?"

"His hand?"

"Yes."

"He's wearing gloves."

"Yes, he is. But there. You can see the outline of a ring. On his right hand."

"Looks like some kind of man's ring. Biggest ring I've ever seen."

The ring was bulky and square, stretching the leather glove.

Tess had seen a clunky ring like that before. She'd seen it on the third finger of the right hand of the cheerful rancher type she'd met at Jaimie Wolfe's place.

How he'd grinned and looked around at the stable yard, at the riding ring, and the barn. "Name's Barnes," he'd told her.

She saw him reach down to lift a potted plant off its saucer, exposing the key to the house. Saw the clunky ring sparkle in the sunlight as he twisted the key in the doorknob, all the while making small talk. She remembered asking him for his contact information so she could talk to him later, and how he'd put her off by asking her to give him her card.

"I'll copy you on the file and the tape," Jenny Searles was saying. "The detective on the original case is Sol Green. I think his number's still good."

"Thanks."

"I'll walk you out."

"Great," Tess said. But she hardly registered the walk back out to the front doors of the station.

She was still back at Jaimie's ranch, watching Wade Poole let the dogs inside the house as he gave her the biggest snow job ever.

~

Tess called Sol Green's number but got no reply. She checked in to a Red Roof Inn off the freeway—on her dime—and called Bonny at home.

"Where are you again?"

"I'm in Phoenix."

She ran it down for him.

"Any progress?"

"I don't know. I thought while I was here I would see what I could find out about Pat Schofield's sister's homicide."

"What's that got to do with it? How long ago was she killed?"

"Eleven years ago."

"I don't see what you're looking for."

"I don't, either. It's probably nothing. But Pat Scofield, George Hanley's daughter, ran into Wade Poole, Karen's husband. She's afraid of him, and thinks Karen was a victim of domestic violence."

"That's not your case. What's it look like?"

"It *looks* like a simple robbery-homicide. A holdup."

"Then why are you still there?"

"I'm sleepy, and I don't want to make the drive."

A pause.

Tess wondered, in that moment, if she'd just driven over the line.

"Good enough," Bonny said at last. "Keep me posted."

∾

The next morning Tess called Danny, who was awake and on his way in to work. "Do you have the Scofields' number?"

"No, but it's in the file."

"Will you text me?"

"Sure."

"How's Elena?"

"Perfect. Although you'd be amazed how such a puny little thing can make such noise. We're in for a long long year."

More than a *year*, Tess thought.

Tess called Sol Green again. This time he answered—on the first ring. "I was just about to call you."

Tess asked if she could come by and talk to him. He gave her directions to an older section of Phoenix. Brick ranch houses, lots of large trees and lawns—something you didn't see in new sections.

Sol Green and his wife were just finishing breakfast when Tess showed up.

They insisted she have breakfast.

Tess asked him a number of questions about the homicide. His wife at that point took the dishes to the sink and rinsed them, as if shutting out what they were saying, then came over and kissed him on the cheek and said, "I'm going to the store."

"Okay, hon."

He leveled his worn eyes on Tess. "So what do you want to know?"

~

Tess was on the freeway by ten a.m. She'd already put in a call to Bonny, telling him what she'd learned from Sol Green. "Bottom line, Wade Poole knew where Karen would be that night, because she was waiting for her nephew to get off work."

"Her nephew?"

"The other victim, David Molroney. He was her nephew—which was not in the cold case file."

She'd learned this from Sol Green.

Tess explained that Karen had been married before she married Wade Poole and was on good terms with David, her nephew from that marriage. In fact, she thought of him as a son. His car was in the shop that week, and while he could get a ride to the store, she agreed to pick him up while his car was in the shop. She did it for a week.

"Sol Green told me they looked at Poole, but he had friends who vouched for him—he was at a bowling alley. Said he cooperated. Everything pointed to a random shooting."

Bonny whistled.

Tess said, "He wanted to get rid of her, so he made it look like a robbery."

"Audacious."

Tess told Bonny about her meeting with Dave Barnes a.k.a. Wade Poole at Jaimie Wolfe's place. Remembering how he'd smiled and looked around the barnyard and picked himself out a nice, unmemorable name. Remembering the chunky ring on his finger. "He was good, Bonny. He was just your friendly neighborhood rancher type looking after a friend's property."

She saw his face now: open, honest, affable. A sunny personality.

Only a psychopath could pull that off.

Bonny said, "Jesus."

~

Driving back, Tess superimposed the image of the man she'd met at Jaimie's over the hooded figure at the convenience store. Fortunately, she could run the tape back in her head exactly as she'd seen it on the video recorder.

Tess recognized his movements.

Subtle things.

The man had always been in control. He knew how to get the upper hand from the beginning—like a good cop would.

And then, there were the gloves, and the bulky ring hidden underneath one of them.

CHAPTER 45

After chores were done, after calling to cancel lessons yet again, Jaimie heard the phone ring in the house.

She was hopeful. Maybe someone had found Adele.

As she walked to the house, she thought for the hundredth time that something might have scared Adele. Dogs did run away. If so, she hoped Adele would find her way back. She'd taken Adele as a trophy, but already loved her like one of her own. The idea of Adele out there on her own, lost, hungry, maybe even *hurt*—was unbearable. Every time the phone rang, she hoped it was someone looking for a reward—she'd gladly pay a hundred dollars. Two hundred, even, if she could just get Adele back.

She was still in shock over Chad's death. She felt as if she'd been beaten around the head. And Michael—she sensed that something was going on with him. Michael, the rock of the family. She sensed that he was holding something back. She sensed that he was scared.

Everything going to shit.

She got to the phone just before the recorder came on. "Hello?"

"Listen carefully."

It had to be a prank. Whoever it was had been sucking on helium. "Michael, is that you? Because it's not very fun—"

"I have your dog."

"What? Who are you?"

"A friend. I found your dog on the road. She's got a collar and tags, and the tag says 'Bandit.' That's your dog, isn't it?"

The weird Donald Duck voice, high-pitched and thin as a thread. She heard whoever it was pause, suck on something, and then he piped: "I want a reward."

"I offered a reward. One hundred dollars—it's all yours."

"Good."

"Why don't you bring her here and I'll write you a check."

"No check—cash. I don't trust the DeKoven family."

That high Donald Duck voice.

"Okay, bring her here. When are you coming?"

"No, you meet me."

"Meet you?" That didn't sound like a good idea. Fear began to thrum in her stomach, in her heart. Was this a crank call? "No, you come here."

"What a shame."

"What do you mean, what a shame?"

"Poor doggie. Looks like Bandit is gonna go to heaven." And the caller hung up.

Jaimie succumbed to panic. She'd blown it! Now this monster would kill Adele. She tried to find the number on the readout, but it was blocked. There was no place to call. How'd they do that? She had to talk to him—had to. The motherfucking bastard was going to kill her dog!

She sat there, trembling. Unable to move, unable to think.

The phone rang again. Jaimie stumbled to her feet and snatched it up. "Who's this?"

Helium Man said, "I'll give you one more chance."

CHAPTER 46

Tess and Danny were once again in the Scofield kitchen. This time the subject was all about Wade Poole.

"So it *was* him," Pat Scofield said, after heating up a plate of tamales. "You want one? They're homemade—Bert made them."

"Thanks," Danny said. They each took one, doled out on dinner roll plates.

"Let's go out onto the patio," Pat said. "It's so nice out there, even though it's sweater weather."

Pat said, "I saw him again. I was sure it was him, but Bert said it was my imagination. Even though he wasn't there." She shot him a resentful look.

Tess let Danny take this. She thought that he and Pat had a better relationship, for whatever reason. Bert looked put out, discounting his wife as usual.

"Can you tell me where you saw him?" Danny said, his voice quiet and gentle.

"Well, I was at the Safeway. And he was in line in the check-out—two people ahead of me."

"Do you think he saw you?"

"He looked back. He tried to hide it, but I'm pretty sure I saw surprise on his face."

"Did he say anything to you?"

"No."

"Did you say anything to him?"

"I wouldn't give him the time of day."

"So what did he do then?"

"He just turned around and stacked his groceries on the conveyer belt. Like he never even saw me."

"So you think he recognized you."

"Oh, he recognized me all right. How do you not recognize your dead wife's sister?"

"Did he react in any way?"

"You could tell he wasn't going to. He thinks he got away with how he treated my sister, but he knew my feelings about him."

"What happened next?"

"He left. I was still in line—I couldn't exactly follow him out! But I watched him go, you better believe I did."

"What did you see?"

"I saw him go out the sliding doors, you could see through them, and walk into the parking lot with his groceries."

"Did you see him get into a car?"

"No. The person in front of me only had four or five items and I was putting things on the belt."

"So you didn't see what he was driving."

"No."

Danny looked at Tess. "Thank you, ma'am. I appreciate—"

"But I did see the truck when he drove by that couple of times. What you'd call cruising."

"Can you describe the truck?"

"It was white."

"Anything else?"

"I don't know anything about trucks. Sorry."

Danny looked at his notes. "Can you tell me about your sister's nephew from her first marriage? His name was David, right?"

"Yes.

"She really liked him. But you have to understand, I wish she'd never met him. If she hadn't, she would have never—" Pat's fingers abruptly went to her mouth and her eyes grew wide. She looked at Tess.

She'd made the connection. After all these years.

Tess could see she was flailing. Her eyes were glassy as she looked from Tess to Danny and back again.

Danny hunkered down so he could look in to her eyes. "Are you all right?"

"I . . ." She glanced around, focused on her husband.

Tess noticed the stubborn look on Bert's face. Had he thought the same thing at one time, but then discarded it as impossible? Tess had no way of knowing.

Danny said, "Do you think that is possible? That she was killed on purpose?"

"By someone, do you mean Wade?" demanded Bert Scofield. "Because that's the most ridiculous thing I ever heard of."

Tess thought that the idea must have crossed his mind before.

Pat said, "You didn't see the way he had her under his thumb. There's a mean side to him, as I keep telling you, but you won't listen and neither would Dad."

Danny shot a look at Tess. Tess said to Bert, "Would you mind—I like those tamales so much. I'm wondering if you can give me the recipe."

"Sure." He led her back into the kitchen. He reached into the cupboard and plunked down a bag of blue corn and husks for the wrapping. "It's pretty straightforward."

"Could you write it down for me? I'd really appreciate it."

"Sure." His voice was gruff. He grabbed a tablet that had been affixed to the refrigerator and got a pen from the kitchen drawer. "You're not fooling me. You just wanted me out of there."

"Yes, that's right. But I do want the recipe."

"Fine. But what you have to understand is, Pat's always been, well, a conspiracy theorist. She's been convinced from day one that Wade killed Karen. Although thankfully, she never said it in public. I don't want to get sued."

"Is Wade the suing type?"

"Who knows? But if you want my opinion, I think she's imagining things."

"But you do admit he'd know where she was at twelve o'clock that night."

"Sure. But that doesn't mean he'd do anything. Look, I know people. I work in business. He and I used to go on hunting trips together, and you get to know a guy. I don't believe it, and I'll tell you another thing, her dad thought he was a good guy. They worked together for fifteen years. George was his mentor. They were like that." He crossed his fingers.

"You sound convinced."

"I know people. Wade's one of the nicest people you'd ever want to meet. Karen was . . . she was difficult. Her first marriage ended, but she got attached to that kid, Dave. Couldn't let it go. No relation, but she was always humoring him. You ask me, she had a crush on the kid. You know, like those schoolteachers?"

"What do you mean?"

"You know, older women and kids barely out of high school. Or even in high school. She was a teacher herself. So . . . it's not a leap to think that she might have had a crush on the kid. Going out there at midnight to pick him up when his car was in the shop? You asked me and I'm telling you what I really think: she was in the wrong place at the wrong time."

Tess heard footsteps behind her—Danny. "Hey, thank you!" he said to Bert. "We've taken up enough of your time, so we'll be going."

"Yeah, well." Bert glared at Danny. "Maybe you should spend more time on solving my father-in-law's murder instead of going on wild goose chases."

"Hey, you might be right," Danny said. He held out a hand. "We'll do our best to find out who killed him. It's important to us."

"Yeah," Bert grumbled. "'Your call's important to us.'"

Tess grinned at Danny.

≈

Outside, Tess said, "What do you think?"

"I think ol' Wade is one hell of a con man."

"Pat's instincts are right," Tess said. "But I can see how the guy can charm the pants off anyone." She thought of the open, friendly face. The guy looked and acted like a big friendly dog. Like he'd bear hug you at any moment. "He's good."

~

Helium Man—that's how Jaimie thought of the son of a bitch—told her to take Harshaw Road out to Mowry, an old ghost town down near the Arizona-Mexico border. It was a remote area, and few tourists made it there. She was to bring a "reward"—ten thousand dollars in cash. He'd wait until she showed up with the money and left it at a prearranged spot, marked by one of those flags on wires they used for cable markers. She was to call him at a certain number when she'd done it. Once he had the money, he'd direct her to where she would find Adele.

Not that she trusted him. But what else could she do?

She knew he was serious, because he called the dog "Adele." So he knew *something* about George Hanley's dog, and he knew she'd adopted her.

This scared Jaimie to the core. She entertained the idea of not playing along, letting him keep her, but he'd anticipated that, too.

He'd told her, graphically, what he would do to Adele, and how long it would take to kill her. He told her he'd cook her on a spit.

She knew he was telling the truth.

"Why are you doing this?" she demanded. "Why hurt an innocent dog?"

His answer: "I know what you did."

~

Jaimie could access the money. No problem with that. Briefly, she thought about calling Michael. But she knew what he'd say. She knew he'd tell her not to do it. And she had to do it. Adele was hers. Adele was more than just a dog—she was the embodiment of what they'd done. Everyone else had gotten a tribute, a prize, except for her. Even Chad, and he didn't even know why. Just for buying the cougar, he had been given a surfboard, stolen out of Peter Farley's house. But what did she get? Nothing. So she took her own tribute, her own prize. George Hanley was going to be hers. *She'd* found him, *she'd* targeted him. So what if she couldn't do anything for at least a year?

He was hers, and she'd been cheated out of it.

She tried to tune out the fear she felt. But her mind kept going back to one question: Who would know about the Survivors Club?

Whoever it was, was male. She was pretty sure of that. Even if he disguised his voice with the helium.

But was she really that sure? Couldn't it be the woman cop?

Was this a trick? Was she trying to lure her out there? Maybe she *should* talk to Michael.

She needed to get the ten thousand out, though. That would take time. But if this *was* for real, Jaimie was not going to let whoever it was kill Adele.

She loved Adele.

Jaimie would go and take out the money, first. Then, if she needed to meet this person, if this was really on the up-and-up and somebody had figured this out and it wasn't the Patagonia cop and if it wasn't the Tucson cop, then she would go out there.

She ran out to the truck. The hand holding the car alarm button shook so badly she missed the first time. Then she was in the truck and taking off for Wells Fargo.

~

"Now what?" Danny asked Tess as they drove back to the sheriff's office.

"I have no idea."

"It's confusing, that's for sure. So what are we thinking here? You really think he killed his wife?"

"It would be hard to prove."

"Yeah, but what do you think?"

Tess said, "I do. I think he killed Karen, and I think that her nephew was collateral damage."

"Why, you think?"

Tess stared out at the blacktop winding through the golden hills. The sun baking the windshield, even though it was only April. "He was tired of her? He wanted to be rid of her?"

"Wouldn't divorce be easier?"

"Maybe. Maybe not. Maybe he liked killing her. Maybe he liked getting away with it—you know, like that guy—"

"Drew Peterson?" Danny said.

"He reminds me of that guy. And don't forget, Karen was five months pregnant."

Danny whistled. "You think he didn't want a kid?"

"Who knows?"

"Damn, I can't imagine that. If that's true, I want to kill that motherfucker."

Tess could feel the violence in her usually easygoing partner. Coiled up, ready to strike. The new father—protective.

He darted a glance at her. "What do you think?"

"What do *you* think?"

"I think he did it. Maybe because of the kid."

Tess could see Danny's knuckles white on the steering wheel. She said, "What about George Hanley? Do you think he killed him, too?"

"If he's a killer, he might get off on it. First the daughter, then come back and finish off the dad. But why now?"

Tess agreed. "There was a long time between the two killings."

"Yeah. Maybe George had figured it out about his daughter."

Tess could see that. "You think maybe George contacted him?"

"What, and told him to come clean? How dumb is that?"

"I don't think George would be that foolish."

"Me either," Danny said.

≈

When they got in, they went straight to Bonny. They shut the door and went through it, piece by piece.

At the end of it, Bonny said, "What about Steve Barkman? You think Poole's good for him, too?"

Tess and Danny looked at each other.

Tess said, "Could be. We're also looking at Michael DeKoven for Hanley."

Bonny leaned back. "You saying you think two people could have killed him. And neither one of them is a cartel?"

Danny said, "Might as well throw in the Zetas, Sinaloas, and Alacráns. Hey, it's a party!"

"Jesus," Bonny said. "George Hanley couldn't buy a break." He looked at Tess and then at Danny. "So who killed Hanley? That's your case. That's who you two should care about."

Tess looked at Danny.

Danny looked at Tess.

"If you had to bet. DeKoven, or Poole?"

She leaned forward. "I could be wrong, but I think it was Poole."

"The question is," Danny said, "how do we find him?"

~

He'd shopped at the Safeway in Continental, so he might be in the Green Valley area. All they had was the description of a white truck—Pat didn't know one truck from another—but fortunately, Tess knew everything about the truck except for its license plate.

That was because the truck had been muddy up to the wheel wells. She didn't see the rear of the truck, but she guessed that he'd either muddied the plate or switched plates. What Tess did know was what he looked like, how he moved, how he talked. That broad red face, that friendly smile—open as the outdoors. He probably would continue to play the good old boy; he fit it so well. The other thing she had to go on was that he had been on Jaimie's property at least once before, because he knew where she hid the key to her house. He had a sociopath's easy way of lying—completely believable.

Tess wondered what he had been doing in Jaimie's house.

She called Danny. After chatting about Elena—"She smiles at me!"—and how well Theresa was doing and the family's participation, his brother surprising them with a homemade cradle—Danny listened to her theory. "So how are we gonna find this guy?"

"I have no idea. We have an Attempt to Locate out there, but unfortunately, there's not much to go on. Wish I'd seen his license plate." She thought about it. "If we're right, he met up with George Hanley at Credo."

"Which meant George went out especially to meet him. In the late afternoon when no one was around."

"We need to get a photo of him. I'm sure there's one from when he worked homicide in Phoenix."

"Or his California DL."

~

A half hour later they had a five-year-old picture of Wade Poole. A half hour after that, Tess drove out see Peter Deuteronomy.

This time the dog must have been inside. When Peter saw her he came out without his rifle. Tess was clearly making progress.

"Peter!" she called from her car, which she had once again parked diagonally so that the engine block was between him and herself. She'd opened the door and stood behind it. Better safe than sorry.

"What do you want now?"

"I want to ask you something about your friend George Hanley."

"I don't tattle on my friends. So you'd better go away."

"Tell you what." Tess rose and walked out from behind the car door and stood there so he could see her hands were away from her weapon. Just in case. "I think a bad guy killed George. The thumb drive you gave me showed that he was investigating someone, and that's who I think killed George. You do want to help find George's killer, right?"

"Hardly knew him."

"But he trusted you. He gave you the thumb drive. He entrusted you with it."

Peter canted his head, thinking.

"Just let me show you these photos, and if you see anyone familiar, you let me know. That's all I'm asking."

"Okay. But you can't make me testify to anything! I will not set foot in a United States court. They're liars and beggars!"

"You won't have to testify," Tess lied. She reached for the small poster board with six photos. "I'm just pulling out these pictures. Is that okay?"

"What do you take me for? Of course it's okay. What do you think? I'm paranoid?"

Tess eased the poster board out and walked toward him, held it out.

He looked at it for one instant and said, "The fourth one, second row."

Tess hid her triumph. "You've seen him before?"

"Saw him maybe two weeks ago."

"Can you tell me where?"

"I saw him down in Credo. I think he was on a scouting mission."

"A scouting mission?"

"I saw him from the road. I heard a noise—I've got really good ears, you gotta have good ears out here. And there he was, sneaking around. I noticed he had a rifle, and I keep track of stuff like that because I was meeting my—" He stopped. "What I noticed, see, was he had an AK-47, like the Mexicans do, only he's Anglo. He went over to a tree and he fooled around some, and when he came back away from the tree he wasn't carrying the rifle."

"Do you mean he put it in the tree?"

He gave her a look that intimated she was completely clueless.

"Of course he put it in the tree."

"You saw him put the rifle in the tree?"

"No, but he fooled around, you know, like maybe he had duct tape or something, and hid the rifle. Like they do. You know. They do it all the time down here—it's their *cache*. Scared me—there are white guys who run with these people but all of them are bad guys, 'cept for a few. I keep my eyes and ears open but my mouth closed." He pulled an invisible zipper across his mouth. "Live and let live, that's my motto."

And preserve your pot connection, Tess thought. "Which tree?"

"One of the oaks. They give a lot of shade, and it's easy to hide stuff."

"Whereabouts? In relation to the cabins?"

"Not too far from the one farthest from the road. The one at the end—on the little hill."

The cabin where George Hanley died. Tess asked, "Which way from the cabin?"

"Down by that little dry creek. There's an oak there."

Tess remembered it. "How long ago was this?"

"I'm not sure. Before what happened to George. I just assumed it was somebody doing something—you know, drug running, gunrunning, people running, that kind of thing. No way I was gonna poke my nose in that hornet's nest."

"Why didn't you tell me this the first time we met?"

He shrugged. "Didn't connect it."

"So you saw him as you were driving by?"

"*Walking* by, and you better believe I kept on going. Eyes forward, you know what I mean? You want to keep your eyes open and your mouth shut around here."

"You weren't driving your truck?"

"Didn't you hear me the first time? I was *walking*. Made sure he didn't see me, either."

"You just went for a walk?"

He looked at her, defiant. "Uh-huh. Just a walk."

"Look, I'm gonna be straight with you. I don't care what you do or whom you do it with. I just want to make sure what you're telling me is accurate. All I care about is George Hanley and finding the guy who killed him."

"Well, that guy is *him*." He tapped the paper with Poole's likeness.

"Sounds like he was pretty far away."

"I have twenty/ten vision. I was a sniper in the army."

"Did he see you?"

"I don't think so. It was getting dark."

"Did you see a vehicle?"

"Nope. My guess is he left it way up or down the road, since he was sneaking around like that. I've seen stuff like that before."

"Did you ever see George Hanley meet someone out there?"

"Only during daytime hours. I don't walk down that road every night, though. Just once in a while."

"Thanks," Tess said. "You've helped a lot."

"That's good. Just being the Good Samaritan."

∾

Tess drove down to the Credo gate. She didn't have a key to the padlock, but it was easy to slip through the four-strand wire farther down.

She walked to the cabin where George Hanley had been killed and then continued on down to the creek and the oak. The oak scattered deep shade on the mosaic of white stones and riverbed. There was a fork in the oak low down, and another place where more branches diverged. She spotted a small patch of duct tape hanging from the higher crook in the tree.

Fingerprints, maybe.

To get a job in law enforcement, you had to be fingerprinted. Wade Poole had been a homicide cop. His fingerprints would be on AFIS. She always carried latex gloves and evidence bags in a case in the back of the Tahoe. She went back to the Tahoe, donned gloves, and brought one of the larger bags. She also carried a knife. Back at the oak, Tess photographed the duct tape, then carefully peeled it off. Gingerly, she dropped the duct tape into the evidence bag, and back at the truck, she marked it.

Any luck, it would come back to Wade Poole.

~

Jaimie drove out on Harshaw Road, which led south toward the Mexican border. It was a graded road early on but then started to wind and get narrower. She was looking for a sign for the ghost town of Mowry. On her right, she passed the graveyard of another ghost town, Harshaw, for which the road was named. A lot of colorful fake flowers, whitewashed stones and crosses, and piled rocks to keep the coyotes away, although the people buried there were from the early part of the twentieth century and long past edibility.

She tried to occupy her mind with stuff like that, but her heart was beating hard and all she could think of was what that thing— Helium Man—said he'd do to Adele.

The road started going up higher, and the trees became thicker—mostly oak.

She was driving into a tight curve when suddenly a white truck pulled out right in front of her. She slammed on the brakes and wrestled with the wheel of her big Dodge Ram, skidding across the narrow road down into the ravine on the other side.

The truck came to rest upright. She took stock: banged up a little but her seat belt saved her. And whoever that asshole was who clipped her—

Someone yanked open the truck door. Somebody coming to rescue her? She was okay, she needed to tell them that, but suddenly her belt was unlatched, a big man leaning over her, crushing her against the airbag that had whopped her in the chest and, she realized, broken her wrist, and he pulled her out by the shoulder and shoved her up against the side of the truck. "Police!" he yelled, and grabbed her arm and wrenched it around behind her back—agony. The next thing she knew, her hands were cuffed behind her back.

She screamed.

The man kicked her legs apart and patted her down, then grabbed her by the arm and pulled her up the embankment and over to his own truck, shoved her inside. "You move, and you're going to jail," he yelled, his red face right in hers. "Got it?"

She nodded mutely. She couldn't think of anything except for the excruciating pain in her wrist. And that she wet her pants.

He drove her truck back out on the road, parked and locked it. Then he came back and got his truck and took off with a slew of dirt, up a two-lane track into the woods.

Jaimie was confused. This guy was dressed like her friends in the ranching community. He drove with one hand on the wheel, slewing along the road, and one hand holding a gun trained on her. She had no doubt he would use it. But another part of her insisted that he was a cop. He treated her as a cop would. With authority.

Cops wouldn't kill unarmed citizens—and that was what she would hold on to.

Her own revolver sat in a zippered bag inside her truck.

Her wrist was screaming. She realized she was screaming too when he took his gun butt and smacked her mouth. "Shut up. Do it now. You are in deep enough trouble already."

They headed up a steep four-wheel-drive road, little more than a trail, up into the hills.

~

They came to a camping spot screened by trees. In the truck, he duct taped her mouth and tied a rope around her neck. He jerked at the rope and told her to follow him. She scrambled to keep up, terrified of being literally hanged—her air cut off. She saw the remains of an adobe building among the trees, roofless, just two walls meeting in a corner, the adobe bricks slumping like a melting candy barn. There was a stake there, driven deep into the ground, and a chain. He replaced the rope with a choke chain and hooked it to the chain. She could only sit in one way, because she was snubbed up pretty close to the stake—about two and a half to three feet.

I'm going to die.

She was sure of that. She also knew he would rape her first, and probably torture her.

He was no cop.

How had she been so stupid? He had her ten thousand dollars and he had her. She could feel the chain links cold and hard against her neck. Could feel her airway close, suffocating her. Realized that wasn't really happening, but she felt it anyway. Panic exploded upward. Her gorge rose. Tears spilled down her cheeks.

The man sat down across from her, cross-legged. His broad face all smiles.

"Please don't kill me!" she said through the duct tape. "I'll do anything you want—anything. Just . . . don't kill me."

He reached over and tugged on the chain. The choke chain pinched her throat.

Suddenly, she had to throw up. She could choke to death.

He ripped the duct tape off just before she vomited.

He watched her like she was some bug crawling along the ground. Fascinated.

"Sorry," he said. "I had to establish the ground rules. You need to speak only when spoken to. Okay?"

She nodded.

He pulled a blade of grass out of the ground and stuck it between his teeth. It was hard to believe this was happening. He had such merry blue eyes. Hard to believe, looking at him, that he wasn't a nice man. Maybe he would just have sex with her, take the money, and let her live.

It was like a tender shoot of a plant inside her, reaching for the sun. Just a slim hope.

"Okay, here are the ground rules," he said at last. "You are my hostage. If you cooperate, you will go back to your family. Got that?"

She nodded. She nodded as hard as she could.

"Okay, where's your phone?"

She nodded to the back pocket of her jeans.

He got up and came to her, bent and slid out her phone. "We're gonna need this for later. The cash is in your truck, I take it?"

She nodded furiously, tried again to speak through the duct tape. Tried to please him. There was hope. She was a hostage. That was okay. Hostages were kept alive.

"Okay, I'll be right back. Don't you move. If you do, you might just end up hanging yourself and you'll be no use to me and none to yourself, neither."

He ran down the hill. She could hear him beating his way through the tree branches and bushes.

She waited. A fly zoomed around and lighted on her nose. She swatted at it with her manacled hands, but it kept coming back. She was in a twisted position, one shoulder high, her head stretched in the direction of the stake. She tried to get her legs under her so she could release the tension in her shoulders, neck, back, and hip. It was easiest just to lie down on her side.

He returned, sounding like an elk stomping through the brush. Smiling.

So weird—the way he smiled. The way he acted. And yet she realized he would kill her without a second thought.

"I counted it. You did good. It looks like I can trust you."

She nodded, hard.

He sat down again, cross-legged in the dirt, and leaned toward her, like he was a friend about to tell her a story by the campfire. "Here's the deal. I want a lot more money than ten thousand dollars, and I think you can get it for me."

She could barely fathom what he was saying. He wanted *more* money?

"See, I know what you, Brayden, and Michael have been doing. I know all about your little game." He tipped his hat up on his head. "That should be worth a lot more than ten thousand dollars. I fig-ure—don't want to be greedy—that the information I have at my disposal, which I could give to the police, with *evidence to back it up*, is worth a cool million or two, at the very least. Just how much is your family's net worth?"

The realization came on her all at once, like a cascade, hitting her hard. He knew about their game? He wanted a couple million dollars? She couldn't seem to process this.

He looked at her—she swore it was in a kindly way—like he felt sorry for her. "I know, it's a lot to take in. How could anybody know? But it's true. I know all about your little game. But hey. We all get our jollies in our own way, and who am I to judge? Thing is, though, I see an opening, I take it. What's good for you folks would be good for me."

He shifted again, his Roper boots stirring up the dust. He sat back, legs crossed at the feet, braced by his arms. Lazy and smiling and terrifying all at once.

It felt like a dream.

"By the way, the name's Wade." He smiled. "Now let's figure out how we're going to do this."

CHAPTER 47

AFIS showed no match for the partial fingerprint on the strip of duct tape that had remained stuck to the tree. It was possible that the duct tape was left by someone else hiding a weapon in the tree, as it seemed to be the best hiding place around there. As Peter Deuteronomy had pointed out, caching weapons in various hiding spots along the border had become a frequent occurrence. Either way, Tess couldn't get Wade Poole on prints. Worse, she had no idea where to begin looking for him. He seemed to have disappeared. So far they had been unable to find an address for Poole in Glendale, California, where he was supposed to have lived. He did not register a vehicle at the DMV. He was not on the tax rolls. He had no phone number.

He had ceased to exist.

But they were on his trail. Danny, working from his computer at home, came across a likely conference earlier in the year, the annual Western Association of Homicide Detectives Conference, held in January. Tess had gone once, herself—there were plenty of good seminars, especially on the latest advances in law enforcement.

"He was retired," Danny said, "but that doesn't mean anything. A lot of those old guys go to this conference—gotta keep their hand in."

Once a homicide cop, always a homicide cop, Tess thought.

"He probably just got together with his old pals and played a lot of golf," Danny added.

It took them all of twenty minutes to get the information from Hanley's records. He had gone to Palm Springs in January.

"So what he said about having too much to drink was true," Tess said. "Bert said if he drank more than one he was a falling-down drunk."

"I can see it. They're hanging out together in the bar, he's having such a good time with his old buddy and former son-in-law he drinks a little too much and spills the beans. He might not have even remembered it. But *Wade* sure did."

"So they decided to team up and prove that the family was killing people," Tess said. "Only Hanley wants to build a case, and Wade wants something else."

"Money."

"Probably."

"He's a mean son of a bitch," Danny said. "It wouldn't surprise me that he'd kill Hanley and try to pin it on the Alacrán. Thirty rounds to make it look like overkill."

"George trusted Peter Deuteronomy to keep his USB disk. He was afraid of what Wade Poole might do."

"Or do to *him*. You thinking what I'm thinking, *guera*?"

Tess was. Wade Poole's next target was the family. If you put yourself in his position, what would he do next?

Extortion.

~

They discussed the possibility that Wade Poole might go after the DeKovens. How would they react to extortion? What kind of pressure would it put on them? And how could Tess and Danny use it to further their own goals?

"This might be the crack in the dam," Tess said.

"Yeah, it could be."

Tess got the feeling Danny was fading. She knew he was beginning to realize that everything had changed now, and would be changed for a long time, and sleep would be one of those catch-as-catch-can deals.

"You sound like the walking dead," Tess said.

"But I'm the happy walking dead."

"Maybe you should get some sleep."

"I'll sleep when I'm dead. What were you saying?"

"What do you think Poole's next move is gonna be?"

"Depends. If he's a hard-ass, he'd start killing people. In the family."

Tess said, "To encourage the others to negotiate, or just because he could?"

"Both, I guess. Maybe he'd kill one of them to scare them."

"Chad," Tess said.

"He'd be the obvious choice. He could show that he had a long arm. That he could get them anytime."

"What about Hanley? I think he killed him because he had everything he needed and he knew Hanley wasn't going to go along with what he was planning."

"Sounds about right." Danny sounded like he was drifting off to sleep. "Tell you what, that family better be scared, if they know what he did to Hanley."

"You think they know how he was killed?" Tess said. "Because if they don't, maybe someone should tell them."

CHAPTER 48

Doris Glazer and her dog Buster rounded the last curve of the trail before the pull-off where she'd left her car. It had been a good hike on a picture-perfect day, but now it was time to head home and take a nap before her shift at Fry's in Nogales. She stooped to leash Buster, and when she looked up she saw a dog standing in the dirt road.

The dog was a sorry sight, but Doris knew it was an Australian shepherd. It had a collar and tags—somebody's pet.

The dog stood in the road, head down, panting. And between pants, it was whining. Doris saw why. The dog was dripping blood from its hind end. Its legs were trembling and splayed out for balance.

"Oh, my God."

The Australian shepherd had been shot in the flank.

~

While the dog was in surgery to remove the bullet, Doris called Animal Control and gave them the registration number on the tag. The dog's name was Bandit, and it belonged to a Jaimie Wolfe, who lived in Patagonia.

Doris had seen Jaimie Wolfe around town, knew her to say "hi" to on the street. Jaimie had that ranch where she taught horseback riding. Her number was unlisted, and since it would be a while before Bandit would be released—and frankly, Doris was worried about paying for the surgery—she decided to drive over to the farm herself.

But no one was there. It was getting late and she had to get ready to go to work, So Doris had to leave it for now. She'd done the right thing, and even if she had to pay out of her own pocket in the long run, Doris would figure out a way to make her dollars stretch a little more.

She doubted it would come to that. Anyone who owned a horse farm had to have some money to pay for their own injured dog.

CHAPTER 49

Michael and Martin had spent the morning shopping and the afternoon sunning by the pool, a light lunch, and a massage for Michael's aching muscles.

As Michael had expected, Martin had forgiven him. Maybe it was thanks to the TAG Heuer Grand Carrera chronometer Martin now sported on his beautiful, lean-muscled arm. His feet were still tender, but Michael knew a foot masseuse at the Los Palmas Resort down the road and summoned him here on his lunch hour. Since the bastinado left no marks, the masseuse suspected nothing.

Michael had told Martin they would "heal together," and Martin was more than willing to forgive him. Now he was agitating to go to a play tonight in town. Michael didn't let on to Martin, but he didn't want to go out. He wanted to stay here and think. And maybe turn the place into a guarded fort. The phone rang. He glanced at the readout—Jaimie.

He didn't want to hear whatever hard luck story she was peddling this time, so he ignored the call.

~

Jaimie had tried several times to raise Michael, but he wasn't answering his cell. She couldn't believe it. Couldn't believe the trouble she was in. And it was getting cold now. Spring nights in the desert mountains could get down into the teens and twenties, and she was wearing a tank top and jeans.

The man—Wade—looked disappointed. "I thought you two were closer than that. He ignores your calls?"

"Maybe he's busy."

He'd stripped off the duct tape, partly because he wanted her to call her brother, but also because it was doubtful anyone would hear her out here.

Wade watched her and massaged his forehead. He'd been covering his right eye and pushing his palm against his temple for a while now. *Migraine.* She knew, because she got them herself. "He'd better get unbusy. This is a limited-time offer."

She shrugged. It was hard to shrug being chained the way she was, but she did it anyway to show him that she didn't care. Every muscle ached. She was cold—shivering. She hated her goddamn brother more than anything on earth except for Mr. Congeniality over there. "What did you do to my dog?"

"I shot her."

"You bastard!"

"Not very ladylike, are you?"

"Fuck you."

Jaimie wanted to kill him. Adele was hers. Adele belonged to her. She loved Adele. She didn't love hardly anyone, but she loved that dog. And now Adele was gone.

Tears slid down her face. She wiped her nose with her good hand, and was surprised when her captor shot up off the ground and kicked her in the ear.

The pain was shattering. She rolled on the ground in agony, the pain flashing through her like a pulsing red-and-black orb, filling her vision, filling her whole world.

He stood over her. "Don't you ever talk to me like that again." He kicked her hard in the side.

Jaimie heard the banging rattle, and suddenly felt him grabbing up links, jerking hard on the choke chain, the metal biting into her flesh. Her air stopping.

Buzzing in her hears. Her vision dimming, little dots like a fuzzy TV screen turning dark, darker, *can't breathe* . . . swimming in agony, needing air—

And suddenly he released her. She fell forward, air gushing into her lungs. Air and dirt—she was facedown and gasping.

"Mind your manners! I've killed women like you for a lot less."

She was aware she was gasping, trying to pull in air. Gasping and sobbing at the same time. Trying to get a deep breath and failing.

"And don't you think I don't know what I'm doing," he added. "Just ask Chad."

~

Tess called Cheryl Tedesco, who was about to leave for the day. Asked if there was anything new on the Barkman case. Her friend at TPD sounded harried. The case remained open, but Cheryl had been discouraged from pursuing it further. There was no evidence that Barkman's death was anything but a freak accident. "There's just not enough *there*, there. Anyway, we're keeping it open but we're directing our resources elsewhere."

Tess knew the directive came from above, and there was no point arguing about it. *Move on.* "We think we know who killed George Hanley."

"Remind me again who that is?"

"The older guy in Credo. The one that looked like a drug hit."

"Oh, yeah, my bad. Sorry." She sounded like she'd had very little sleep. The new case must be a bear.

Tess described Wade Poole. "He's former homicide. We think he killed his wife and made it look like a robbery—this is a really bad guy. I just wanted to give you a heads-up—he may be after the DeKoven clan."

Cheryl knew about Tess's theory that the family was targeting people like Alec Sheppard, people who survived accidents.

Tess realized it required a leap of faith to believe that. Half the time she didn't believe it herself.

So crazy, on its face.

Cheryl said, "So you still think it's true? They're still playing that game?"

"I think right now the shoe's on the other foot. I think they're running scared. We have an Attempt to Locate out on Wade Poole."

"Guy sounds like a phantom."

"The main thing. I wanted to go up to Michael DeKoven's and warn him about Poole. I didn't want to step on any toes."

"No toes stepped on," Cheryl said. "Be my guest—I wish I could help but I'm *inundated* here. We have another shooting in midtown—and this time it's one of ours who got shot."

"I'm sorry."

"Yeah, me too. Didn't know him, but he had a wife and two kids."

They talked a little about it until Cheryl drifted off. Nothing more to say. She'd just disconnected when a call came in from Will Fallon, a deputy out of Patagonia. "Something's happened I think you'll be interested in."

"Oh?"

"There was an accident out on Harshaw Road, up near Mowry. Somebody driving by spotted a truck that crashed into the woods. It belongs to Jaimie Wolfe."

∼

Tess drove out to see Jaimie's truck. It was scratched up but possibly still operable. The driver's-side door was open. She peered in, careful not to touch anything. The airbags had been deployed, but Tess could see a dog leash and a pile of bridles and halters on the passenger-side floor.

Other vehicles had been on the road, so it was hard to see the tracks because the graded dirt road was hard ground, like a washboard. But she could see where the truck left the road and plunged down the embankment. She also saw a spot where a vehicle had stopped, slewed, and scattered gravel and rocks. And a place where the tires had dug in the dirt, two divots, as a vehicle laid scratch.

Jaimie Wolfe was gone.

∼

Tess was worried that Jaimie might be disoriented from the crash. She could have tried to walk home or hitched a ride. Or she could be wandering in the forest. Tess drove in the direction of Jaimie's place. On the way she called the sheriff's office and asked for them to pull together a search team. There was a sheriff's substation in Patagonia, and they were already looking. But they might need to send a search and rescue team. "I'm on my way to Jaimie's," Tess added.

"Walt's there. No sign of Mrs. Wolfe."

Tess was almost there, so she pulled in anyway.

Walt Aronow was driving out. He rolled down his window. "She's not home," he said. "We've got a search and rescue team on the way out to the crash site."

Tess decided to look at the farm anyway.

Everything was quiet. She went to the house—just as Walt had told her, everything was buttoned up. Next, she walked to the barn. The barn was typical of a horse farm: two rows of stalls fronting an aisle wide enough to drive a pickup through. The barn could be closed on both ends—two sets of double doors. She walked into the cool shade, and horses put their heads over their stalls and one nickered at her. They had hay and water, so they were all right.

She walked back outside and scanned the property. The only vehicle here was the ranch truck, a sun-blistered 1970s GMC.

This time, she walked around to the back of the farm truck and took note of the license number.

～

When she called in, her detective sergeant, Joe Messina, confirmed they were mobilizing search and rescue. "If she's up in those mountains and disoriented, she's going to be in trouble. It'll get cold up there tonight. We can't wait."

Tess couldn't imagine even a disoriented Jaimie Wolfe climbing uphill, but if she was frightened by something. Or someone . . .

It had been sitting right in front of her all this time.

What if she'd been run off the road?

What if Wade Poole was after her? What if he had her?

They could be anywhere by now.

Joe seemed to read her mind. "You think it was Wade Poole?"

Tess had filed her most recent report earlier in the day by e-mail. Joe and Bonny knew about Wade Poole.

"You saw photos of the scene."

"Yeah, those boot prints. There was a scuffle."

It had been hard to see, because the surface of the road had been baked hard. But you could draw that conclusion.

"Okay, I'll get Danny on it, too. You stay out in the field, if you think that's where you need to be."

~

Michael awoke from his nap to the ringing of the phone. He was entangled in Martin's arms. Someone had been calling him at intervals all last night, but they never left a message, and he didn't recognize the number.

The last rays of the sun streamed in through the blinds, striping Martin's magnificent body. Michael smiled down on him. Martin was his possession. He knew that not only did he possess Martin's body, but his soul. Martin's love for him was absolute, but sometimes he played games—withholding his affection, like that argument about his audition. He could be annoying sometimes. Michael didn't want to be trapped—ever again. His marriage to Nicole

313

taught him that. But it was flattering. And there was no more beautiful man on the planet than Martin.

And he was good. Very good.

I own you, Michael thought with satisfaction. *You beautiful, beautiful boy. You're mine.*

He picked up the phone and answered.

First there was nothing. Then, Jaimie started babbling. Babbling and crying. It took a while for him to figure out what she was telling him. And when he realized what had happened, his blood froze.

She was a hostage.

Michael decided to pretend that nothing had happened. This was way too big for him to assimilate all at once. So they went out on to the terrace and they had dinner as usual. He said nothing, of course, to Martin. He stared out at the pool and let it sink in. He had to understand it first.

Martin was prattling on about New York, his new timepiece, and some New York designer. Wondered aloud about the *Les Mis* production he would be attending tonight. Michael stared into the lighted pool as if the answer could be found there.

Jaimie he could do without. He didn't care, frankly, what happened to her. Yes, she was his sister, and there was blood to consider. But his siblings had always disappointed him. He'd loved Chad but never took him seriously. Who could? Jaimie was obnoxious, embarrassing, a man-hunter, a drunk—acting out constantly, even though she had a very good life, thanks to the DeKoven inheritance. Jaimie and her stupid horses. Jaimie and that dog—he still didn't understand how she could pull something like that.

The women in his family had been weak—except for Brayden. Michael allowed that she was tough and smart. She sure didn't get that from their doormat of a mother. What a pathetic weakling. Their mother never once stood up for them. She knew what their father did to them but she was too meek to say a word. She acted the plain, long-suffering housewife, pretending she was too sick to help anyone, but it wasn't really that. She wasn't just weak. She was selfish.

She didn't care about anyone but herself.

He hated her even more than the old man.

Michael knew he was trying not to think about the subject at hand. The problem was not that this guy had Jaimie, that she was his hostage. The problem was that he *knew*.

How did he know?

Michael had no idea. But the guy had demanded two million dollars to keep quiet.

Which was bullshit.

Michael would have found a way to pay the two million (and that would not be easy), but he knew that blackmailers always came back to the well. They wouldn't stop. The threat would hang over his head forever. He'd never know when he'd get another phone call to replenish the coffers.

Plus, there were . . . *issues,* laying hands on money like that. Their financial assets were complicated—blind trusts, offshore accounts, a real house of cards. These days it paid to keep a low profile. They had spending money—they were fine, all of them—but so much of their fortune was tied up.

Michael had a pretty good idea who was doing this. Who'd have the brass to do it. And if he was right, he could just go ahead and take him out.

He pictured Sheppard as he was the last time he'd seen him, at the Houston center.

He remember sipping his Starbucks and watching Sheppard, and how Sheppard had caught his eye.

Now, Michael did what he'd done on that day. He formed his right hand into a gun, and squeezed the trigger at the pool.

Second time counts for all.

～

Michael had done his due diligence on Alec Sheppard at the time he'd prepared to kill him. The problem was, Sheppard checked out of the Marriott two days ago. He could be anywhere. Michael was about to call the office in Houston to see if he could sweet-talk his way into finding out where Sheppard was here in Arizona, when Brayden called.

"Did you get that crazy phone call?" she demanded.

"Which one?" He laughed, but even he could hear the worry in his own voice.

"The man who's holding Jaimie hostage, that one!"

"A crank. Don't worry about it."

"He knows, Michael. He knows about Houston. He knows about California—this guy knows what we did."

Michael closed his eyes and saw the white truck on Kitt Peak, saw the note under the windshield wiper of his 4Runner: I KNOW WHAT YOU DID.

And it was then that he realized he'd seen the white truck before. And the guy in it.

Maybe a week or two ago, at the little general store down the road. The guy grinned at him when he was coming out the door. A rancher guy. He walked to his truck—a white truck—and got in. Michael remembered because of what the guy said to him before he stepped off the porch of the general store. "Do I know you, friend?"

Michael had replied, "I don't think so."

"I guess I must've got you confused with someone else, then." His smile was affable.

And he'd patted Michael on the shoulder.

Which reminded Michael of something. How he'd said almost the same thing to Peter Farley in LA.

When he was stalking him.

CHAPTER 50

Wade Poole was disappointed that Michael DeKoven hadn't taken his first offer seriously, but it didn't surprise him much. Negotiations often started on a negative note.

Time to go back to Jaimie's. He needed a place to go to ground with her, so why not to her house?

Besides, it was past time for him to get the DVD.

He'd checked on it once—right under the woman cop's nose—but it was possible that Jaimie might have hidden it someplace else.

Doubtful. Jaimie probably wouldn't even think about moving it—her mind didn't work that way. She was lazy and overconfident, and he was sure she believed her home was her castle and inviolable.

Still, when it came to that family, you couldn't trust anybody.

He put her in the truck and bumped down the lane—a back-side loop that bypassed Harshaw road. It was little more than a cow track, but it got him to a ranch road that came out pretty close to the highway to Patagonia. His right front bumper was smashed up some, but he took the chance. No one was on the road for most of the way—it was only a mile or two—and on the one occasion when headlights did appear, he pulled off the road at a diagonal and turned off his engine and lights. He doubted anyone would see the crimp in the bumper by the way he parked.

He watched as the vehicle went by—a search and rescue truck. What were the odds they were looking for Jaimie?

It was going on midnight when he turned in under the WOLFE MANOR sign. He stopped about a quarter mile down the road and checked the place out. Aside from a snort or two from the horses, no one was there. The place was dark. There were no vehicles. Still, he reconnoitered. Looked in all the places where he'd have set up surveillance if he'd been the one watching. It was easy to think like a cop because he was one.

Finally, he drove in and parked behind the dark house. A couple of dogs barked and then they all got up from the porch and the yard and came toward them. He dragged Jaimie into the house. He'd given her a couple of Xanax to take the edge off, so she stumbled a little as they walked in. He was a little shaky on his feet as well. His feet numb, probably from sitting cross-legged all that time. At least that was what he chose to think. The dogs funneled in after them. He herded them back outside by pouring dry dog food on the porch. The good thing was, they'd alert him to anyone coming.

After securing her in the bathtub, hooking her collar to a chain wrapped around a water pipe, he went back outside and drove his new truck into the center aisle of the horse barn and closed the doors. Back in the house, he donned latex gloves and went straight to the TV set.

It didn't take long to hit the Mother Lode. Jaimie kept it right by the TV set—in a stack of DVDs. There were six DVDs—various movies and a workout video—and at the bottom, a Maxell Gold DVD, unmarked. The DVDs had been stuck in the back of a small cabinet, made to look like an afterthought.

He was pretty sure this was what he was looking for.

He pulled out the DVD on the bottom—the only one that wasn't marked—put it in the player, and cued it up.

He wasn't disappointed.

These kids were amazing. They thought they were invincible. They thought they could get away with anything. They honestly thought they were entitled to anything. Just crook a finger or give an order, and some poor peasant leaped up to please them.

~

Assholes.

The video (it was poor quality—she must have burned it from a video she took off her cell phone) had gone all the way to just short of the end. He cued to the beginning and played it. There was some footage that looked as if it had been tacked on. A sullen gray sky. Tall cliffs, green bushes and trees, and dark jagged rocks, slick with water from eddies around them. The video panned down to the dark water, where a yellow inflatable boat sat, two people looking up. The camera panned around to the inside of a roofed platform with bench seats and pulleys—tight quarters. Athletic-looking kid, couldn't be more than twenty, clipping some kind of harness to another kid's leg. The camera panned down to the water and the people in the boat. There was a break in the video and then a close-up of a woman smiling. She looked both nervous and excited. There were the pulleys and ropes and the athletic-looking kid.

Another break.

He got the idea that the video had been patched together from different sources.

Now the camera panned to the sky, the cliff.

Screaming.

Jerky video. Something hurtling down, a figure, landing hard on the bank.

"Pow!" someone yelled.

A woman's voice.

A smile, a tanned face, upturned nose, dark hair, ribboned with yellow streaks, sunglasses. Just one jerky moment—the expensive lipstick, the broad smile.

Jaimie.

But that wasn't the best thing on the homemade DVD. The best was something even older. Maybe four or five years ago. Michael younger, Jaimie younger. Taking turns with the camera.

They were all either shit-faced, or drugged. And they were laughing. Hysterical. Michael was on something, that was obvious, and he was sprawled on a bed in what Wade assumed was his ancestral mansion. Lying there like a pasha, in a striped button-down shirt, open and loose on his chest. Pushing on the head of some woman giving him head, looked like a bleached blonde. Jerky movements. Another scene, out by the pool, tottering around drunk, talking into the camera. Waving his finger at whoever was videotaping him.

"We did it, Dad, you fucking son of a bitch!"

Jaimie holding on to his shoulder, laughing. "We survived you, and now *you're* moldering away! You couldn't survive *us*!" Paroxysms of laughter.

Jaimie pretending to hold a microphone. "How many have you killed, Michael? Just give me an estimate!"

He looked sleepy, a sweet smile on his face. Sprawled on a chaise by the pool. Started counting on his fingers. "One, two, three . . . ?"

Jaimie homing in on him with her fake microphone. "What was your favorite? Who did you like killing most?"

He grinned. "That's easy. Dear old Dad."

Thought about it for a second. "Putting Mom out of her misery, that was pretty good, too."

They both dissolved into laughter. Shared hits off a bottle of champagne. Got celebratory and opened another bottle, which Michael sprayed all over Jaimie. Brayden was there, too, and they took turns teasing her, encouraging her to talk into the camera, but she just folded her arms and hopped back.

There was a lot more of it, but that was enough.

Wade had enough to get his payday.

CHAPTER 51

When Michael's phone rang (his ringtone was, appropriately, "When the Bullet Hits the Bone") and he saw Jaimie's name on the readout again, his first inclination was to ignore her, as he usually did. But he knew it was the rancher guy, and that the rancher guy meant business. He wanted to ignore the call, but he couldn't.

He'd make it clear. There would be no two million dollars. The rancher guy could kill Jaimie. It didn't matter to him.

"Guess where I am?" the rancher guy said.

"I don't give a damn."

"Oh, but you should. I'm at Jaimie's."

"So?"

"Are you familiar with her television and sound system?"

Michael felt his first stirring of unease. He said nothing.

"Really, you should have a talk with your sister. She was dumb enough to leave the DVD she burned of your party out in plain sight. Well, not plain *sight* exactly, but close enough for horseshoes."

"I'm hanging up now."

"Don't you want to see the video?"

Michael felt his pulse race. Did Jaimie really just leave it out for anyone to see? Was she that stupid?

The answer was yes. She was that stupid.

"One thing I've learned," the guy said, "in this long life of mine, is that people do what's easy. When nobody's looking, when they feel like they can let their guard down, that nobody will know how smart they are, they do dumb things. Like put a DVD right next to the DVD player. Maybe put something on top of it, oh, like a bunch of movies, to hide it, but I can't tell you how many times people have fucked up on some little turning point like that."

Michael didn't reply.

"There's even writing on the case. 'TSC.' That's what it says on here. Sound familiar?"

"No."

"This is just a guess, but maybe TSC is short for The Survivors Club. Oh, wait, she mentioned that somewhere along the way. Maybe it was on the drive over. Hard to hear her with that choke chain pulled tight."

"You know what I think? I think you're full of shit."

He was about to thumb the phone off when the guy said, "Nice party you guys had. Let me send it to you. Hold on."

It came through.

"I'll wait while you watch a little, okay?"

Michael watched. He couldn't help himself. It was from about five years ago. They were celebrating another killing. He couldn't remember which one it was. And looking at himself, so completely out of it, his heart sank. Everything seemed to cave inside of him.

Leaving only terror.

Prison.

And then one day, they'd strap him to a gurney in a little room and give him a lethal injection.

Fear kited up into his throat, but disciplined himself by thinking, *I have lawyers.* He said, "So what?"

"So what? Hey you got monster ones, my friend. *So what.* This goes viral. I can transmit it anywhere. I can transmit it to the local gendarmes, I can transmit it to the FBI, it can go all over the world with a touch of a button. So what? You really want to push me?"

Michael's vocal cords barely got purchase, but he said, "Fuck you."

"Fuck me? What a terrible thing to say. You just hurt my feelings, friend."

Michael could barely feel his fingers holding the phone. He could picture the little room at the prison in Florence. There was a window, and people behind the window, and they'd all be peering in at him like kids with their faces to the glass. Like his death was a TV show. But facts were facts. "If I paid you two million dollars, what would stop you from extorting me again and again?"

"Hmmm." The man paused, then said, "Would you trust my word? I'm a man of my word. You would have to trust me on that."

Michael said nothing.

"Just a little pressure from my thumb and this goes all over. The first place it goes is to the FBI."

"It doesn't mean anything. It's just some of us joking around about killing our parents. A fantasy."

Another pause. Then, "There are facts to back it up, bro. Peter Farley. The woman in New Zealand. Santa Cruz County and TPD is already on your trail, bud, they're already looking at you. You think they won't act on this evidence? You think it won't show them where and what to investigate? You're toast, my friend. Unless you pay me to shut up. And I'll even throw in Jaimie."

Michael almost hung up. But he couldn't. His fingers were slippery with sweat now. He clamped harder on the phone.

"Two million, bro. Worth the price of admission, let me tell you."

But Michael knew this wouldn't be the end.

Still, he had to do something. "You come here. Bring it. Bring Jaimie. We'll talk then."

"Gonna take you some time to work out the details, friend. Put in a call to your bank. I have a number for an account in Belize for you to wire it to. These days, it should take a couple of minutes tops, once you say the word."

"It's after hours, bud. Tell you what. You come here and we'll talk."

"I'm not going there."

"Then we're done here." And Michael disconnected.

CHAPTER 52

Tess had finished a late dinner when she got the call—searchers had discovered a camping area above Mowry, on a hiking trail in a remote area. There was a stake in the ground and a chain, and footprints that appeared to match the partials they'd seen down below, where the truck had crashed off the side of the road. It looked as if Jaimie had been kidnapped and held there.

Tess thought that was probably true.

Whatever had happened, Jaimie and her kidnapper were gone.

It sounded like a crime scene to Tess. She spoke to the head of the team, a neighbor and a former cop himself, James Tarbel. They agreed that since it was dark, they could easily trample whatever evidence there was. The next day they would send a detective and crime scene techs.

She sat there in the dark, thinking. She was sure it was Wade Poole, sure he had Jaimie. But where were they now? Why did he take her up here?

It had been a temporary hiding place, but it could have been more than that, from the description. She guessed—and she could be wrong about this—he had photographed her to scare her family.

Now she thought she knew why Poole had kidnapped Jaimie.

Poole knew about the family—he knew what they were doing. He'd killed George Hanley because of it. Because they'd disagreed on what to do with the evidence. Hanley wanted to turn it over to the authorities. But he'd made the mistake of letting his old partner, his son-in-law, in on the deal.

Poole didn't care about bringing the DeKovens to justice.

Tess was pretty sure that all Wade Poole cared about was money.

She got ready for bed, but couldn't sleep. Finally, she decided to go back to Jaimie's one more time and see if there was anything to point to where Wade Poole might go next.

~

It was full dark now, and cold. When Tess drove onto the ranch, she saw immediately that something was different.

Should have secured this as a secondary crime scene, she thought.

Tired. Too much going on.

Tess stared at the spot where the ranch truck had been—the old, root beer—colored GMC.

It was gone.

She stood there, arms crossed, feeling the chill down to her bone. Cold at night in the desert, especially in the spring. The heat was absorbed by the earth and the atmosphere felt thin and chilly.

And dark. She heard horses stirring in their stalls, here a grunt and neigh. She had her Maglite and her service weapon, and that was it.

The barn door was closed. It had been open before.

Tess held the Maglite in her left hand and drew her weapon. She felt the familiar adrenaline rush. Where she'd been tired and sleepy a moment ago, she was all nerve now. Every sense bristling.

Maybe he'd taken the truck.

Or maybe not.

She made her way around the barn. The couple of windows were too high, and no way to get up to them. She heard a snort. It wasn't a frightened sound, more like a horse just . . . sighing. She listened through the wall and heard a rhythmic munching.

A horseman, though, wouldn't scare these horses. A ranch guy—and Wade certainly looked as if he'd spent time on a ranch somewhere—would not raise any alarms.

Tess decided not to take any chances. She called for backup, and within ten minutes a couple of deputies arrived from the substation in town.

They took it slow. They were careful. Weapons drawn, one going low—Deputy Walsh—and one going high–Tess. And one standing on the other side of the double doors, Deputy Agel.

Tess pulled the right hand door to the side—it slid on a groove.

Agel, from the left, covered them. Yelled, "Police! Don't move!"

One single lightbulb cast light from the rafters. No hayloft—Tess had seen the separate feed shed away from the barn.

The horses looked over their stalls. Four on one side and three on the other. The last stall empty. Or someone hiding in it.

Walsh duckwalked out from under Tess, aiming to the right. Tess to the left, along with Agel. Checking each stall.

"Clear!"

"Clear!"

"Clear!"

The last stall was empty.

But they had something—confirmation.

Backed in to the far wall at the end of the aisle was Wade Poole's stolen Ford truck—the front bumper mashed against the wheel well.

"Looks like he's been in a fender-bender," Tess said.

~

She called it in. "No license plate," Tess told her detective sergeant. "He must have put it on the farm truck."

She gave him the VIN number and waited.

Twenty minutes later it was confirmed. The white Ford F-350 belonged to a construction site in Nogales, Arizona—Redline Construction. The truck had been stolen eleven days earlier.

"They didn't lock it up?" Usually construction sites, even out in the boonies, set up chain-link fence enclosures for temporary parking lots.

"Apparently not. Where do you think he's headed?"

Tess didn't know. But she could guess. "Wade Poole is after the DeKoven family. I think he's planning to shake them down. So I would send a TPD unit to Brayden DeKoven's address, and Pima County should check out Michael DeKoven's place out on the Spanish Trail." She rattled off both addresses.

"You remember them?" Messina said. Added, "I guess you would, huh? That's handy."

He still wasn't used to her, still saw her as a freak. But she was a useful freak.

"I would set up surveillance if he's not there yet," Tess added. She made a mental note to call Cheryl Tedesco. Cheryl would want to know what was going on, and might even be able to move things along at TPD.

"We have an Attempt to Locate in both counties now for a brown 1978 GMC pickup." He read off the license plate belonging to the white Ford.

"Sounds good. I'm on my way."

"What address?"

"Michael DeKoven's."

Tess thought, if she were Wade Poole, that was where she'd go.

~

Tess was almost to the Vail exit outside Tucson when her detective sergeant contacted her again.

"We have a description of the truck, but the license plate isn't the same."

He'd switched plates again? The license plate didn't come back to the ranch truck or the stolen Ford. Somewhere along the line, he'd stolen another plate.

One jump ahead.

"Where is he?"

"He's on Spanish Trail. Pima County Sheriff's unit is following."

"Ask them not to alert him."

"Will do. I'll tell him to turn off."

Tess's heart was beating so hard she wondered if it would burst through her chest cavity. Wade Poole was armed and dangerous. If he was cornered, he would not hesitate to kill.

He was a killing machine.

~

Wade saw the Pima County Sheriff's car coming in his direction. He saw the body of the car feint slightly—a reflex action—and continue on smoothly. He guessed that someone had put out a BOLO on the ranch truck. He watched in his rearview as the radio car slowed and pulled off onto the verge. Knew it would turn around and pursue. There was no place to go to ground. But he was close to Michael DeKoven's castle on a hill—probably not three miles overland. He could see the lights up on the hill. He thought about ditching the truck, but he wanted Jaimie as a hostage. He kept his gaze glued to the rearview mirror. The curve in the road hid the sheriff's car. Any minute he expected headlights to appear. But they didn't.

Maybe he was hypersensitive. He kept driving. The turnoff was up ahead, and he wanted to keep Jaimie with him. He glanced at her. She leaned as far as she could away from him, up against the passenger side. From her posture you'd think she was cowed, but he saw the hatred in her eyes. Even in the dark of the night, he could see it. He would not take her for granted. Hatred like that could overcome a lot.

Momma didn't raise no fools. He'd have to watch her every minute.

Wade knew that Michael would call back. He was sure that Michael would be frozen, that he wouldn't know which way to jump. The rich little turd couldn't get help from law enforcement. He couldn't get help from anyone. Michael thought that he could draw Wade to go to him, that on his home turf he'd have the upper hand. But Wade had all the cards.

~

Tess's Tahoe was a plain wrap. But she knew, if anyone had antennae for a plain wrap, it would be Wade Poole. She pulled off the road at the little general store, now closed, and waited. She knew where Wade was headed. Meantime, the Pima County sheriff's deputy who had spotted him rolled in. He introduced himself as Wiley Moran.

They discussed what they were going to do. There was time for backup.

But that wasn't the only consideration. Wade Poole was loaded for bear, and Jaimie Wolfe was almost certainly his hostage.

"What do you think Poole would do if he was turned down?" asked Deputy Moran.

He knew the right question to ask. Tess had been a deputy not too long ago, and she knew how important it was to think a situation through. Especially if you were ambitious, and Deputy Moran clearly was.

Tess said, "He'd kill them both."

Deputy Moran's eyebrows rose in an arch. He didn't have to ask a question.

Tess said, "He'd kill them and take off. Cut his losses."

"And if he couldn't get away?" Moran asked.

"He would kill as many as he could. And then he'd kill himself."

Deputy Moran nodded. "That's what I figured."

Tess liked him. He had been very quick to stop and take stock of the situation, and had not turned around to go after Poole. He'd thought his actions through with the information he had at the time.

One word from her, and he'd pulled over to the side of the road. He could have been a much different type.

Tess was glad she'd found him.

"He knows you pulled off," Tess said. "Either he thinks you were just patrolling—routine—or that you'd been called off. Any way you look at it, he's going to be wary. But at least we haven't scared him off. I'm thinking I should go ahead. My Tahoe's unmarked. He won't necessarily be looking for a car like this."

"Then I'm going to have to wait for backup, ma'am."

"You'll call it in?"

"Yeah. SWAT."

"SWAT," Tess said.

He was right. They would need SWAT.

Deputy Moran said, "I'm worried about the hostage."

"Me, too." Tess was certain Wade Poole planned to shoot Jaimie if Michael DeKoven didn't cooperate.

"Think we should get closer?" Moran asked.

Tess decided to share her real fear with Deputy Moran. "We think that Poole is going to extort money from the DeKoven family. He's using Jaimie as a hostage, but what would scare a guy like DeKoven the most? What ultimate threat?"

"That he'd kill her right in front of him," Moran said. "As an example."

Tess nodded. "I agree."

He said, "The message would be that DeKoven would be next. I think we should get closer. I think we've got probable cause."

"Or at least 'possible cause,'" Tess said.

Moran laughed at that. "'Possible cause.' Sounds good enough to me."

Tess looked up the road. From where they were they could see Zinderneuf's lighted windows. The Moorish-slash-Pueblo-style building dominated the landscape. At one time, there was no Thunderhead Ranch, there were no homes anywhere nearby. That was before some of the land was sold off and subdivided. At one time, Zinderneuf had dominated the valley. But now it didn't look all that different from the McMansions farther down the road. Clinging to the top of a hill, lighted windows. Except that Zinderneuf was all by itself.

"Wouldn't take much to climb up there." Moran nodded toward a shallow wash that crossed under the road and meandered between two scrub-covered hills. "We follow the wash around that hill and then go up cross-country."

There was a moon already, and it was almost full.

Moran called in and said they would be observing, and when SWAT came, they would identify themselves. The estimated time for the SWAT team was inside twenty-five minutes.

They followed the arroyo along the hillside and found a horse trail leading up. They kept low to the ground and tried to stay as quiet as possible, stopping often to listen.

It took them about fifteen minutes to traverse the distance. They reached the blacktopped area where Tess had first seen Michael's expensive Fisker Karma. It must be garaged now. Jaimie Wolfe's ranch truck was parked closest to the gate. Poole and his hostage hadn't been here long.

They worked their way toward the side of the house. The only noise was the sound of crickets. A bat fluttered past them and dipped down into the pool and up. Tess saw low decorative lights at intervals through the sparse mesquite limbs. They followed a dirt path along the ridge, lighted occasionally from recessed lamps set into the low wall of the pool area. The pool reflected the lights from the house. Across the way, screened by a garden and a royal palm, the guest house was dark. Tess wondered if Michael's estranged wife and children were in residence. It was a little early to be asleep. They might be out somewhere.

They duckwalked along the desert side of the house and under a massive eucalyptus tree. Two windows were lighted on the far end, casting rectangles of light on the bushes and cactus. There was a space of about two and a half feet below the window, so they crawled under, careful of the thorns. They reached the corner and followed that around. No windows on that side. On the far side was an entrance—locked, and a porch overlooked the city lights. They went from dirt to flagstone paving and came upon a kitchen entrance. Tess checked the door: unlocked.

She looked at Moran and he looked at her. She tilted her chin in the direction of the city, and he gave her a curt nod: they would wait for SWAT.

They followed the porch around to the garden entrance, with steps down to the pool.

The house had been large for its time but not by modern standards. The buildings followed the profile of the ridge. Everything was quiet. No movement across the long pool area or at the guest house. The wife's house was still dark. Tess hoped she was gone.

The only sound was the hum of the pool filter. The adobe walls to the house were probably two feet thick.

They circled the house again. Heard voices from one of the rooms on the east side.

Getting louder. Garbled. Angry?

Tess and Moran looked at each other. Weapons at the ready, drawn and at their sides.

"*Possible cause.*" It had been a joke, but now it wasn't.

Then they heard a crash, echoing through the thick walls—

A gunshot.

They couldn't wait. They were going in.

CHAPTER 53

Michael had been in his study looking at his bank accounts online when he heard a door open and close.

He almost called out Martin's name.

But Martin had wanted to go to a show at the convention center in downtown Tucson, and Michael hadn't felt like it. He was too tied up in knots. He looked at his watch. The show had only been going for about thirty-five minutes—no way it could be Martin unless he decided not to go at all.

He thumbed his phone and tapped in Martin's number.

"How's the show?" he asked when Martin answered.

"It's okay. The production values need some work—"

"Something's come up," Michael said. "Got to go."

He kept quiet, his ear tuned to the front door. It was the front door. Jaimie knew the combination to the keypad by heart. Maybe

Poole had been lying. Maybe Jaimie was fine, and maybe she'd run here so he could protect her.

But he didn't think so.

He could feel his stomach tighten. Could almost feel his organs shrink, as if they were clenched in gelid fingers—fingers of the dead. Blood seemed to race from his extremities, and adrenaline poured through him. An electric river of fear.

He'd never been afraid before.

Even when his father raped him.

Even when, a couple of times, he thought someone might catch on to what they were doing. There was always that danger of slipping up. Which made it scary, but also fun.

But now he knew that the man called Wade Poole was in the house. He had Jaimie and he was creeping around, looking. Opening doors—he heard one creak—and coming his way. Seeing the light under the door. The light to his office.

Part of him yelled *Run!*

But he was no coward. He'd killed people and watched the light die in their eyes. He wasn't going to run now.

Not many people could summon up the wherewithal to kill. He was one of them. He could look in someone's eyes and kill them—and enjoy it.

He got up slowly. His Ruger .44 was in the locked drawer of his desk. He got the key out and wriggled it into the lock. Had trouble with it. Felt the first stirrings of panic. His hands weren't shaking, exactly, just a little tremor—

The door burst open.

Of course he hadn't locked it.

And there was Jaimie—her face a white fright mask, mascara running down her cheeks. Looking like she'd been unearthed out of a fresh grave. Like a zombie. His sister, the zombie.

All these thoughts ribboned through his mind, and he saw the black hole of a very-large-caliber gun. Pointed right at his face.

And he saw the man behind the gun. The man who held Jaimie as if she were a rag doll. The man was strong, brutish, and stupid.

Stupid.

Like a guy who fell off the proverbial turnip truck.

An ox.

A rancher type, the kind Jaimie fucked. Blue work shirt. White straw cowboy hat. Round face. Sunburn. Blue eyes. Local yokel grin. Graying blond hair.

Except his eyes were like blue marbles. Cold.

Suddenly, it occurred to him that he might have underestimated the man.

He understood that when the man shoved Jaimie facedown on the desk and pushed the gun muzzle into her hair.

Smiling as he did it.

"Here's how it's gonna go, friend."

He was the cowboy he'd seen outside the general store. The Okie.

"I'm gonna kill her right in front of you. It's gonna make a big mess. This is a large-caliber weapon. She'll blow chunks and so will you. She's gonna mess up the nice finish on your desk. All that blood'll soak into the grain. Now I know you're not afraid of blood or killing. But you're gonna see her close up, and then, being human nature and all, you'll picture what *you'll* look like. Just remember, friend, dead's forever. There's now, and then there's nothing."

Michael steeled himself. "Go ahead and kill her."

"Look, bud, all I want is you to wire that money to my account. You can do it in two minutes tops. Don't you care about your sister at all?"

"No."

He shook his head. "Okay, then."

And he pulled the trigger.

CHAPTER 54

Tess checked the kitchen door—unlocked. She said, "I'll go low right. You go high left, okay?"

"Roger."

They took their positions on either side of the door, weapons at the ready. Moran's pointing to the left, Tess's to the right. Moran turned the knob and pushed the door open with his foot.

Nothing greeted them.

The shot had come from the right. Moran went left, Tess went right, and they cleared the rooms immediately in front of them. Tess, the kitchen, Moran, the parlor. They zeroed in on the room where they'd heard the shot.

Noise—a commotion—someone banging into furniture, the screech of wood against tile, and then the loud shock of something repeatedly hitting the floor.

Michael's study.

The sound of a gourd breaking. Again and again.

The door was open and Tess could see a woman's body sprawled face-down over the desk, blood oozing out from under her head, a clot of it burrowed into her slightly upturned cheek.

Long dark hair with blonde highlights.

Jaimie.

But the horror was so much worse. Michael DeKoven was crawling on his hands and knees, his head a bloody mess. A man in Wrangler jeans and a blue denim shirt bent over him, slamming his head repeatedly into the floor.

Poole.

"Police! Hands behind your head! Do it now!"

Tess heard her own voice, but it sounded foreign in her ears.

"Do it now!" yelled Deputy Moran. His voice strong and loud in the room.

Poole kept pounding DeKoven's head into the floor. "How do you like *that*, motherfucker? How do you like *that*?"

Blood spraying—a red mist. A solid chunk of DeKoven's head smashing into the floor once more before Moran was able to get hold of one of Poole's blood-slippery arms in his, wrenching it behind the man's back.

Michael DeKoven's body slumped, then caved.

Tess thought he was dead. He *had* to be dead.

Tess had to hopscotch over Michael's body to give Moran a hand. Poole was staggering, bellowing like a maddened bull, trying to twist around and head butt Moran. "I'll show you, you prissy little fucker!" he yelled at DeKoven's corpse. "I'll show you who's boss!"

Tess latched on. He roared and shook her off, swung his head back and forth, blood flying like an oscillating lawn sprinkler.

Enraged. His eyes red rimmed. She latched onto him again. It took both of them to restrain him.

Abruptly, he stopped struggling.

All three of them huffing like freight trains.

Blood snared his mouth and dripped to the bottom of his nose and splashed on the tile.

Suddenly he dropped to his knees, almost pulling Tess and Moran with him. Tess stumbled and went to one knee just to stay up.

Poole shook himself like a big dog and blood flew. He raised his face to the ceiling and howled. He howled like a wolf.

Moran looked at Tess. "What the—?"

The howling morphed into laughter. Jagged, manic, loud.

It went on and on and on.

CHAPTER 55

Jurisdictional hell.

Everyone wanted a piece of Wade Poole.

Pima County Sheriff's got the nod—they had the best case. Fortunately, Tess and Danny would sit in on the interrogation, along with Cheryl Tedesco of TPD.

They'd need a bigger interview room.

While they cooled their heels at the Pima County Sheriff's Adult Detention Center on Silverlake Road, Danny made a call to his wife.

Tess listened as they talked, overheard him crooning a lullaby to his new little girl. How his voice softened. How his face changed. Tess found herself wishing that she had a family like that, had that dimension to her life. *A child*.

She'd never thought about that possibility before.

As Danny disconnected, he looked at her, puzzled. "What?"

"Nothing."

Danny pocketed his phone and leaned forward, elbows on knees. Clasped his hands and glanced over at her. "What you think is going to happen in there?"

"What do *you* think will happen in there?"

"I think he'll reserve his right to remain silent. I think we came all this way for nothing."

Tess agreed. As a homicide cop, Wade Poole had been on the other side too many times. He knew all the tricks. He knew what they would say before they said it.

Plus, he was an asshole.

He'd stonewall them.

He knew he was going down, but he'd still get the last laugh.

It was a victory of sorts.

~

The room was cramped, stale, and warm. There were enough people there for a poorly attended city council meeting. Tess, Danny, and Cheryl were merely observers.

There were two Pima County sheriff's detectives. They came to the party armed with an arsenal of evidence. In Michael DeKoven's house alone, two people were dead by Wade Poole's hand, and a Pima County Sheriff's deputy and a Santa Cruz County homicide detective had witnessed Michael DeKoven's murder.

Poole sat easy in his chair, despite the fact that he couldn't stretch out. His hands were cuffed and chained to the interview table. He smiled: the jovial hayseed.

Detective Phil Arenas leaned forward. "You know we've got you dead to rights, Wade. You're smart enough to know that. So why don't you tell me your side?"

Wade shifted in his seat.

He grinned. "Yeah, you got me." He leaned forward. "So what say I tell you everything?"

The surprise was plain on Arenas's face.

Wade leaned back. The chain rattled. "'Course I want something in exchange. I want a cushy place, one of those country club prisons."

Tess was aware she was staring at him. And she wasn't alone. The secondary investigator on the case, Eric Spindler, opened his mouth wide enough to let flies in.

"Wade," Spindler said. "You know that that's not the way it w—"

Poole kept his eye on the lead, Phil Arenas. "That's the deal. I'll clear this case for you and a bunch of others, because I know *exactly* what those kids did." He grinned, all corn pone. "You give me a good place, and I'll tell all."

"We'll do our best, Wade," Arenas said. "But you know as well as I do. There aren't any country club prisons in Arizona."

"You know what I mean. I want the best of the best. Whatever that is." He leveled his gaze at Arenas. "But you gotta give me hospice care."

~

Arenas left the room. They waited, but they didn't have to wait long.

"Okay, Wade," Arenas said, settling into the chair close to Poole. "If everything you say checks out, we can do that. So you're sick? What is it you have?"

"Brain cancer. My doctor's name is Clarence Pogue." He rattled off the number. "Got it on the speed dial inside of my head."

"How are you feeling?"

"Not too bad. Headaches, mostly. My balance sucks. The vomiting is the worst. You gonna make that call?"

Spindler pulled his phone from his pocket and left the room.

Wade sat back and grinned. For a man with a death sentence, he looked as if he didn't have a care in the world.

Spindler came back. "We'll get you into hospice."

And so Wade Poole began to talk.

He confessed to killing George Hanley. "What'd he think? He'd serve up proof about those kids killing people and tie it up in a nice little bow? You think they'd take him seriously? Stupid old fool, throwing away a chance to make a fortune with both hands. So I shot him, made it look like a cartel did it."

"Just curious, Wade," Arenas said. "While you're getting things off your chest, what about your wife, Karen Poole?"

He grinned. "That was mine."

"How about Chad DeKoven? You know anything about that?"

He held up a manacled hand. "Guilty. While I'm in a talkative mood, I can tell you I killed Steve Barkman, too—my most creative work yet. Kind of an experiment, but surprise-surprise, it worked." He grinned. "Guess this good ol' boy is a one-man crime wave."

"Why did you kill Steve Barkman?"

He leaned forward. "That greedy little son of a bitch wasn't interested in helping out Sheppard. He wanted a piece of the DeKoven pie. Can you believe that? Poor dumb fuck thought he could mess with me and mine."

He sat back again, grinning from ear to ear.

"Had a dog like him once, sneaky little shit, used to skulk around and steal hoof parings when I was shoeing horses. Ate 'em right up. Always looked ashamed of himself, but he ate 'em. That's what Steve Barkman reminded me of. A hoof-eating dog." He leaned back even farther in his seat and stretched his legs out. "But there was another reason. You want to know what it was?"

"I'd appreciate anything you can say that will help us understand what happened here," Arenas said.

Poole grinned. "I bet you would. I killed him for the same reason I killed Hanley and the surfer dude. Because my best girl asked me to."

Phil Arenas looked at his partner. Cheryl looked at Tess and Danny and they looked at her.

"You should see your faces," Poole said. "You didn't know that, did you? You want to know who she is?"

He leaned into the microphone.

"Brayden.

"DeKoven.

"McConnell."

~

The interrogation went for hours. Wade Poole had a lot to say and nothing to lose. Although he was forthcoming, even jovial, there was an undercurrent of rage Tess could feel. It was always there, behind the friendly mask he wore.

"I lured Hanley out to the ghost town. It was an ambush, pure and simple. He backed up onto the porch and I just kept walking and shooting, walking and shooting. Like that old fifties show, *The Rifleman*. Bam bam bam bam! Perfect place for a drug hit. When in doubt, always muddy the waters."

By that time, he told them, he liked the idea of playing vigilante. He'd planned to pick off the DeKovens one by one. "I decided to mess with their heads first. Scare 'em. For sport, you know? The hunter becomes the hunted." He grinned.

"How'd you meet Brayden DeKoven?" Phil Arenas asked.

"I was on to them all, but I figured Brayden would be the weakest link, being the youngest and a female. Jesus, was *I* ever wrong. That simpering little bitch has ice water in her veins!" He laughed. "She made me an offer I couldn't refuse. She wanted her two brothers and her sister dead. Gave me this song and dance about how she'd waited for a guy like me all her life, batted her eyes real pretty, did things to me you can't imagine." He winked. "Told me if I killed them she'd split the inheritance with me."

"You believed that?" Arenas asked.

His eyes turned to stone, and once again Tess could see the real man behind the friendly mask. "Hell, no. What she didn't realize, though, was, she was next."

"No interest in marrying her?"

"It wouldn't last long, would it? I'm a dead man! Plus, who could live with a crazy bitch like that? And her kid? Jesus. Nope, I wanted money up front and she paid me good. I've still got a lot of life left in me and I've got one hell of a bucket list. If you're gonna die, you might as well go out in style. So I figured I could blackmail Michael DeKoven as easily as she could."

They were just finishing up when he turned pale. "I'm gonna pass out. You got a bed in here somewhere? I need to lie down *now*."

But he didn't make it as far as the door.

CHAPTER 56

On a warm spring day, Elena Christina Rojas was christened at the Sacred Heart Catholic Church in Nogales.

Danny invited everyone to the house afterward. Tess wandered through the rooms of their brick ranch, balancing her plate of blue corn tamales, apple empanada, and barbecued flank steak with her cup of punch. She now knew the exact definition of the word "beaming," because Danny embodied it. His smile seemed permanently affixed to his face—pride, joy, and gratitude all wrapped into one. He stuck like a burr to his wife and his baby, his jokes a little less off-color.

His focus had changed. He was the same Danny Rojas who teased Tess and called her *guera*, the same Danny who looked for humor in every situation, but he now wore a mantle of fatherhood on his shoulders and Tess was acutely aware of it. *Father. Dad.* There was more to him now. Being a father was number one, just ahead of being a husband.

Tess threaded through knots of cops and friends and family, the low babble of voices, thinking that for all Danny's wisecracks, he had this one very important part of his life nailed down.

He had someone.

He had two someones.

Tess had a new someone herself. Last week she'd visited Adele at the vet hospital and ended up paying the bill and bringing her home. Adele wouldn't fit in Tess's glass case of mementos, but she'd been precious to two homicide victims: George Hanley and Jaimie DeKoven, and was quickly becoming just as precious to Tess.

Peter Deuteronomy had somehow got wind of it and called her extension at work to offer her his extra coupons for PetSmart.

Tess walked out onto the patio, which had a view of the hills in Nogales, Mexico, and the golden grassland.

The sky an aching blue above.

It was beautiful out here—quiet. But Tess realized how tired she was.

She was haunted by nightmares. The violence she'd seen in Michael DeKoven's house clung to her and would not let go. She'd always been good at compartmentalizing, always been good at filing things away. But Wade Poole beating Michael DeKoven's head against the floor replayed constantly in her mind.

The sheer savagery of it left an indelible mark.

Meanwhile, Wade Poole was being treated better than ninety-five percent of the prison population. His brain cancer wasn't advanced, and he still had days—even weeks—when he wasn't affected by his illness.

Tess and Danny were still working to nail down all the murders the Survivors Club had committed. The killings spanned several jurisdictions—including New Zealand—but only one possible killing here in Arizona. The ex-soldier shot by a sniper. The DeKovens had been careful not to kill in their own backyard.

Brayden DeKoven was questioned but so far there had been no arrest. She'd lawyered up big-time. Tess thought they'd better hurry; the youngest DeKoven was certainly a flight risk.

Even on the incriminating tape of the family boasting about their crimes by the pool, she had managed to appear innocent. Tess had run the tape through her head many times: Jaimie and Michael drinking champagne, completely out of hand—and Brayden, trying to avoid the spotlight. Brayden, embarrassed by her drunken and drugged siblings, even shy—seemingly astonished at what they were saying. To anyone watching, it appeared that Brayden had just walked onto a strange movie set and had no idea what was going on.

That plain, innocent, sweet dumpling face.

There was a lot of ground to cover. Tess and Danny had no idea how many people had been killed by the DeKovens, but she guessed at least four, since one of the DeKovens had slapped the number five on Alec Sheppard's chest.

She owed Alec a call. They'd been playing phone tag the last couple of days. She tapped in his number, and this time, he answered on the first ring.

"I want to catch you up," Tess said.

It was a long story and it took some time.

Finally, they disconnected. Tess stared at the oak-covered hills of Mexico, cluttered with brightly painted houses that seemed to pile one on top of the other. Traffic whispered on the freeway below, but she listened for cars on the road outside Danny's subdivision. She inhaled the sweet scent of star jasmine spilling over the parapet.

She heard tires on gravel and the sound of a car door opening and closing. Greetings inside the house, heard Danny's voice floating out of the open sliding glass door. "I think she's outside."

Tess was aware that her heart was beating hard, pulsing in her ears. She hadn't felt this way since grade school.

She turned to the doorway just as Max Conroy stepped outside to greet her.

THE END

Acknowledgments

Many thanks to the experts who helped make this book a reality: John Cheek of Cops 'n Writers; US Border Patrol agent Simon Keller; Ed Love, forensic firearm examiner; my wonderful husband, Glenn McCreedy, for his insights on cycling as well as his loving support; John Peters, weapon and skydiving expert; Sabine Peters, skydiving expert; Barbara Schiller, who helped me envision the DeKovens' home in the Tucson foothills; William Simon, computer forensics expert and cheerleader, as needed; and Aleta Walther, San Bernardino County Parks Ranger and dear friend.

It takes a village to raise a book, and I am grateful to every one of the Thomas & Mercer team. Thanks to Courtney Miller, my acquiring editor, who has shepherded me through three books now, and to Kevin Smith, whose remarkable editing skills made *The Survivors Club* a much better story. And many thanks to the wonderful Thomas & Mercer Author Team: Danielle Marshall, Marketing Manager; Jacque Ben-Zekry, Author Relations (boy is she good at that!); Ali Foster, Merchandising; Reema Al Zaben, Production; Leslie LaRue, Marketing; Kaila Lightner, Merchandising; and Rory Connell, Marketing.

As ever, I owe a great debt of gratitude to Deborah Schneider and to all the folks at Gelfman Schneider who have helped guide me safely through the whitewater of publishing.

About the Author

GALEN EVANS

Hailed by best-selling author T. Jefferson Parker as "a strong new voice in American crime fiction," J. Carson Black has written fourteen novels. Her thriller, *The Shop*, reached #1 on the Kindle Best-seller list, and her crime thriller series featuring homicide detective Laura Cardinal became a *New York Times* and *USA Today* bestseller. Although Black earned a master's degree in operatic voice, she was inspired to write a horror novel after reading *The Shining*. She lives in Tucson, Arizona.